Waterproof

Lee DuCote

ISBN: 978-0996643290

Edited by: Merrell Knighten
Alice Sullivan
Cover Designer: Marianne Nowicki

Raccoon Bend Publishing Services rev. date: 8/1/2015

To: My Father

Acknowledgements

My most humble and heartfelt thanks:

To a family that is more supportive than I could ever ask for. Alicia, my wife, thank you for the support and encouragement that I can do all things. Dylan, my son, thank you for being a better man and having the utmost respect for others.

To my editor, Merrell Knighten, who keeps me in the boundaries of grammar, punctuation, and spelling, and adds a flavor of imagination from his Louisiana roots. Aren't you glad you didn't have me as a student?

To my coach and editor, Alice Sullivan, who has helped the creations of my writings come to life with her dedication and talents.

To a very special team of readers that is honest in their critiques and encouraging in the creation. Randy Allums, Chrissy Tubbs, Katie Holmes, Janet Nolan, (my precious mother), and my father Leo DuCote.

To my readers and fans, none of this would be possible without your inspiring messages and sweet reviews.

Chapter 1

The chant "Fight!" rang through the air as the children congregated to witness the one-sided battle between Spencer LeJeune and the school bully, Jimmy Pastadoria. And all because of two ducklings.

The altercation started when Jimmy snatched the two yellow ducklings from Spencer's childhood crush, Toni Benoit. Spencer and Toni had been riding through town on their bikes with two little yellow heads stuck out of the basket mounted to Toni's handle bars. When they stopped briefly at Gentry's convenient store, Toni held onto her ducklings, Skip and Mac, and Spencer disappeared inside for two icees. Coming back out, Spencer found Jimmy holding both ducks up in the air and out of Toni's reach. "Say goodbye to these two little quackers," he taunted.

The ducks were an Easter gift for Toni, and when they were grown, she wanted to release them in the city park pond. But standing in front of the convenience store, she was now possibly witnessing the demise of her two beloved pets.

"Put 'em down, Jimmy." Spencer growled at him. Jimmy just laughed at his persistence.

Spencer had grown up in the small town, and as an only child, his father, Steve, had sheltered him and stepped in to interrupt many of his conflicts, but his dad was nowhere around this day. At the age of ten, he had not developed as fast as the other kids and was at least three inches shorter than the next shortest boy in his class, so his size was definitely hindering his chances in today's fight.

Toni lived only a few streets over from Spencer and had known him her whole life, all ten years of it. They had spent countless hours running the coastline and levees while fishing, catching frogs, and setting nets for crawfish. At an early age, though, she was already catching the attention of boys in her class with her long dark hair and hazel eyes, and being the captain of their peewee cheer squad heightened her popularity. Toni carried the disposition of a little girl, but packed the punch of the toughest linebacker; however, she was no match for Jimmy Pastadoria.

She retrieved Skip and Mac, but at the expense of witnessing her best friend receive the worst beating of his life.

Jimmy, who was now sitting on top of Spencer, had gotten tired of punching him in the face and had begun applying as much pressure as he could muster to Spencer's arm, seeing if he could snap it in half. Just before Spencer thought his arm was going to be torn off—

"Hey! Get up from there!" Old Man Gentry, the store clerk, snatched Jimmy off Spencer.

"Hey, let go of me! I'll get my dad and he'll teach you not to touch me!" Jimmy yelled at the old gray-haired man who held a tight grip on him.

"You go get your daddy. He needs a beatin' too just for letting you out of your house! Now you go on from here, and if I catch you back around I'll let the sheriff deal with you. You hear?"

Jimmy pulled his arm from the death grip the old man had on him. "Come on, they're just a bunch of losers," he told his two wanna-be friends that followed everywhere he went.

Spencer's eye had already closed with the swelling, and blood dripped from his lips and nose. "Spencer, I'm so sorry. Here are your glasses," Toni said while cuddling the two little balls of yellow feathers and handing him a broken pair of rimmed glasses.

"You kids come in the store and let me get some ice on that there eye," the man insisted. Spencer wanted to cry, but was too scared that his eye would hurt worse, so he fought back the tears. He grimaced at the pain as the old man helped him into the store, followed by his secret crush and two ducks.

"My daddy is gonna be mad at me," he said, looking at his glasses.

"I don't think so. That was a brave thing to protect your friend. I suspect he'll be proud. I know I am." The old man tried lifting Spencer's spirits.

After sitting him on a stool and placing a bag of ice on his eye, the old man put down a bowl of water for the ducks. Once he saw the mess they were making, he handed Toni a towel and she began to dry off the ducks while ignoring the puddles on the dark old wooden floor.

"I give you that towel to clean the water off the floor," the old man smiled.

"I know," she replied, clueless.

"She doesn't like for 'em to get wet," Spencer spoke up, referring to the ducks.

"Them birds are waterproof—you don't have to worry about 'em getting wet."

"I know," she shyly replied again.

Just as the man pulled the bag from Spencer to examine his eye, they noticed a dusty white truck pulling up to the front door with a center-console boat on a trailer behind it. It was Spencer's dad. Before the rig could rest at a stop, the front door swung open and in walked a tan-faced man with sunglasses dangling around his neck. "You OK, boy?" his father asked.

"Yes, sir," Spencer replied in a soft tone.

"What happened?" Steve asked the clerk.

"Your boy took up for this young lady and her ducks. He got the worst end of it, but stood his ground."

Steve pulled the bag from his son's bruised face and looked at his painfully swollen eye. "You're gonna have a black eye for a while. Let's get to the house and put some meat on it."

"Thank you for your help, Mr. Gentry," Steve said to the old man.

"Any time," the old man replied with a chuckle.

Steve loaded the two bikes into the back of the truck and with two kids and two ducks, they started home. They passed the marina where Steve worked out of, the white dust kicking up from the mud tires on his truck as they sped down the seashell road. The boat behind them weaved side to side as they drove over the speed limit—the only outward indication of Steve's anger at the situation.

Steve spent most of his time in the 22-foot center-console boat as a marine biologist; he made many trips up the marsh and through the canals that led to the other small local towns. One town he passed on a regular basis was Lafitte, and Spencer loved hearing the stories of the old Haitian voodoo woman who lived there, Lebreaux Papillon. His dad claimed to have met her once and didn't trust her mysterious flair. The next town north was Jean Lafitte, named after the famous pirate. The stories of treasures and battles that were passed around through the oyster boat captains never got old for Spencer and Toni. To Spencer, his dad had the greatest occupation in the world.

"All right, Toni, I'll get your bike," Steve said, parking the truck outside her house.

"Bye, Spencer, and thank you," she said with her arms still around the two ducks. He waved with the bag still on his eye.

"Tell your mama I bring you home, OK?" Steve said in his thick Cajun accent.

"Yes, sir," she said pushing her bike up the gravel driveway.

"Let's go take care of that eye and find your other pair of glasses," he said climbing back in the truck. The tires on the half-ton truck spun out, shooting shells and rocks under the boat and leaving a dust cloud as they jetted home.

Chapter 2

After a few days, Spencer had a bright black and blue left eye, swollen and still so sensitive that he elected not to wear his glasses. He was sitting in front of the TV squinting his right eye and trying to focus on the screen when a light knock came from the front door. Opening it, he found his friend with her two sidekicks.

"Hey, Toni. You can come in, but Dad wants the ducks to stay outside. He says they poop too much." He couldn't see her expression, but could hear her giggling.

"OK, you come outside then." Her soft voice was alluring, so he ducked back inside for his spare pair of glasses and fought through the pain of them resting on his swollen eye.

"Do you want to go search for treasure?" she asked in an excited voice. She could tell he still wasn't his normal ambitious self, but knew he was always interested in hunting for treasure. After a quick discussion, they decided to leave the ducks behind and head to the docks to ask the oyster boat captains if they knew of any. Many times before they had asked the captains for stories, and in response the old men would entertain the two young kids with big stories of sunken Spanish riches and areas haunted by pirates.

Reaching the docks, they noticed Spencer's dad's truck and empty trailer in the parking area—nothing out of the ordinary. With the exception of a couple of vessels that were in for repairs, most of the oyster boats were already out fishing.

Spencer and Toni walked down the dock toward the remaining boats. Only one deckhand was working, but that didn't stop them from asking; surely the captains would share their stories with their deckhands.

"Hey, Mister! Do you know of any sunken treasure?" Spencer asked.

The deckhand, in his late twenties, was covered from head to toe in grease and sweat.

"Where did you get that shiner?" the deckhand asked Spencer while lighting a cigar.

"In a fight."

"Did you win?" he asked. Spencer lowered his head, and the deckhand knew instantly he had asked the wrong question. "Well, next time hit 'em first. Treasure?" he asked, then paused to think for a moment. "No, I can't say I know of any treasures. You two need to ask the old-timers. They ought to be back at dark."

As the two turned to walk back to their bikes, an old Haitian woman stepped in their path. "Treasure, you say?" she asked.

Toni was startled by her appearance—with long gray hair and a long embroidered duster, she looked as if she had just stepped out of a fairytale.

"Yes, ma'am. We're searching," Spencer answered.

"Searching for what?" she quizzed the pair.

Toni grabbed his arm and tried to pull him toward their bikes. "Well, we have heard stories from some of the old-timers about Spanish treasure. Do you know of any?" he asked.

A smile formed across her face as she nodded. "I do."

Spencer looked at Toni, her hand still holding his arm, "Stop pulling on me. She knows where we might find some." He turned his attention back to the old woman. "Where is it?"

"I tell you of great treasure, so big dat da Spaniards couldn't take it in three ships. Right here in Barataria Basin. Come and I show you." With that, she held out her hand to them.

"No, Spencer! We don't know her," Toni objected.

The old woman looked a little offended, but gave her mysterious smile once again. "I am Lebreaux Papillon." She held her hand out further.

At first, Spencer thought he misunderstood her gesture, but then it sank in. He was standing directly in front of the old voodoo woman. Nervously he shook her hand, "I'm Spencer, and this is Toni." He took a deep swallow and asked, "Are you the voodoo woman?" Toni's eyes widened with his question.

Again she smiled. "Some might say dat. But I know no harm. You don't have to go if you don't want." Her expression was nonchalant—take it or leave it.

"We can't be gone long," Spencer said, a hint of uncertainty in his voice.

"We be back before de first gull fly inland," she replied.

Spencer wasn't sure what time that was, but it sounded good to him. With Spencer still pulling Toni by her arm, they stepped down into the wooden skiff. As the old woman cranked the motor, she said, "You two sit, and I'll tell you a story of da barge."

Toni and Spencer spun around on the wooden bench and faced the old woman as the three of them motored slowly toward the Barataria Basin. Pulling past the dock, the deck hand looked on, confused as to why two kids were riding with an old woman.

A few moments after hitting the open bay, she started her story. "Long time way before Jean Lafitte, der was a Spanish expedition dat moved silver and other treasure from Mexico to Spain. One particular fleet came through da gulf; it must have been in da early 1600s. Most people say dey was twenty-eight ships, but dey wrong. Der was thirty-one ships." She held up three fingers. "When all twenty-eight ships sailed from Mexico, dat's where they loaded da treasure, trois ships remained. Now dees Spaniards had in mind to bring all dis treasure back to Spain to der king, but da plunder was so great dat da trois ships couldn't carry it all."

"I've heard this story," Spencer interrupted.

"Ssssh!" Toni elbowed him in the side. She was intently listening.

The old woman laughed at Toni's aggressive curiosity. "Well, you see, dees men ... dey built a big barge dat would hold all der gold and silver, but da barge was so heavy dat it was slow sailing. Dey take da northern route close to da coast so dat no pirates would steal from dem. It was so slow dat dey would sail maybe fifty miles a day. But 'bout da time dey got by Grand Isle, a big storm brewed up from da sea and blowed hard against dem. Da storm sank all trois ships and killed everyone on board."

"But someone survived?" Spencer tried to add to her story.

"Yes, yes, one did make it. A captain of one of doze ships had set two conquistadors on da barge to fight off any pirates if dey came across any. One got himself washed over during da big storm and da other, he hid with da treasure. For four nights he got himself tossed and turned until da fifth day he found himself sinking with da barge in Barataria Bay. He know dat da barge would soon be gone, so he grab a handful of silver coins and swam north. He came across many native people—da first was Houma Indian people, and he tell dem of da barge and bring dem da silver coins, all but one. It take him three years to reach East to a Spanish fort. Dey thought he was native, but he show dem da silver coin. Now dey send him back to Spain and he tell dem his story. For five years those Spaniards try to find da barge, but never did."

She stopped the skiff and turned off the engine. "You see, da barge … it's out der." She pointed toward the bay.

"Do you know where?" Spencer asked.

"You gonna find it."

"OK! When and how?"

"You will know," she added.

"If you don't know where it is, why did you bring us out here?" Toni asked.

"Because, child, too many ears on dat dock." She paused a moment, looking at the pair. "Boy, you will need dis." She handed him a badly tarnished and dented silver coin. "Don't tell nobody about this," she said. Both Spencer and Toni stared wide-eyed at the coin that now rested in the palm of the ten-year-old boy.

"Why isn't it round?" Spencer examined the coin.

"Dat's for you to find out," she answered.

Catching their attention, she gave them a firm stare. "Now look at me eyes and show me your palms." Spencer tucked the old silver coin into the pocket of his faded old blue jeans and volunteered his hand first for the old woman to examine. Toni reluctantly lifted her palm to the strange woman's gaze. "Ahh, you two will be together." She lowered their hands, still holding them in her firm grip. "You two hold da secret. Keep it dat way."

She looked West at the sun as it started to settle into an orange glow. "We better be getting back."

"One more ting—de mark ... is on da *Potosi*."

Chapter 3

Toni wanted to become a veterinarian more than anything in her childhood world. She was going to fix the stray problem and help dogs and cats all across the country, but for the time being, she was having trouble keeping her two ducks out of trouble—and dry.

"You know ducks are *supposed* to be wet?" Spencer said, stopping his bike just shy of her front porch.

"I know," she replied still drying the scrambling bird. The other duck was standing close to the cage with feathers tangled and sticking up in all directions from being dried off with Toni's towel.

"You want to go check on our hidden coin?" he asked.

She gave him a funny look. "It won't be much hidden if we go check on it all the time."

"OK, what do you want to do?"

"I don't know," she said, releasing the second duck with messy feathers.

Just then, a dusty white truck slid to a stop in front of Toni's house. "Hey bud, climb in. You're going with me," Steve shouted from the rolled down window.

"Toni, are your folks home?" he asked.

"Yes, sir," she shouted back.

"Tell them a big storm is coming and to batten down," he said, stepping out and loading Spencer's bike in the back.

Once they were in the truck, Spencer asked, "How big is the storm?"

"It's not huge, but it's like a buzz saw. It's coming across Florida right now. Let's go help get the docks ready," Steve said.

At the docks, the news had already spread, and many of the oyster boats were pulling out and heading up the canals deeper into the mainland. The coastal captains knew their chances of saving boats were higher if they went inland, hoping the winds and surges were not as bad. Already the wind had picked up, and people were scrambling on the docks to get fuel and board up what they could.

"Say, you're that kid who asked about treasures the other day. Where did that old lady take you and the little girl?" the deckhand asked as Steve and Spencer walked to the marina store.

Steve stopped and looked at Spencer. "What old lady?" he asked.

"We went with a lady to look at the marsh the other day," Spencer answered. He didn't want to tell him who he had been with, in fear of getting punished.

"What have I told you about riding with strangers? We'll talk about this later." His dad pressed on to help board up the marina store.

Spencer was hoping his dad would forget about the whole incident, but it wasn't five minutes before Steve brought it back up. "Who was the lady?" he asked.

Spencer had learned one thing early in life, and that was not to lie to his father—but this time was tempting. "She said her name was Lebreaux."

"Lebreaux Papillon!?" his father exclaimed in a loud voice.

Spencer lowered his head. "Yes, sir."

"Out of all the old ladies, you choose a voodoo woman to go with!?" He put down the hammer in his hand and paced in a circle on the dock. It was obvious to everyone around he was mad about something. "I promised your mother on her death bed that I wouldn't let anything happen to you. And this? A voodoo woman!?"

It was no surprise to Spencer that his dad was very superstitious. It was also obvious that his punishment was coming, so he said a quick prayer and then waited. But nothing happened.

Finally Steve took a knee in front of him. "Never again ride with someone you don't know. OK?" Steve said.

"Yes, sir."

"I've lost your mother, and I'm not interested in losing you too." As Spencer looked up into his dad's face, he saw his dad's eyes begin to water.

Two years ago, when Spencer was eight years old, his mother had passed away from an infection she developed from a deep gash in her thigh. She was in Steve's shop trying to pull out a shovel when she tripped over a hose and landed on a lawn mower blade that Steve had been sharpening. He never expected anyone to go in the shop and held himself responsible for leaving the blade sticking up from a block of wood. He spent many sleepless nights blaming himself—if only he had put the blade on the wall, he would not have lost the love of his life. Now two years later, Steve's boat carried the name "Magi," after his wife of nearly fourteen years.

The LeJeune family had resided in south Louisiana since their ancestors came down from the Chicago area in the mid-1800s. Steve had received his degree in marine biology at LSU, and he met Magi, who was from Monroe, during his last year. They dated a few years before they decided to marry and move to Buras for Steve's new job with the state as one of the biologists in the southern marsh. They had been through many storms together, but this would be his first without her.

"Dad, do you think everything will be OK?" Spencer asked, sensing his dad's urgency.

"Yeah, sport, everyone will be just fine. We just want to make sure." Steve believed in working hard and that a little sweat was good for everyone. Now he was a ball of sweat as he helped the fishermen and the marina workers prepare for one of the worst storms—hurricane Andrew—to hit Louisiana.

It was early in the morning when the eye of the storm passed west of Buras leaving plenty of damage, but thankfully not as bad as most people had prepared for. Spencer never went to sleep that night. With the howling winds beating against the shutters that covered their living room windows, every loud noise brought visions of their house being sucked into the sky or swept away.

The house rested on stilts to protect it from storm surges, and with the high winds that Andrew brought, the stilts paid off with water accumulating a foot deep underneath. Steve stood at the back door for hours staring out at the rain steadily falling, and the debris that would occasionally fly by. Once, Spencer heard him whisper, "Thank you, Magi." He thought his dad was thanking her for watching out for them.

"Dad, do you think Perino road is under water?" Spencer asked.

"Yeah, I bet it is. Why?" Steve asked.

"Dang it!" Spencer said getting up from the couch. "Me and Toni hid something there."

"What's that?" his dad asked.

"It's nothing." He didn't want to tell him about the coin and remind him of Lebreaux.

The rest of the day they watched as more rain fell and debris floated by. The water would claim many of the low-lying houses, but they were safe—father and son, silently watching their world change before them.

Chapter 4

Once Andrew sawed through the area and moved north, and the water had receded enough that only puddles were left, Spencer walked his bike down the steps of his house and rode to Toni's. Peddling through the streets and around trees and debris, he couldn't believe what he saw; he had been through a few storms, but nothing like this.

The closer he got to Toni's, the more worried he became with all the destruction, and soon found himself standing up to peddle faster. Turning the corner into her driveway, he saw that the water hadn't reached the house, but part of the roof was missing. Her father and older brother had already nailed blue tarps over the opening and had started piling debris in the front yard.

Toni, who seemed blissfully oblivious to her surroundings, was sitting on the front porch playing with Skip and Mac. "Hey we need to check on the coin! Dad thinks that Perino Road was underwater."

"Did you tell him about the coin?" she asked.

"No, you wanna go?" he persisted.

She stood to her feet and picked up her two yellow-feathered friends. "OK, let me put them in their cage," she said, disappearing inside.

Running back out, she jumped from the porch, bypassing the steps, and grabbed her bike. Racing toward Perino road, Spencer was finding it harder and harder to keep up with her on his bike.

"Slow down," he yelled.

"Come on, Spencer. You got to go faster," she replied, barely out of breath. He was starting to become frustrated with the fact that a girl could outride him.

Pulling down Perino Road, they saw evidence that the surge had reached the bush where they had hidden the silver coin. They had both agreed that it would be safer in a leather pouch and sealed in a ziplock bag, but they never thought the area would flood. Toni pulled back the piles of limbs and seaweed that had accumulated around the bush and started digging, but didn't have to go far: Their fear came true once they realized it was gone. To their disadvantage, the ziplock bag had become buoyant, and once the water rose, the coin went with it.

"What are we going to do? We'll never find the treasure now!" Spencer paced in circles, very similar to what he had witnessed his father doing the day before.

"Calm down and let me think." Toni was studying the layout of the land and the debris.

"You see how all these sticks and seaweed are facing away from the bushes?" she asked Spencer, who wasn't calming down.

"Yeah, so?"

"Well, that means that it floated that way." She pointed southwest.

"That's a lot of that way," Spencer replied, looking toward an open bay.

"I bet if we find Lebreaux and tell her, she'll help us find it," Toni replied.

"No way! We tell her and she'll put a curse on us, and if her curse don't work, then my daddy's belt will. Screw the treasure!" Spencer was set.

"Spencer LeJeune! You watch your mouth and stop being a scaredy cat! We are gonna find her." She pointed her finger at him.

He knew the wrath of his dad's leather belt and was obstinate about not looking for Lebreaux. But now he wasn't sure who had the stronger spell, the voodoo woman or Toni Benoit's hazel eyes. After kicking a few big rocks and thinking about how he could pad his butt without his dad knowing, he agreed to follow the little dark-haired girl to find the one person his father warned him about.

On their way to the docks, they rode on the side of the road looking out over a long field. It was lined with a few medium-sized boats that had washed ashore during the surge. Once they reached the docks, Spencer saw something he wasn't anticipating—his dad's truck and trailer. *Maybe he's already out in his boat,* he thought. Having the luck of a ten-year-old boy in the middle of mischievous behavior, though, instead he found his dad standing on the dock, all tall and noticeable.

"Hey kids, you shouldn't be here," Steve said as soon as they rode their bikes up. Spencer instantly knew something was wrong; his dad always started his conversation with the word "sport."

"Why?" he asked.

"Well, son, things didn't turn out as we would have liked them to." He started walking them back to the parking lot as they slowly peddled their bikes.

Toni looked over her shoulder and saw the skiff being raised out of the water. "Hey! That's Lebreaux's boat."

Spencer hit the brakes on his bike, causing his dad to trip over him. "What are y'all doing with her boat?" Spencer asked.

"Kids, I'm sorry to say that Lebreaux was caught out in the storm, and we don't think she made it."

"She died?" Toni asked wide-eyed as she stood staring at the boat.

"Probably so. A few of the fishermen found her skiff floating near the big island."

"But she wasn't in it?" Toni continued.

"No, but that water was pretty bad, so odds are she didn't survive. You two head home, and I'll be there shortly." He gave them a slight push. Steve had grown impervious to death since losing Magi and didn't realize how his lack of emotions affected others.

"Man, I can't believe our luck," Spencer said as they peddled off.

"Our luck! You're always worried about treasure and not others. Lebreaux *died*! Doesn't that bother you? I swear, Spencer LeJeune, sometimes I wonder why I hang out with you!" she snapped at him, shooting him a fiery look. Then she flipped her hair in the opposite direction and pointed her bike home.

"I didn't mean anything by it!" He shouted back at her, but decided not to pursue her.

Within another block, Spencer heard the familiar sound of his dad's truck tires roaring from the road as he slowed down to collect his son.

"Where's Toni?"

"I said something dumb and made her mad."

"Well, I'm sure you two will work it out," Steve answered.

"Is the sheriff gonna go tell her family?" Spencer asked. That question made him remember the visit he got when the sheriff picked him up from school the day his mother passed away.

"I don't believe she had family. That would be up to the Jefferson Parish sheriff, where she supposedly lived."

"I thought you said she had a brother?" Spencer asked, thinking back on a story he once heard.

"Well, she claimed to be the sister of a man named Jean-Francois, but when locals looked into it, they found that he was a rebel slave that lived in the late 1700s. She was a little crazy. But I am sorry she died."

Spencer sat quietly looking out the window at part of the ruins of Plaquemine Parish and thought about the missing coin. He was disappointed; Lebreaux had trusted them and they had let her down. Now she was gone, and he wouldn't have the opportunity to tell her he was sorry for losing it. He also thought about Toni and how he could make it up to her for making her mad. She was spending more time with the cheerleaders, but maybe once school started back, they would be eating lunch together again.

Little did Spencer realize that the chaotic day would begin a slow fading of their friendship. Toni was beginning to hang with the popular crowd, and he still hadn't grown any taller, leaving him at the lunch table with a few other boys and girls that didn't fit in. Their days of treasure hunting, bike riding, fishing, and riding in the boat through the marsh would soon be replaced with cheerleading, sports, and boyfriends. The vision of her riding away angrily with her hair flowing back and forth would be painted in his memories for a long time to come.

"Maybe you and Toni can go with me to check on my traps in the east bay tomorrow," Steve commented.

"Yeah, maybe so," Spencer replied.

Chapter 5

Years later, as a sophomore in high school, Spencer hadn't grown much taller than he had in the eighth grade, and with his stature came the absence of his popularity. He found himself with the other outcasts during lunch. In sharp contrast, Toni's popularity only grew, now that she was dating the star football player, Jimmy Pastadoria. The friendship between Toni and Spencer had grown from spending almost all their free time together to exchanging hellos in the hallway of Buras High School. Toni had become a beautiful young lady that every boy in school dreamed of dating, but in fear of Jimmy most boys wouldn't acknowledge her.

Thankfully one thing hadn't changed from Toni's youthful demeanor—her love for animals and her goal to one day practice veterinarian medicine. Skip and Mac had been turned loose in the city park pond years earlier, and she made frequent trips to feed them and their family.

Spencer had never lost his crush on Toni and spent days watching from a distance, wondering if they would ever return to the friendship they once had. With few friends, he began spending his time writing down the stories he had heard while growing up on the docks and the mysterious dreams he had about Lebreaux since her disappearance. His stories started off short and simple and quickly grew into novelettes about pirates, treasure, voodoo queens, and there was always a princess in need of rescuing.

He had become fascinated while studying the histories of Henry Morgan, Jean Lafitte, and even Jean Francois Papillon. Though he would often research the family history of Jean Francois in search for Lebreaux, he would always come up empty. Still, countless hours were spent daydreaming of finding evidence of Lebreaux during the days of Jean Lafitte. The hours that weren't spent planning his short stories about pirate treasure were spent on Toni and what could have—and should have—been.

Steve, who had remained single, encouraged Spencer to write and paid to have his first book, a compilation of short stories, published. *Pirates and Voodoo* became the best-selling book in old man Gentry's store with fourteen copies sold. Spencer wasn't concerned that people weren't interested in his book, but he did keep track of everyone who bought it. By the end of the first year, every book was accounted for but one, and he was determined to find out who bought the missing copy.

Spencer had also fallen in love with his dad's occupation and continued to accompany him on most trips to the marsh, helping record the growth of marine life. It seemed the fastest growth of marsh life was one that many didn't want, the nutria rat. It had been brought to Central America in the mid-nineteenth century by fur farmers, and as their business became extinct, they released their rats, not knowing of their rapid reproduction. Now, the furry critters were destroying the marsh and most of the vegetation life that once was more than abundant.

But, out of the many jobs his father had in the marsh, Spencer's favorite studies were the dolphin population of Barataria Bay. After his dad upgraded his 22-foot center-console for a 32-foot Yellowfin center-console with twin 300 Verados engines, they would run the bay in search of dolphin pods, often attracting them to swim under the hull.

It was on a fall day of his sophomore year when Spencer returned home from school to find his dad waiting for him at the kitchen table. The table was normally the spot where they would have life lessons and family business, along with many frozen meals. But this day, things would change.

"What are you doing home so early?" Spencer asked, throwing his backpack on the counter top.

"We need to have a talk," his dad replied.

"I gassed the boat up last time I used it," he responded.

His dad smiled. "It's not that. I have been offered a job with a larger salary," Steve started.

"That's great!" Spencer said, clueless about why that was so important.

"Yes it is. The thing is that it's in Jacksonville, Florida."

Spencer stopped searching the refrigerator and looked back around the door at the table. "Really? Wow!" He sat down.

"Now, if you don't want to go, then I'll tell 'em no and we'll stay here."

"I don't know, I mean, I don't have much here. But Jacksonville, wow!" Spencer was fathoming the idea.

"When would we leave?"

"Two weeks."

"What about our house?"

His dad smiled again. "We'll keep it—we'll be able to afford it. Plus we'll need a place to stay when we come back to visit," his father answered.

"As long as we can come back to visit … then I say, yes. Let's go." Spencer began to get excited.

"And you're sure you're good with this?"

"Yeah, let's call it our adventure." Spencer reached out to shake on the deal.

Later that night Spencer thought about their decision on moving and the repercussions it would have on the few friends he had. *Ahhh, who's going to miss me anyways? I can write about the pirates on the Atlantic coast.*

It was the beginning of his last week, and he had planned to tell Toni about his plans of moving to Jacksonville.

Pulling his tray from the cashier, he glanced over to see Toni sitting at her normal table with Jimmy's arm around her waist. Spencer wound his way through the tables that littered the cafeteria where other high school students were eating lunch. Toni noticed Spencer walking up to their table and greeted him with a warm smile, one that he hadn't seen in a while.

"What do you want?" Jimmy asked, not paying him any attention.

"Do you have a minute?" he asked Toni.

"Sure." She climbed out of her seat.

"What? You can't say it for all of us to hear?" Jimmy spouted off.

"Chill," Toni said, looking at Jimmy.

The two of them walked the short distance toward the double doors leading out of the cafeteria.

As soon as they were alone in the hallway, Spencer turned to face her. "I wanted to tell you that my dad and I are moving to Jacksonville, Florida."

"Wow, when?" she asked.

"Next week."

"This is quick. Did you just find out?"

"No, I've known for a couple of weeks," he replied.

"Why didn't you tell me sooner?" she asked, confused.

"Well, we really don't talk anymore," he answered. Toni looked down at the floor, and with her expression—was it sadness or guilt?—Spencer knew she was agreeing.

"Good luck to you, Spencer. I hope everything works out for the best, and please promise you'll come back and visit."

"We will," he replied.

Toni reached around him and drew him in for one last hug, sending the wrong message to her boyfriend. Just as they embraced, the door swung open as a girl exited the cafeteria and Jimmy's table had a perfect view of the childhood friends saying goodbye.

"You going to let that book geek hug your girl in front of everyone?" another boy taunted Jimmy.

"Hell, no!" he replied, picking up a roll covered with mashed potatoes and gravy. Pieces of potatoes and gravy splattered the cafeteria as the roll hurled toward the back of Spencer's head. An explosion of food erupted on impact as the roll slammed into Spencer's dark curly hair. The cafeteria went silent, then surged with laughter once everyone saw the mess.

Spencer helplessly looked at a very surprised Toni. "You know, I'm not going to miss this place," he replied, wiping the potatoes from his hair.

"Jimmy! That was cruel!" Toni yelled at Jimmy, who was approaching them.

"Sorry, LeJeune," Jimmy said, laughing.

"That's OK—I know you can't help being an asshole," Spencer said.

The laughing stopped as Jimmy grabbed Spencer's shirt. "What?" He picked his feet off the ground.

"Stop it, Jimmy!" Toni pulled at Jimmy's arm.

"Tell this little fruitcake to apologize and I will." A firm tap on Jimmy's shoulder from one of the teachers forced him to turn to find a grim look and a motion for him to follow.

"This isn't over, LeJeune." He released Jimmy and followed the teacher out the double doors.

"What do you see in that jerk?" Spencer asked.

"I'm sorry," Toni replied, not answering the question.

"Well, have a good life," Spencer replied as he walked out the cafeteria doors and out of Toni Benoit's world.

The following Saturday, Steve hooked up their boat, the Magi 2, and followed the moving truck out of Buras, Louisiana. Spencer watched as the welcome sign vanished in the distance and then turned to face the road ahead, wondering what his new life would hold.

Chapter 6

It had been just over twenty years since Spencer had been back to Buras, and now in his mid-thirties he was amazed at the growth and change. Remnants of buildings and structures that Hurricane Katrina had claimed in 2005 were slowly disappearing with the construction of new homes and businesses.

Spencer was astonished at the deterioration of the marsh due to the oil spills and nutria rats, and drove slowly to take it all in as he crossed the waterways and bridges driving toward his hometown. His four-door three-quarter-ton truck came to a crawl as he passed the docks that once housed over a hundred commercial boats. Now there were only about twenty sitting idle until oyster season opened in September.

Spencer loved the attitude of the Cajun people—no matter what storm or oil spill was in front of them, they would never give up—but unfortunately some were going broke.

He parked his red truck and his matching red 42-foot Yellowfin center-console boat outside the marina store. He immediately recognized the owner as he walked out of the weather-beaten marina store. "Boy, that's a nice boat! Four Yamaha 350s should get you here to Grand Isle and back in the blink of an eye," the man greeted him.

Spencer realized the man didn't recognize him, and he could understand why; when he left Buras at the age of fifteen, he wasn't much taller than a middle-school kid. Now standing 6'2" and having spent the last fifteen years in the gym on a daily basis, he had transformed into the man he was now—the man he'd always wanted to be. Just like his dad.

"You want to dock that vessel here?" the man asked.

"Yes sir. You don't remember me?" Spencer asked.

The man looked him over. "No, I'm sorry."

"Spencer LeJeune. Steve was my father," he replied.

"Holy cow, son. You grew up! How's your father?" the man asked.

Spencer looked down at the shells that were crushed to pave the parking lot. "Dad went on to be with Mom six months ago," he responded.

He thought the news would have made it back to Buras, but it obviously hadn't made it to the marina.

"I'm sorry to hear that. Your daddy was a good man and did a lot of good here for the oyster boats. What are you doing back?" he asked Spencer.

"Following in Dad's footsteps. I've been hired to help with the population of bottlenose dolphins and to help keep records of the oyster beds."

Steve LeJeune had built up a great reputation as a marine biologist, and the work he had done in Florida preceded him. With Steve's reputation, the combination of the state of Louisiana, and the oil companies, Spencer had been hired to return to his home and help with the oyster industry.

The man walked beside the 42-foot beast that was waiting to be launched with an admiring look. "Man, this sure is a big boat for biology work."

"Yeah, Dad always said go big," Spencer said, pulling out his wallet. "What do I owe you to launch?" he asked the man.

"Nothing, and the first month is on the house—glad to have you back." He patted Spencer on the back.

Once he got the monstrosity in the water and tied up to dock #4, Spencer headed to their old house—now his. Pulling up to the small blue house on stilts, Spencer's memory kicked in, and flashbacks of his childhood flipped through his mind like a slide show.

The house had been used as rental property the last twenty years for fishermen who came to Buras for vacations. It had been well kept up and freshly mowed, and as he looked at the front porch, he remembered the countless times he pushed his bike up and down the stairs that led to the sliding glass front door.

Now standing on the front porch, he could see the bay with the sun starting its descent into the water. He had seen thousands of sunsets, but had never grown to appreciate them—except for one.

Leaning on the railing, he thought back to when his mother had passed away. Many people, including the local priest, had tried to comfort him, but everyone seemed to be filled with words and ideas of what to do, and as a young boy direction wasn't what he wanted.

One evening he snuck away to the pier that stretched into the bay farther than any others in town; just down the street from his house. He found himself alone, the very thing he wanted. Sitting on the end of the dock with his legs hanging over the side, he had watched, heartbroken and lost, as the sun began its track to disappear beyond the horizon. He never heard the light footsteps approaching from behind.

"Hey, Spencer," Toni softly spoke.

He didn't want her to see the tears in his eyes and quickly wiped them away.

"Can I sit beside you?" she asked.

"Sure."

With her legs hanging over the side beside his, she remained silent, not moving, not saying a word—just sitting quietly beside her best friend.

As the sun dipped into the bay she placed her hand on top of his, turning his palm up so their hands locked. Moments later, once the sun had disappeared, he wasn't sure why, but tears began running down his face uncontrollably until he found himself sobbing.

Still, she didn't say anything. She simply moved closer and put her arm around him and let him cry on her shoulder—a kind act that burrowed deep into his heart and a sunset that burned into his memory.

That was a long time ago. I wonder where she is now, he thought. He had heard that she had graduated from LSU with a veterinary degree, returned home to run the parish clinic, and had remained single. He was surprised at that last bit of news—a trait they had in common.

Spencer didn't try to make contact with her and wasn't sure if she even remembered him. But he knew that in a small town they would definitely run into each other, and he didn't have a clue what he would say.

Walking into the house, he was surprised to find the furniture in the same place with the wall colors unchanged. He set his soft leather briefcase down on the kitchen table and made his way to the back bedrooms, his eyes beginning to water up. *Wow! I didn't think it would bother me. Mom, Pops ... I sure miss you.*

He walked back into the kitchen and examined the 1950s refrigerator he'd had delivered prior to arriving. *I bet they struggled getting that up the steps.* With it empty, he climbed back into his truck and headed toward the local store to pick up a few things until he could get to a grocery store.

Passing by what was left of the high school, he thought about the times he had there, nothing he missed. Easing the three-quarter-ton red truck to a stop outside the old brick, tin-roofed store, he noticed the name *Gentry's Store* was still on the building. *Surely Mr. Gentry isn't still alive?*

"How ya doing?" the old man said from behind the counter as he walked in.

"Mr. Gentry?" Spencer asked in disbelief.

"Yes?" he answered Spencer.

"You don't remember me?" Spencer questioned him.

Mr. Gentry squinted his eyes and studied him for a short moment. "I sure do. Why, it seems like just the other day I was putting ice on that eye of yours."

"Yes sir," Spencer laughed.

"You're big enough now you won't be needing any ice," Mr. Gentry replied.

"No sir, don't plan on fighting," he said, making his way to the bread.

"Glad to have you back. Sorry to hear about your dad; he was a good man."

"Thanks." *I guess they did get the news.*

"How long you back for?"

"A while. I accepted a job here with the state." He grabbed a few bottles of water and two sticks of beef jerky.

"That little girl you ran with back then has made a pretty good vet now. Saving all the animals she can. Pretty thing, too." Spencer just smiled and placed the items on the counter.

"You want me to start a tab?" Mr. Gentry asked.

"No, I'll just pay as I go. Thank you, though." Spencer looked back at the rack that still held three of his books. *I can't believe he still has them out.* He grabbed the brown paper bag, nodded goodbye, and pushed on the wooden screen door leading out.

After returning to his house and setting the bag on the kitchen counter, he walked to the front porch to watch the final sunset. Leaning over the railing and admiring the sky exploding into a bright fire-touched orange, he said a little prayer about meeting Toni again.

When the sun had vanished, he stood up and reached into his left pocket and pulled out a tarnished old silver coin. He chuckled to himself. *Thanks, Lebreaux!*

Chapter 7

Spencer idled slowly up to the dock holding a white line in his hand. With a few inches from the boat touching the dock, he stepped off and pushed against the hull to keep from ramming into the pier. After tying to the cleats, he jumped back down into the 42' Yellowfin and gathered his gear.

"So I heard young LeJeune has returned to pick up on his dad's work," a dark leathery skinned captain said. His cigar was unlit and hanging from the side of his mouth.

Spencer looked at him for a brief moment, trying to recall the familiar face. "I guess so."

"It's been some time and I've weathered a bit," the man said, knowing he wasn't recognized. "I was the deckhand here for a few years while you ran the docks as a little boy."

Then it hit Spencer. "Yeah, I remember you now. You've got your own boat, I see. Dusty, right?"

"Good memory, Captain Dusty McCormick." They shook hands.

"I'm glad to see a LeJeune here. These oyster beds need better reports than we've been getting. I believe there's more than they lead us to believe," he said, lighting his cigar.

"Well, I hope I can help."

"Heard you're gonna help with the dolphins too."

"Yes, that's the plan," Spencer replied, wondering where Dusty got his information from.

"You'll have a good vet to help with that. You two still talk?" referring to Toni.

"No, I haven't talked to Toni since high school."

"She's a good girl. I coached a little after you left and got to know the kids pretty well. I was sure glad when she broke it off with that Pastadoria boy."

Spencer laughed. "How long did that last?" he asked.

"For a couple of years during high school. He chased her to college, but I think he got the message after a couple of years that she wasn't interested." He took a long drag off his cheap cigar.

"Well, I've been gone a long time. I don't know a whole lot of people here anymore."

"We can change that. A few captains are having a crawfish boil tonight; bring your beer and appetite around 7:30." He turned to walk back to his boat.

Spencer hadn't had crawfish in a while, and to him there was nothing better than hot crawfish and cold beer. He watched as Dusty slowly walked back to his 48' custom trawler. The sun and hard work of the fishing industry had taken its toll on him and he looked and acted much older than a forty-something-year-old should. *Nice guy, though. Always had been.*

Spencer finished covering the console in his boat, picked up his two duffle bags, and stepped out onto the dock. He thought that he had better run by the store to grab his beer before heading home. *If I hurry I can still get in a run*, he thought, tossing the bags in the back seat.

After setting the beer in the 1950's fridge and changing into his running clothes, he tied his shoes and stretched on the bottom two steps of his house. Then, lifting his arms up, he rotated his head in a circle, popping his neck. With a slow jog he ran to the end of his street and then toward the city park.

He had turned his smart phone to his favorite radio station and listened to the theme songs to *Pirates* and other movies by famous composers. His favorite composer, Michael Curry, was the second song and it inspired him to make his run a little longer than planned.

Ten minutes into his run, he was in the zone. He thought about the latest book he had written—it was the sixth book in the series he had started in high school, *Pirates and Voodoo*. Publishing his own books for years now, he enjoyed writing about pirates, treasure, and the mysterious voodoo woman who frequently visited his dreams. Another inspiring musical piece started, and the timing couldn't have been better as he turned into the park and toward the city pond.

He jogged down one of the paved paths and noticed a beautiful woman sitting on a park bench with a loaf of bread in hand, throwing small pieces toward a flock of white ducks. Some of the birds were walking under her legs, eating the crumbs that hit the ground below her. As he got closer, he could see she was wearing white shorts and a gray tank top, with hair dark hair pulled back and aviator sunglasses blocking his view of her eyes.

She looked in his direction and then looked back down at the ducks that were gathered under her. She didn't recognize him at first. But he knew her in an instant. As the music in his ears became louder, the piano and violin dueled against each other, creating the perfect crescendo to their meeting.

It had been nearly twenty years since they last saw each other, and he figured she would be like everyone else and not recognize him. But something about him was familiar—too familiar to forget.

She watched him approach as she pulled a slice of bread apart and broke it into small pieces. Her skin was dark and flawless, and her hair was as long and shiny as he remembered; he wished she weren't wearing sunglasses so he could see her hazel eyes.

Coming closer, he smiled as she pulled down her sunglasses. "Spencer?"

You've got to be kidding me! It's been twenty years. He wasn't sure whether to play it cool and act as though he didn't recognize her, or say hi. He pulled up and stopped. "Hi, Toni."

"Oh, my gosh! It *is* you! I heard you were coming back. Look at you; you look great." She stood to hug him.

"I'm kinda sweaty," he said, giving her a side arm hug.

"How have you been?" she said with a hint of excitement in her voice.

"Good. And you?" he asked.

"Sit down and talk to me. It's been a long time. I heard you finished grad school in marine biology."

Wow, how would she know that? "Yeah, following my dad's footsteps."

"I'm sorry to hear about your dad."

"Me too. So Dusty tells me you're a vet now," he said playing it cool, although he was nearly giddy at seeing her again.

"I am. Chasing that childhood dream." She smiled.

He pointed to the white ducks swimming in front of them. "Are these from Skip and Mac?" He asked.

"Yeah, can you believe that?" she said.

"They survived Katrina?" he asked.

She smiled. "Yeah, with me in a hotel room in Bossier City!"

"That sounds like you, always saving animals," he said. She laughed.

"So LSU?" he asked.

"Yep, love purple, live gold. I enjoyed my time there. I pledged Zeta and did the Greek thing for four years. I had planned to move to north Louisiana after graduating, but this position came available, and well, you know, home is home."

He knew home was home—all too well; he had memories, but they weren't great. But for him, moving to Jacksonville had turned out to be a positive move. He had started running track for the high school and turned out to be a decent runner his first year.

"So what was Florida like?" she asked.

"The water was clearer," he began. "It was good—I spent most of my time on the water." He looked at his watch and realized it was close to 7:00.

"Oh, I didn't realize what time it is. I have plans later so I'd better finish my run," he said, standing. "It was good seeing you."

"Yeah, you too," she answered. "If you're not busy tomorrow, you should come by the clinic."

39

He shook his head to confirm. "OK, I don't know what time I'll be back in, but I'll try."

Turning to finish his run, he put his ear buds back in and picked up his pace. *Wow, she looks good,* he thought. Then just as quickly, his mind corrected his heart. *Stay on task; don't let feelings make you wander from your task.*

Chapter 8

Remnants of the crawfish boil from the night before littered the dock as Spencer pulled his equipment to his boat. Most of the shrimp boats had already left the docks to get an early run before the heat set in.

Spencer had been thinking about seeing Toni at the park and was questioning whether he wanted to stop by the clinic. He walked back to his truck to gather his side-scan sonar and laptop that was neatly tucked away in a waterproof case.

Lugging the equipment back, Dusty stopped washing his boat and called out to Spencer. He'd been cleaning the grease that had accumulated on the floor from his repairs. "That's some sophisticated equipment for checking oyster beds?" His cigar was hanging out of his mouth.

Spencer smiled. "Hard to believe that you haven't blown yourself up with that stogy around all these fumes," he replied.

Dusty just laughed. "Where you heading today?"

"I'm running over to Hackberry Bay."

"Hackberry, in area 13? Is that going to be open this year?"

"I don't know—I just do the reports," Spencer smiled.

Dusty had good reason to ask; the area had been closed to oyster fishing due to the oil spill in 2010. As the third generation of his family to fish the Barataria area, he had survived many storms including Katrina, and nothing was pushing him out.

"What's the dive gear for?" he asked Spencer with a curious look.

"Oyster bed research and recreation, but mostly for oyster beds."

Dusty shook his head in acknowledgment. "You going to the clinic to see that girl today?" he asked.

It threw Spencer that Dusty would know she asked him to stop by. He shrugged. "I've got a long day today."

"So?" Dusty asked.

"Why would you think I would be interested in her?" Spencer asked, wondering if he was overstepping polite conversation.

"Shoot! As a little boy you chased that girl all over the docks and streets."

Smiling, Spencer replied, "Well, that was a long time ago."

"Huh!" Dusty grunted out a sly smile. "You mentioned her four or five times at the crawfish boil last night. But it's none of my business. Be safe out there." He turned to walk back to his boat. Spencer did the same.

Did I mention her too much last night? I did have a few more beers than normal. I hope I didn't say too much. Standing there holding his duffel bag, he wondered, *Did I mention the treasure?*

As Spencer fired up his boat, he thought about how many times he and his dad had left the very same dock, and that thought stirred his childhood memories of returning in the evening. Dusk was Spencer's favorite time, when the water would glow with the lights from other boats and oil derricks scattered throughout the basin. He spun his hat around and throttled down toward a northern bay called Adams, the four Yamaha 350s barely sounding strained as he jetted across the choppy water.

Spencer slowed his speed just as he entered Adams Bay and let the boat drift to a stop. With the sun beaming down, he took off his hat long enough to pull his t-shirt over his head.

To look at him now, you'd never know he used to be a scrawny kid. With a new city and a determination to never be picked on again, Spencer discovered a love of fitness in his late teens. He was well toned and had earned a defined six-pack while swimming and working out. He had even taken up surfing while on the East Coast and spent many days on the beach, drawing attention from quite a few girls. Still an awkward kid at heart, he ignored them for the most part.

In the heat of the afternoon, he made several passes along the shore, dragging the towfish and concentrating on the computer screen as the sonar took three-dimensional pictures of the bay floor. As he made his seventh pass, the sonar picked up on an object that was out of place. *Could that be it? Is this what I'm looking for?* He took a snapshot of the picture and turned the 42' around to make another pass. Looking closer, he could see a square object extruding from the mud, no deeper than fifteen feet.

Spencer pulled out his scuba gear and snapped a bottle to the back of his buoyancy compensator. Blowing up the BC with air, he threw it over the side, picked up his fins and mask, and dove in after it. Once he strapped himself in, he released the air from the BC and kicked toward the structure that his sonar had uncovered.

Within minutes, the wooden structure came into view. It was long and square, sinking farther into the bay floor. Spencer grabbed on the end and pulled himself closer to the wood, his heart pounding and his breathing rapid. He fanned the soot from the wooden object and saw it was intact, but then he saw something small and shiny. The object was round and silver and pressed against one of the wood planks. Pulling himself closer, he saw that it was a screw. He had found a victim from Katrina—someone's sunken pier.

He shot back to the surface, and breaking the water line, he pulled his mask down to his neck. "Well, hell!" Floating behind his boat for a moment, thinking that there would probably be many false alarms, he ran his finger and thumb together, realizing the water seemed slimier than when he was a kid.

Then he heard the faint sound of an outboard motor. That wasn't unusual at all, but the longer he listened, he noticed the motor had a particular tick in the engine. *Where have I heard that before?* he thought.

Growing up around water and all types of boats, Spencer had learned to recognize boats by the sound of the engines. This motor had a familiar sound to it that he hadn't heard since his childhood … the same sound made by Lebreaux's motor on her old wooden skiff. As his mind registered the connection, his eyes widened and he spun in the water looking in all directions, but no boat was in sight.

He wrapped his fins around his wrist, climbed up the ladder on the back of his boat, and let his gear rest on the floor while he wiped the water from his face and hair, still looking for the boat, but finding nothing.

His dark skin shone with the water beading off, thanks to the sunscreen he had applied earlier. Putting his aviator sunglasses on, he saw a white crane flapping its wings in the water. *That's strange,* he thought, and motoring closer, he could see the bird was in distress in only a foot of water. His boat resting gently on the bottom, he leaned over and grabbed the bird that was weak and out of breath.

"Well, buddy, with this broken leg you don't have much chance." With a smile, he looked around, and then back to the bird. "I guess we're going to the veterinary clinic after all."

Chapter 9

As the 42' boat drifted to a stop in front of dock #4, Spencer was greeted by a tall, overweight man with a thick beard and receding hairline. At first Spencer thought he was just admiring his boat until the man put his right foot on the bow.

"So Spencer LeJeune decides to come back," the man said.

Spencer studied the man, trying to recall the familiar voice. Then with a knowing smirk and head gesture, the man smiled, revealing his crooked tooth. "Jimmy?" Spencer asked, shocked.

"You sound surprised," Jimmy replied.

Spencer *was* surprised and started to ask him a question when the white crane began thrashing in the towel he was wrapped up in.

"What'cha got there?" Jimmy asked.

Spencer wasn't sure how this welcome was going to turn out; the last time he saw Jimmy was twenty years ago, and it wasn't on good terms. In fact, Spencer had maintained a mild aversion to mashed potatoes ever since.

"I found this critter near Adams Bay, broken foot," he replied.

"Ha, you always had a thing for birds. Hell, you oughta just shoot the thing."

"That's not how I was raised. What are you doing here?" Spencer asked.

"Someone's gotta field all the complaints about this oil spill that happened three years ago," he answered in a shrewd tone.

"Ah ... so you work for the oil companies?"

"Why else would I care about it?"

Some things never change! Especially this guy, Spencer thought. "Well, I won't keep you from your business," Spencer hinted for him to leave.

But not catching on, Jimmy asked, "What's all that equipment for? Marine biology must have gone all techy," he said, looking into Spencer's boat.

"Well, if there hadn't been such a mess down here with the oil spill, I wouldn't need all this." Spencer was doing his best to get rid of Jimmy.

Jimmy squinted his eyes at the offending remark. "You been gone a long time. Don't get any ideas of coming back and giving these fishermen a bunch of crap that the oil has hurt their fishing ... and don't think Toni is as available as people say," he said, pointing a finger at Spencer.

What? Toni? Where did that come into the conversation? This guy is a bona fide dumbass!

"I'm not sure I understand your idiotic babble, but if you think the oil spill didn't hurt the fishing down here, then you've got some learning to do," Spencer popped back. This time he stepped out of the boat and approached Jimmy; he wasn't losing any more fights to this bully.

Jimmy stood up, surprised by the response he had just heard; he had been the top dog and had his way for the last twenty years on the docks. "You didn't grow up enough to face me!" he snapped back.

"I see you two kids have reunited!" Dusty stepped in between them.

"McCormick, you don't need to be in this!" Jimmy pushed against him.

"I don't think you need to be here," Dusty replied.

"You two are perfect for each other," Jimmy stepped back. "And leave her alone!" he added and walked off.

"That was just weird," Spencer said, looking at Dusty.

"Not for him."

Spencer stepped back down in the boat and tightened the towel around the wounded crane to prevent it from hurting itself.

"Once he graduated from college, which was a miracle in itself, his dad got him a big job with the oil company, and he let it get to his head," Dusty said. "But he's got some pull around here with the bigwigs."

"I don't think I have anything to worry about."

"Well, be careful around him. He put a deckhand in the hospital a few years back and ended his fishing career for asking Toni out. He's crazy!"

"More like dumb," Spencer replied.

"That too," Dusty laughed. "You need help with that bird?"

"Nah, once I get this equipment put away, I'll run him over to the clinic," Spencer said.

"That's a good reason for needing to go to the clinic," Dusty said with a smile, walking back to his boat.

Spencer pulled up to the clinic and barely got parked before the crane thrashed his way free from the towel. After rewrapping him, Spencer walked in, and finding the waiting room empty with no one behind the counter, he hit the silver bell that was sitting beside a waiting list. Before anyone came out, something caught his vision out of the corner of his eye, but turning around, he didn't see anything.

A young girl came to the front. "What can I help you with?"

"I found this crane out in the bay with a broken leg," he replied.

The girl looked confused. "Um, hang on." She disappeared to the back. The mysterious flicker came again at the corner of his eye, and again turning to look, he still found nothing.

Another lady returned with the girl. "Hi, so you found a crane with a banged-up leg?" She took the towel from him. "We normally don't tend to wildlife; have you contacted Wildlife and Fisheries?" she asked, looking at the bird's leg.

"No, I just thought this would be the best place."

The lady looked past him and said, "Tucker! Get down from there!"

Spencer turned to find a raccoon climbing on the table, trying to get a closer look at what they had wrapped in the towel.

"You have a pet raccoon?" Spencer asked, surprised.

"*I* don't." The lady turned and hollered toward the back, "Toni! Tucker is back out front."

"I hope he isn't bothering anyone," Toni said, walking out. "Spencer! Hi!" She sounded as if she couldn't find the right words to say.

"He brought you a critter." The lady handed her the crane in the towel.

"Aw, poor guy. Come on back." She opened the door for Spencer to enter.

He turned to find the raccoon following them. Toni unwrapped a granola bar and put it on top of a cabinet to occupy Tucker.

"Not a whole lot I can do other than splint the leg and cage him for a few weeks till it heals," she said, examining the leg closer.

"I'll pay for his stay," Spencer said.

"Nah, we have room. So it takes a wounded bird to get you in here?" she smiled.

"I guess," he laughed.

"So how's being back? Weird?" Toni asked.

"No. Different with so many things that have changed."

"Yeah, we can thank Katrina for that."

"What was strange was that I ran into Jimmy today," he said.

She rolled her eyes. "Mr. Big shot," she replied.

"You two dated for a long time—what happened?"

"High school drama." She turned, trying to avoid any more questions.

Taking the hint, he asked, "How is your dad?"

"He's good. Still working." She wrapped blue vet tape around a small makeshift splint on the crane's leg. "That should hold for a while."

Spencer watched as she gently took the overexcited bird out of the towel and placed him in a dog kennel. Her baggy scrubs hid her toned figure. She was as beautiful as he had expected, and her sweet demeanor still reminded him of the little girl he had a crush on growing up. He caught himself smiling and quickly changed his expression.

She backed up to the counter and with one jump pulled herself up and sat with her legs dangling off the edge. Just like when they were kids.

"When was the last time you went out on the bay?" he asked.

She smiled. "It's been a while."

"Do you have anything tomorrow?" he continued.

"I think I can knock off."

"Would you like to go out then?" he asked.

"Sure."

"I'll stop by around nine," he said with a smile.

She smiled back. "I'll be ready."

He walked back to his truck, unable to hide a childish grin. Then the thoughts came. *What are you doing? You don't need any distractions and you certainly don't have time.*

Chapter 10

The following morning Spencer pulled up to the vet clinic to find Toni sitting outside on the stone wall that lined the pathway leading to the front door.

"You're late," she said, climbing in the passenger side.

He looked down at the clock that read 8:51. "Late?" he answered.

She grinned. "Wow, nice truck. Science must be paying off," she joked, snooping in the back seat as she scanned the truck.

"So how in the world did you end up with a raccoon? I know you were going to save all the strays in the world," he asked, starting a conversation.

"Someone brought him in as a baby, and after weeks of bottle feeding, he just stayed around."

"He stayed? Or you kept him?" he picked at her.

"I don't know—I guess mother instincts," she laughed.

The marina was busy with fishermen competitively fueling their boats and heading out for the day. Spencer stopped shy of parking and then, looking over his shoulder, backed up close to the dock.

"Man, look at that boat! That's some serious fisherman," she nodded at the red 42' center-console boat floating a few stalls behind them.

"Yeah, really. Who would bring such a hideous boat down here?" he said, still picking at her.

"I didn't say *hideous*; pretty nice is more like it. What in the world are you doing with so much gear?" she asked, helping him unload his truck.

"It seems I've heard that a time or two," he replied as she followed him with one of his duffle bags over her shoulder. Then he stopped at the front of his boat. "So here's my hideous boat."

"You got to be kidding me!" She stepped in before he had a chance to invite her.

"I'll get the rest," he said sarcastically.

"OK," she replied, not paying him any attention while looking at the monitors on the console. Locking his truck, he thought about how long it had been since they were together on the bay.

The four Yamaha 350s fired up, and Spencer walked around the boat, untying from the cleats and throwing the loose line onto the dock.

"You kids be careful," a familiar voice said from the front of the dock.

"Hey, Cap!" Toni said to Dusty, who was wearing his usual white t-shirt, cutoff jeans, and ball cap with his company logo.

"Did your dad finish with that flaying knife I loaned you two days before yesterday?" Dusty asked.

"I'll get it back to you tomorrow," she said.

"See you after dark," Spencer yelled back as they backed out of their slip. Motoring slowly through the marina, he kicked off his flip-flops and propped up in the captain's chair.

Once they cleared the harbor, he asked, "You ready?"

She smiled and turned her ball cap backwards, "Let 'er rip, potato chip!" she yelled over the motors.

He hadn't heard that phrase since they were kids and it made him laugh.

Throttling down the 350s, the engines caught a low gear, and the force pushed the boat almost out of the water, Toni stumbled back, not expecting the quick take off. Spencer reached out and with one arm, snagged her from falling down. "Hang on," he said over the rumble of the engines.

She found her face within inches from his, and locking eyes for just a split second made her realize he wasn't that geeky kid any more.

"Thanks," she spoke softly, almost in a spell. With his smile in response, she thought it would break the awkward moment, but to her surprise she found herself in a place she didn't expect.

"You want to drive?" he asked, noticing her silence and wondering what thoughts were racing through her head.

"Scoot!" She forced herself in the chair.

He laughed and let her win the pushing war, thinking she had grown up in the familiar waters and probably knew them better than he did. Her hair blew back from under her baseball cap. The wind pushed past the windshield on the console, and for a short boat ride, the past caught up with them, as he remembered the countless times his father had taken them on the same route.

The engines slowed as Toni pulled up on the throttles and allowed the boat to come to a drift, and a few Roseate Spoonbill birds flew overhead. "It's good to see the Cajun Flamingos again," he said, looking up.

"Tell me about Florida," she said, still sitting in the captain's chair. "You didn't tell me much when you were out jogging."

He made his way to the front of the boat where his sonar equipment sat. "It was good, high school was fun, and working with the marine life was awesome," he said, pulling his computer and the towfish back to where she was sitting.

"I bet. How come you never married?" she quizzed.

"Never met the right girl."

"Girlfriends?" she asked.

"Oh, I dated some in college. But to be honest, no one really fit with my love for the water. They were more interested in shopping and gabbing." He was tying a knot to the towfish scanner.

"Hey, now, nothing wrong with shopping," she smiled.

"Idle toward that small island." He pointed to their left. Spencer lowered the towfish in the water while she turned the wheel to line up with their point. After he adjusted his equipment to the correct depth, he turned back in time to find Toni shedding her tank top, revealing her light blue bikini top. Caught off guard, he stared for a moment, thinking, *Dang! She grew up!*

"Is this fast enough?" she asked, breaking his stare.

"Uh, yeah. We're good." He plugged the cable into the back of the laptop that was nestled in the case.

"*Waterproof?*" she asked, referring to the name that was printed on the back of his boat.

He smiled. "Good name for a boat," he answered.

"How did you come up with that name?" she asked, wondering if it had something to do with her childhood ducks.

"Boats are waterproof," he said, lying. The name had stuck in his mind ever since old man Gentry told her that her ducks were waterproof years earlier, every time she insisted on drying them off with a towel.

"What are we doing out here?" she asked.

"Starting a recording on the computer," he explained. "I'm using sonar to delineate potential oyster bed areas and noting the depth. Exciting, huh?"

"Anything out here is exciting." She stepped out from under the canopy and sat on a bench seat in front of the console.

"I have also been asked to help with the research on the dolphins and a possible lung disorder since the oil spill," he said, knowing that would catch her attention. As a child her favorite thing was to ride on the bow, waiting for bottlenose dolphins to break the surface. It seemed every time Steve would bring her, they would see more dolphins. She was their good luck charm.

"I want to help!" Her eyes lit up.

"I figured you would. Once the other biologist shows up, we'll start. You'll be the first to know," he said.

He took off his sunglasses long enough to remove his shirt, unaware of the eyes fixed on his chest and ripped abs.

Dang! He grew up! She hoped he wouldn't see her expression through her sunglasses. She also hoped his shirt stayed off as long as possible.

They spent the rest of the day trolling the water alongside the other biologist, and recording data on his computer. As the sun started to set, he pulled up his equipment and stored it.

The two of them made it to the bow, and lying one on either side, they watched the sun as it disappeared into the horizon. Right before the light of day was completely gone, he stole a glance. She was lying back with her long hair cascading off the bow and into the boat. Under the purple sky, his expression softened and he thought, *She is so beautiful.* With his next breath he looked back at the vanishing sun just as a light wind picked up on the water.

Sighing in contentment as the cool air brushed against his warm skin, he never heard her whisper, "I'm glad you're back."

Chapter 11

The rain pounded on the docks, leaving Spencer and a few other captains sitting in the marina store. There were a few tables in the back next to the windows that allowed the fishermen to drink their coffee and watch the trawlers unload their catch.

Tapping an app on his smart phone, Spencer looked at the radar, determining that he had an hour at the most before he could head out. He propped his feet in the chair facing him and looked back at the coffee cup that was steaming with a fresh pour. The cups hadn't changed since he was a kid, reminding him of the many times he sat with his dad waiting out rainstorms at that very table. Wondering where it rained the most, southern Louisiana or northern Florida, he drifted off to a memory of his father two years after they'd relocated.

"Hey, Sport!" his dad called as he entered the coffee shop across the street from the pier.

"Hey, Dad."

"How was school?" Steve asked. Spencer was then a senior, and Steve asked the same question every day; early on it bugged Spencer, but in time he got used to it.

"Good, starting track practice soon," he said as he opened his backpack and pulled out his laptop. With it pouring down outside, they weren't going anywhere soon.

"How's that book coming?" his dad asked.

"Really good—I think this one will top the first three." Spencer was writing the fourth book of his *Pirates and Voodoo* series. He had turned one of his vivid dreams into a great story about Lebreaux and one of Jean Lafitte's buccaneers she was in love with.

"I have some exciting news for you," Steve said.

Spencer pulled out his earbuds. "Oh, yeah, what's that?" he asked.

"We are studying something else starting tomorrow; I'm holding you out of school to help." Hearing that he wasn't going to school, Spencer expected that to be the exciting news, but it was what came out of his dad's mouth next that floored him. "I've been hired to run side-scan sonar in a search for an old Spanish ship for an expedition group." Steve smiled.

Spencer blinked a few times. "What!?" he finally managed to get out.

"You heard me."

"We're joining a treasure hunt?" Spencer knew what Spanish wreck plus expedition really meant.

"I don't know about joining, but we are going to be helping," Steve answered.

Spencer couldn't think straight with the excitement running through his veins. "Dad! That is a dream of mine."

"I know." Steve smiled while sipping his coffee.

"The *Griego*?" Spencer asked.

His dad formed a confused look. "Yes, how did you know? Never mind," he said with a smile. Steve knew. His son had already spent years devouring any history he could find about pirate ships and treasure.

"Did you know that she was one of the flagships of the New Spanish fleet?"

"New Spanish fleet?" Steve realized Spencer knew more than he did. With a look of interest from his dad, Spencer began a brief history of the ship.

"There were many fleets that hauled silver from Central America to Spain from the mid 1500s to the late 1600s. The New Spanish fleet was one of them. As the fleet sailed back to Spain, they were caught in a storm and several ships sank. Spain lost most of its treasure, including the *Griego*." Spencer pulled up the story on the Internet to show his father. "You see, after they would load the silver, gold, and other treasures on the ships in Central America, they would rendezvous in Havana. The fleet left Havana during hurricane season, and once they got around Florida, they met a storm head on. Several ships sank." Spencer had his dad's full attention. "So during the hurricane, the *Griego* was last seen sailing north along the banks of Florida. Rumors had it that the captain faked the sinking of the ship and stole the treasure, but others say the ship was so badly damaged that it sailed itself off course and sank. Who knows? It was a long time ago. And now we're part of the expedition!" Spencer was so excited he could barely contain himself.

"Hired on to help. I'm not sure about being *part* of the expedition," Steve said, trying to buffer his son's emotions.

A few months later, the *Griego* was found with the help of Steve and Spencer, who were greatly rewarded for the help. It was the start of their career in treasure hunting.

Steve agreed to partner with Spencer in their quest to find other wrecks and treasure, but only with the understanding that Spencer would graduate from college, no matter what. It wasn't a hard decision for Spencer, since he was still in love with his father's occupation and the work he encountered. His interest in marine life grew so much that he continued on to get his graduate degree.

Torn between two loves—history and marine biology—Spencer spent the last nine years chasing the history and studying the tactics and routes of the early Spanish captains of 1600s, while enjoying a lucrative marine biology career alongside his father.

Just six months ago, he and his father had planned on traveling to Spain and spending a summer at the archives of the Barcelona Maritime Museum researching a wreck they had found mentioned in an old letter they came across in an estate sale. Before they could buy their plane tickets, though, Steve suffered a massive heart attack, and at the early age of fifty-nine, he went on to be with the love of his life, Magi.

For the first time in his life, Spencer found himself alone. Debating over continuing his career as a marine biologist in Florida, heading home to Buras, or chasing the dream of treasure hunting, Spencer decided to head to Spain to research the letter as a tribute to his father.

Still in deep mourning at the sudden loss of his father, he traveled to Barcelona and began his research for the *Compostela*, the ship that was mentioned in the letter. The letter bore the crest of a family in Spain, the Cardona family.

In Barcelona he met an old historian whom he couldn't understand, but he learned that he needed to travel to Seville, Spain to the Maritime Museum for the possible manifest of the ship's cargo. Once he got to Seville, he realized that his native language wasn't going to get him far with the museum historians. Spencer made a grave mistake by hiring an interpreter from the restaurant behind the museum.

He didn't find the information he was looking for, but the young interpreter he had hired suggested more information on the ship might be found in the Galicia Museum of the Sea in Vigo, Spain, just a few hours south from Santiago de Compostela. Renting a car, he drove to Vigo, unaware that he was being followed by the young man he had hired to interpret, who had realized that Spencer was on the search for something that had been missing for many years.

The young man was the grandson of Eduardo Vargas, one of Spain's most notable organized criminals and the descendent of Gaspar Vargas, a man hired by Spain in 1622 to find the sunken ships from the Tierra Firme Fleet. Despite years of searching and using up much of the family's resources, the ships had never been found and the family had been disgraced as a result. Every generation since had been tasked with finding the treasure and exonerating the family's status.

It wasn't long before the young man contacted his grandfather, Eduardo, with the information. Immediately Vargas sent four of his men to find Spencer at any cost.

Walking through the long, quiet hallways of the museum in Vigo, Spencer admired the model ships and artifacts that had been collected over the centuries, but it was the strange encounter he had that made the trip mysterious.

In one exhibit, he was approached by a lady who spoke English. "You are here for da *Compostela* manifest?" she asked in what reminded him of a Creole accent. But that couldn't be right. Not here in Spain.

Still, Spencer stood speechless; he was halfway around the world by himself, yet this lady knew why he was there. His only thought was that the historians in Seville might have called ahead of him. "Yes, I am," he responded.

"I have it here." She handed him an old leather-bound notebook.

"You're giving it to me?" he asked, confused.

"Yes, and one other ting. I was told to give you dis and to remind you that da mark is on da *Potosi*," she replied in a thick Spanish accent while handing him a tarnished silver coin.

"Where did you get this?" he asked.

She ignored his question and grabbed his shoulder. "Now go! Dey will be here soon."

"Who?" he asked, still confused.

"Go! I was told dey mustn't find you!"

Looking past her and down an aisle, he saw four men dressed in black suits burst in the front door. "Go! I will hold them a while." She pushed him toward the back.

Quickly walking toward the back, he turned briefly back to the lady, who smiled at him. *What is going on? Potosi? How does she know this?* he wondered as he quickly exited the museum.

As the door closed behind him, he could hear the men shouting to each other in their native language, looking for someone—for him—so he ran to his rental car. He drove to a parking lot blocks away from the museum and quickly parked for a look into the old leather-bound notebook. To his surprise, as he unrolled it, he saw it wasn't the manifest to the *Compostela*. It was an old weathered bamboo map outlining the Gulf of Mexico and Barataria Bay. There were several holes notched out and a signature on the bottom right— Nicholas Cardona. Mental puzzle pieces all clicked into place. The voodoo woman was right.

His heart pounding in his chest, Spencer rolled up the map and looked back in the direction of the museum. Not seeing anyone pursuing him, he cautiously drove to his hotel with the silver coin in his hand.

Chapter 12

Washing the last bit of salt water off his boat, Spencer threw the tangled hose in the back of his truck and climbed in the driver seat to back the boat and trailer into a parking spot. Once unhooked from the trailer, Spencer felt his phone buzz in his front pocket of his cargo shorts.

He pulled his phone out to see a text from Toni, "Whatcha doing?"

"Cleaning the boat," he replied.

"Hungry?" she texted back.

"Always!"

"Oyster Bar at 9 p.m.!"

Before he could respond, his phone buzzed again, "We have a co-ed softball game tonight, and you're in the line-up! It's a vet clinic team, and I figured you qualified. Unless you're scared?"

"What time?" he replied.

"In an hour. See you at the city ballparks." She added a smiley face.

Cool of her to invite me out. I'd like to see her again. But why is she being this nice?

The dust hadn't even settled from his truck tires before he raced up the steps to his house. He had his glove but he didn't have cleats. He stopped in his room and thought about where he could buy some at such a short notice.

These will just have to do, he thought, grabbing a pair of running shoes from the closet. He walked through the hallway and paused at his father's room to look in. The quietness seemed eerie.

Setting his shoes and baseball glove on the table, he opened the 1950s refrigerator he had purchased online; it resembled his grandparents' when he was a child. He remembered going to their house and playing card games, and the old refrigerator always stuck out in his memory.

As he devoured a ham sandwich and chips, his phone buzzed again with a picture from Toni and a text that asked, "Is this OK?" It was a picture of a red jersey with the number 12 on the back. Another text followed: "It's a small."

Small?

"Just joking." She quickly added. He chuckled and threw his phone into his bag, thinking that this was the Toni he remembered from their childhood.

The city ballparks had been rebuilt since Katrina and housed four playing fields, two for little leagues and two for adult leagues. A small sea of red jerseys was congregating on one side of a field. Walking toward the field, Spencer pointed his key remote back at his truck and locked his doors.

Toni met him halfway to the field with his number 12 jersey. "Thanks for coming, I didn't know who we were playing until I got here. I hope it's not a problem." She pointed at the opposing team. One player stood out more than the others—Jimmy Pastadoria.

"Not a problem to me," he said, looking at Jimmy. They'd walked through the cinderblock dugout and were almost across the field to the opposite side before Jimmy noticed him.

"Well, I guess I get to crush the clinic team with little LeJeune," Jimmy spouted off.

"I guess so," Spencer smiled back at him, intentionally provoking him.

"We'll see if you're still smiling after tonight!" Jimmy shouted back with all the bravado he could muster.

Toni stopped and hollered at Jimmy. "Now look, I didn't invite Spencer to play just for y'all to ruin the night with macho attitudes. So shut up." She pointed her finger at Jimmy. He turned back toward his team, laughing.

"I can handle him," Spencer said, a little embarrassed.

"You shouldn't have to," she stormed past him to their dugout.

Spencer shook hands with his teammates—employees of the clinic and their spouses—then slipped on the jersey and grabbed his glove.

"Warm up?" he asked Toni.

She followed him out onto the field with her glove in hand. Still fuming, she ripped a fastball at him, and Spencer barely had time to get his glove up and catch it. "It's OK," he said, throwing it back, trying to calm her down.

"I'll be fine ... but we better win!" Her next throw was just as hard and fast as the first. It sparked a memory of their childhood—she was always a tough player and overly competitive.

With sunset still a few hours away, the evening was hot and the sky had begun to turn an ember red when Spencer heard the click of the lights as a park official turned them on. The umpire called for team captains and Toni and Jimmy faced each other over home plate. Spencer chuckled at the sight of them meeting with an umpire in the middle; it looked like a Saturday Night Fight between David and Goliath. Spencer wanted to shout, "Let's get ready to rumble!" but didn't want to get Toni more fired up.

It was bottom of the third when Spencer got up to bat, and the game wasn't going anywhere near the way Toni wanted. To make things worse, Jimmy was pitching and taunting everyone who got up to bat. Most of the players and spouses had made comments that it wasn't very much fun with the jerk on the mound.

"Finally! Little LeJeune," Jimmy shouted as Spencer walked out of the warmup box.

"Just pitch!" he replied.

First pitch, strike.

Second pitch, strike.

Spencer's blood was boiling with the heckling, but he was determined not to let Jimmy see.

On his third pitch, Jimmy floated a high ball. Spencer eyed it all the way in, and swinging as hard as he possibly could, felt nothing but air as he heard the ball settle into the catcher's mitt.

The remarks and laughter from the pitcher's mound only fueled Spencer's anger; he hadn't felt this mad in a long time.

"It's OK—you'll get it next time," Toni said as he walked by.

That's the last thing I need, Spencer thought, *to relive middle school!*

Toward the end of the eighth inning, the clinic team started a rally, and before they knew it they were only two runs down.

In the ninth inning, the clinic held Jimmy's team to no runs and had the last at bat with two runs down, but still Jimmy never shut up. He was obnoxious at every opportunity. He hollered at his team, at the umpire, at the fans, and at anyone who was listening.

Spencer was fifth up to bat. The first batter had hit a single and the next two had struck out, leaving the fourth batter to hit another single. Two on, two down, and Spencer was next up to bat. Things weren't looking good.

The heckling started before Spencer even walked out onto the field. "This game is in the bag!" Jimmy shouted back to his dugout. Even his own team was tired of hearing him and looked ready to head elsewhere.

Spencer walked up to home plate and dug in as best he could with his running shoes, thinking, *Please, please, please let me hit one!* Spencer glared at the ball that Jimmy was rolling around in his right hand, and with knuckles facing home plate, Jimmy wound up and let the ball go with a wicked spin. Everything suddenly got quiet, and the ball seemed to travel in slow motion. Spencer watched as it passed by one of the field lights and came back into focus just feet from the catcher's mitt.

Stepping forward with his left foot, Spencer took a crushing swing toward the spinning ball. The crack of the bat was the only sound on the field for a brief second, and Jimmy could do nothing but look over his head as the ball sailed toward center field and disappeared behind the fence. At the sound of the ball hitting something in the parking lot behind the fence, the dugout from the clinic side erupted into cheers, emptying onto the field, yelling and celebrating Spencer's home run and the winning run.

Spencer looked back at Jimmy as he stepped onto second base, but Jimmy was staring past center field. "My truck! You hit my damn truck!"

"Holy crap! It doesn't get any better than this!" Toni yelled as she jumped into Spencer's arms as he touched home plate.

You've got that right! Spencer was thinking. *It's been a long time coming, but that'll shut his pie hole.* Everyone shook hands on center field with the exception of Jimmy, who was already out in the parking lot, staring at the dent in his hood from the winning hit.

"Drinks on me!" a guy yelled as the clinic team gathered to grab their gear from the benches.

"Oyster Bar it is!" another yelled.

"Give me a ride?" Toni asked Spencer.

"You didn't drive?"

"No, I rode with Cheryl."

"Come on," he replied.

"I get to ride with the hero," she joked back at him, carrying her bag over her shoulder. Leaving the field and walking beside him, she gave him a strong hip bump, throwing him off balance. He glanced at her to find her smiling with a glimmer in her hazel eyes he hadn't seen in a long time. *What are you thinking?* he wondered, smiling back at her.

Toni rattled on about the game, her clinic, Tucker the raccoon, and everything else that came to her mind from the fields to the Oyster Bar. She was still on a high from beating Jimmy's team.

Spencer sat quietly, enjoying every second of listening to her ... but wondering what it all meant. *We didn't exactly leave things in the best way twenty years ago, but she doesn't seem to even acknowledge it. I wasn't expecting this. But I like it.*

Chapter 13

Spencer lifted the towfish for his side-scan sonar onto the tailgate of his truck. The mud and oil residue from the water had discolored the sides, so he washed it off with a bucket of soapy water and sprayed it down with silicone, so it wouldn't collect the oil residue as easily. He looked out over the dock into the bay as a cool northern breeze blew in. *That's an unusually cool wind this time of year,* he thought, packing up the remaining part of his gear.

He didn't have to turn around; the smell of a cheap cigar told him Dusty was close. "LeJeune, you carry more equipment than I have ever seen," Dusty said, never removing the cigar from his mouth.

"You know, you'll never see sixty if you keep smoking those things," Spencer said.

"Huh! I'll probably die before then anyway—either a mean oyster or jealous boyfriend," he laughed. Without asking, Dusty grabbed one of Spencer's duffel bags and headed toward his boat. Spencer quietly accepted and followed with the towfish in hand.

"Heard all about your game. Seems the whole town is all happy with you showing up Jimmy," Dusty said.

"Yeah, I'm not too excited about people saying those things. Stirs up drama."

"Yep, I knew I liked you," Dusty said, handing the bag down into the boat. "Still, I wish I was there to see it," he added.

Spencer's phone buzzed with a text, "Have a good day!" Toni left a smiley face. Spencer smiled.

"From Toni?" Dusty asked, seeing him smile.

"Yeah."

"You two are meant for each other."

"Oh, I don't know about that. Just friends," he lied, knowing his feelings were rapidly changing.

Spencer walked around the freshly cleaned boat, untying it from the dock, "Where you heading today?" Dusty asked.

"Snail bay."

"Snail Bay? That's close to my farm," Dusty answered. Most of the oyster boat captains were known as oyster farmers, and many claimed their leased areas from the state to be "their" farms.

"Yeah, I figured I would work that way," Spencer replied.

"Well, don't piss off my oysters! They need to grow."

"I won't," Spencer laughed.

With a kick off from the bow by Dusty, Spencer found himself floating in the marina while his engines warmed up. He pulled out his phone and replied to the text, "You too! Tell Tucker hi!" he typed. He eased the throttles forward and began to idle out of the docks and into the open bay. Before he opened up his boat on the water, another cool breeze blew through, this time a little harder.

"We don't get this often! Not good for fishing," a captain yelled at him about the cooler weather as their boats passed. Spencer pulled his phone out and checked the weather again. *Well that's weird. Nothing out of the ordinary forecasted.*

He kicked it into high gear, and the roar of the four 350s sailed his center-console across the water. He turned his cap backwards and set his feet up on the console aiming toward the area where Dusty's camp was located.

Dusty's camp house had been in the family for three generations; his great-grandfather had moved over from Europe to begin a lifelong career in oyster farming. Once he established his camp house and his boat, he brought over Dusty's grandfather, and together they fished the areas of Barataria Bay. Dusty would often refer to his great-grandfather as a Taco, but Spencer never understood and didn't ask. Later he learned it was what they called the earlier settlers and their sons.

Passing by the camp, Spencer noticed the front screen door open and flapping in the northern wind. He circled around and geared down, approaching the makeshift dock that seemed to have survived the last hundred years of storms. The camp had been rebuilt several times, but the old dock had remained.

Throwing a rope around one of the pylons to secure his boat, he walked up to the camp, calling "Hello!" to make sure he was the only one there. The thought briefly ran through his head that if someone answered, it would scare the crap out of him.

Walking through the camp house, he noticed someone had been there recently. *I bet Dusty just didn't latch the bolt.* He pulled shut the old wooden screen door and bolted it closed. As he walked toward the dock, another cool breeze blew past him, but this time he heard a faint whisper. Spencer stopped and looked around. No one else was there. *I must be hearing things.* But before he reached his boat, he heard it again, this time making out a few words, "with de girl." *I must be going crazy!* Looking at his watch, he realized precious time was getting away, and he still had a long trip to Snail Bay.

Pushing down on the throttles, he finally reached his destination, and feeling windblown, he searched his backpack for his ChapStick. The air was cool, but he could feel the sun beating down on his already burned shoulders from a few days ago, even through his t-shirt.

The choppy water settled down once he passed by a small island, so taking advantage of the smooth water, he rigged his sonar and computer for the day. After easing the boat forward, he dropped the towfish in the water and set the depth.

Spencer hadn't even had time to open a bottle of water before he felt the boat catch, and quickly turning to check the line on the sonar, he could see that it was dragging something. He put the engines in neutral and pulled the towfish up to see what it was hung on. Along with the towfish came a green fishing net. *Dang!* he muttered to himself. He pulled his knife out and had just started to cut the line when he noticed an old piece of wood tangled in the net just below the water line.

He pulled the towfish into the boat and dragged in the rest of the net. Once he reached the old piece of wood, he cut the rest of the line and threw it in the corner of the boat. Even with mud and silt covering the piece of wood, he could still tell that it wasn't driftwood, and once he washed the mud away, he saw the old nails still buried in the wood. With his knife he pried one of the nails out until the head and ¼ inch of the shank landed on the deck of the boat.

It was a square tapered nail with a rosehead top, but tapered down only two sides of the shank. Spencer studied it closely, remembering the lesson he and his father had on the early 1600s nails from their time spent searching for the *Griego*. Even as old and weather as it was, it still appeared to be handmade, meaning that it even predated the 1600s. He made a mental note to send it to his friend in Jacksonville who worked for the university in their metallurgy department to be sure.

He filled the live-well tank on the boat with water from the bay and sank the piece of wood into it for safe keeping. He hadn't done any work yet and had driven a long way, so his excitement about the nail and anticipation of sending the pieces in that he had discovered would have to wait until that evening. He set his GPS to record the spot and continued with his work.

After several hours of mapping the bay and making recordings, he packed up his sonar equipment and throttled down toward Buras, leaving Snail Bay and the orange glow of a setting sun behind him. Thoughts ran through his head, finally allowing his excitement to take over. He sent a text to his friend in Jacksonville about the nails, and to his surprise, the return text said he could find another professor who knew even more about metallurgy at LSU.

Just over halfway back, he spotted a bottlenose dolphin break the surface just ahead of him, and within a few minutes he had a pod riding the bow of his boat. He leaned out and watched them play in the wake and blow water from their snouts toward the hull. *Toni should be here,* he thought. *This is right up her ally.* He snapped a picture and sent it to her ... unaware of the old wooden skiff just off his starboard side.

Chapter 14

Driving back from LSU, Spencer was a little disappointed. He would have liked to have spoken to the professor instead of leaving the sample nail and wood with a twenty-year-old college student, but the professor was stuck in a meeting. Stuck behind slow traffic on the two-lane highway back to Buras, he got a chuckle out of the name on the back of the fishing boat being towed in front of him—*No Work.* "That's the perfect name for a boat," he said out loud.

It had taken most of the day to get to Baton Rouge and back because of his frequent stops at the small mom-and-pop tackle stores he came across. He was bound and determined to find a certain fishing lure he had read about. A local fishing guide had been out fishing with others most of the year and was finally sharing his secret, a chartreuse red tail with gold specks and a red-tinted Colorado blade. It sounded normal to Spencer except for the gold specks. *Amazing how picky fish are,* he thought.

He had just turned his satellite radio to a pop station when he heard his phone ding. Reaching through the clutter on the front seat and pulling out his phone from under a pile of paper, he saw a text.

"Whatcha doing tonight?" Toni was asking.

Trying not to weave across the road, he typed back, "Nothing. What's up?"

"When was the last time you had good Southern cooked gumbo?" she replied.

Where is all this coming from? Why is she being this nice? he wondered, reading the text. "Been a while," he texted back.

"Do you want to come over tonight and eat?"

He studied the text for a moment. "I'll have to take a rain check tonight," he finally responded. "Sorry."

"It's OK, another time," she replied.

He dialed Dusty's number. "Hey, LeJeune," Dusty replied without saying hello.

"You busy?"

"Nope, what's up?"

"I need to talk to you," Spencer said.

"Head to the marina. I'll be at my boat in a few." He hung up.

Spencer stopped by Gentry's store for a twelve-pack of beer, and before the door could shut behind him, he was facing an entire rack of the secret fishing lures he had been searching for.

"Dang! I drove all over looking for these today," he said to Mr. Gentry.

"Oh yeah, there was an article in a magazine about them. I called the guy and he sent me that rack," Mr. Gentry answered, unaware of the popularity of the lure.

Spencer gathered a few other items he needed at home and set them and the twelve-pack on the counter.

"How's the oyster season going to look this year?" Mr. Gentry asked.

"I believe pretty good."

"Boy, we sure need one. That oil spill screwed things up for a while," he answered, putting the items in a paper bag. Spencer looked around the store, thinking how nice it was that it hadn't changed much at all. Stepping into Mr. Gentry's store would take anyone back fifty years with the brick walls and faded old wooden floors.

"Have a good evening," Spencer said with his back on the door as he pushed it open.

"You too. Nice hit the other night," Mr. Gentry replied with a thin smile.

Spencer smiled as the door shut, not knowing if Mr. Gentry was at the game or if small-town gossip was making its way around. Setting the twelve-pack in the back seat, he heard a vehicle come to a sliding stop on the loose gravel beside him. It was Jimmy's truck.

Jimmy stepped out and headed toward the doors. "LeJeune," he said with a nod.

"Jimmy," Spencer answered.

Jimmy disappeared into the store. Spencer stood in shock for a moment. *Wow, that's a change from his other greetings.*

Spencer's red three-quarter ton pulled into the marina parking lot that was rapidly emptying with fishermen heading to their usual evening spot, the Oyster Bar. He could see the light puffs of smoke coming from Dusty's trawler as he sat in a lounge chair with his typical cigar.

"You spend a lot of time on this old lug," Spencer said, stepping down onto the boat.

"She's the only faithful gal I got," he grinned with the cigar stuck between his teeth.

"You brought my flavor. Throw me one," Dusty eyed the twelve-pack tucked under Spencer's arm. "What's on your mind?" he went right to the question. "Wait! Don't tell me—Toni," he added.

"When I left twenty years ago, she was dating Jimmy and would have nothing to do with me, but now she acts like we're best friends and nothing ever happened."

"What's your complaint?" Dusty asked.

"Well, I don't have one. I don't know why I'm hesitant about her being so nice; I can't put my finger on it."

Dusty took a long drag off his cigar and stretched his head back to release the smoke in the warm evening air. "You don't know, do you?" he looked at Spencer.

"Know what?"

Dusty slowly shook his head, looking in the sky. "Here a few years ago, a young, good-looking guy blew through town. Musician, folk music, but mostly country. He was good, too. Well, they started dating and before everyone knew it, they were pretty serious. Pissed Jimmy off, but nothing he could do." Dusty took a swig of cold beer. "Anyway, he got discovered by some record company and started touring around the South, coming back here every two to three weeks. That poor girl moped around here when he was gone. He would come back and promise the world, then take off again. I think he must have cheated on her half a dozen times, but she was bound and determined to settle him down. Then one day he left, and well, haven't seen him since."

Spencer lit one of Dusty's cigars and settled back in the chair. "So she's on the rebound?"

"I wouldn't say that. But I haven't seen her this giddy in a while."

"Why?" He looked at Dusty.

"Hey man, I'm an oyster farmer. Not a date doctor. You chased that girl all over these docks, and now she's showing you some interest and you look afraid. Or you have other agendas?"

"No agendas," Spencer answered in a defensive tone.

"I have a crazy idea," Dusty said.

"What's that?"

"Ask her out," he answered.

"I don't know if I want to go down that trail," Spencer said.

Dusty leaned closer to him and looked him in the eye. "Then why are you asking?" He smiled. "Here's your opportunity," Dusty said, sitting back up.

Spencer just looked at him, then toward the parking lot as Toni's jeep pulled up and parked under the light of the marina store. He watched in silence as her shadow made its way down the dock toward Dusty's trawler. *Damn, she's good looking,* Spencer thought.

"I figured you two would be out here solving all the world's problems," she smiled, stepping down onto the boat.

"We're working on it," Dusty replied.

"So you turned me down for beer, cigars, and Dusty?" Toni grinned.

"Yeah, sorry. He wanted to talk," Spencer said, lying.

Dusty held up his beer, "Girl problems." He smiled with his cigar in his mouth.

"You have a girl?" Toni questioned in excitement.

"Nope. That's the problem."

"I can help with that."

"No, no, I'll fix it myself." Dusty stood up and handed her a beer, "You kids don't stay up late."

"You're leaving?" Spencer asked.

Dusty looked at him and then at Toni and then said with a smirk, "I don't think she'll bite." He laughed, walking onto the pier. Spencer played it off, offering Toni his chair.

"It's nice tonight—let's head out for a while," she said.

I have to keep my mind on the treasure, not a girl, he thought, debating her invitation.

Giving in, he said, "OK, let me go get my keys from my truck." Within minutes, he was back, and Toni held her hand out for the keys. "You sure are pushing with my boat," he grumbled. She stood her ground with her hand out, not saying a word, until he smiled and handed them over. She cranked the engines and let them warm up while he untied from the dock. Before he could reach port side of the boat, Toni was backing out.

They idled quietly away from the docks and into the opening of the bay. "Whatcha say we cruise the coast line?" he asked.

"Sounds good," she agreed.

They spent the rest of the evening on a slow boat ride toward the town of Empire. Spencer took the wheel on their way back, and the half-moon lit the water just enough for him to see his path and the figure of his childhood crush sitting in front of him. She sat quietly, looking up at the stars in deep thought while Spencer continued to struggle with his feelings for her and with mustering up enough bravery to talk to her about them. *What is she thinking? It's been a long time, and we've seemed to have picked up where we left off as kids. Just ask her. Dang it! I don't need any distractions.*

Waterproof pushed through the calm waters and the cool night air of Barataria Bay as the two childhood friends each quietly reminisced about their past—and their current feelings.

Chapter 15

As the boats rested in their stalls, the morning dew burned off in the rising sun, and a white cloud of dust hovered over the parking lot as Spencer's truck came to a rest. He stepped out and stretched his arms above his head. After reaching back in the truck for his aviator sunglasses and his coffee, he headed toward Dusty's boat.

"Well, good morning! I wasn't sure if you were going to make it after a long night on the bay," Dusty greeted him, leaning on the railing of his trawler.

"You keeping track of us?" Spencer asked.

"So there is an 'us'?" he picked on Spencer.

"I don't know what there is. Friends, probably. Did you come back up here last night?"

"Yeah, I couldn't sleep, so I got an early start." Dusty answered.

Dusty had worked throughout the early morning hours reassembling the diesel engine he had taken apart, and he had asked Spencer the night before if he had time to help. Spencer had learned many things from his father, but one important thing was always to help others, especially the other boat captains.

By the looks and smell of Dusty, he had been hard at work for some time. Spencer stepped down onto the trawler, making ripples in the calm morning water. A few white cranes walked alongside the shore fishing for their morning breakfast before joining the other birds headed toward the marsh.

"Well, how far did you get last night?" Spencer asked, placing his glasses inside the door of the wheelhouse.

"I think we'll finish it this morning."

"Seems you spend more time working on this lug than fishing."

"Nah, once season starts everyone else will be broke down but me." Spencer knew he was probably right. He leaned down and saw that Dusty had replaced the heads and had only a few other parts to attach, so he wondered if he was needed or if was he was really there to keep Dusty company.

Close to mid-morning, Spencer could feel himself begin to sink from staying out so late. Leaning back against the railing with hands and arms as greasy and dirty as the engine, he struggled to find a clean spot on his shirt to wipe the sweat out of his eyes.

Magically, a white towel draped over his shoulder and seemed to suspend in the air, but as he looked back, the sun blinded him from seeing the face that belonged to a petite figure.

"You're a mess," Toni said.

"Well, well. Look who decided to come help," Dusty said, looking over the engine.

"I don't know about helping, but I brought more coffee." She handed each of them a tall cup. Spencer leaned over the side and washed what he could off his hands and arms and dried his face and hands with the towel.

"I needed this. Thank you," he said as he took the cup.

"You about ruined the boy for this morning keeping him up all night; been dragging the whole time," Dusty said, not looking up.

"Yeah, he's kinda a light weight," she punched Spencer in the arm.

"Look, I need my beauty rest," Spencer joked back. Toni took a swallow of her coffee and quickly turned toward the water, spitting it back out.

"You OK?" Spencer asked.

She wiped her mouth, "Yes, it's hot." She began blushing.

"I'll be right back," Spencer said, heading to retrieve another shirt from his truck. Dusty peeked over, catching Toni watching him walk to his truck.

"You like that boy?" he asked.

She turned to Dusty. "No, we're just friends."

"Keep telling yourself that. And hand me that 9/16 wrench." After handing him the wrench, she backed up to the engine cover, dusted it off, and jumped up, sitting with her legs dangling on the side.

"Spencer and I are just friends, always have been. It would be like dating my brother," she replied.

"Well you're not kin. The brother thing is out, so what other excuses do you have?"

She gave Dusty a smirk. "How come *you* never married?" she asked.

"Oh I don't know. I guess I never could find the right girl who liked oyster farming," he replied.

"I bet they're out there. What about Marsha who works at the parts store?"

Dusty looked back over the engine at her with a funny look. "Married twice and six kids!"

He looked up at Spencer, who was walking back with a fresh shirt. "Will you hurry up? Your girlfriend is trying to be matchmaker.com," he yelled.

"Shhhh, I'm not his girlfriend," she replied in a loud whisper.

The trawler rocked back and forward as Spencer stepped down onto the bow and sat back down beside the engine where he had been most of the morning. He wondered if it was coincidence that she chose to sit on the cover above him or if she had planned it. He began handing the bolts back to Dusty and trying his best not to stare at the tan legs dangling within a foot from his face. Cocking his head sideways and looking up, he shot a smile at her, and she drew her legs up and sat with them crossed.

Was that a "Your legs are too close" smile or just a friendly smile? she wondered.

After a few minutes and with the sun now beaming down on them, Dusty said, "That should get it. Let's fill this puppy with oil and give it a crank," wiping his hands with an old greasy rag.

Toni hopped down and began taking the quarts of oil out of the box, opening them and handing them to Spencer. Once they finished, Dusty hooked up the batteries and said, "Well, here goes nothing." As he turned the key, the engine turned over two times, then fired up, white smoke settling over the water as the engine idled down.

Dusty walked back to the cover, giving Spencer a high five. "Untie us, kiddo!" he said to Toni.

She walked around the railing untying the trawler and chucking the ropes onto the pier. As the oyster boat pulled out and motored around the docks heading toward the bay, Spencer and Toni walked together to the bow to catch the fresh, cool wind coming off the water.

"Something about these boats," she said.

"What's that?"

"I don't know, I guess growing up around them." She flipped her hair to allow the wind to cool the back of her neck, catching Spencer's eye again.

"It seems like yesterday we got in trouble for coming out here with that old woman," she said.

Spencer was watching the pelicans fly inches from the water. "Lebreaux Papillion," he said.

"You know people started a rumor or a wives' tale that after she died, they would hear her motor or see her in her wooden skiff. Crazy locals," she said. "I know where she lived," she added.

The words didn't register at first with Spencer. "What? Where?"

"She lived in an old white house in Lafitte. There's an old store with a wooden porch, and the road that runs beside it led to her house. Not sure if it's still there, but my dad showed me one day when I was in middle school," she replied. Spencer wasn't sure why she volunteered the information.

"That's crazy. I wrote about her in my books."

"Are you still writing?" she asked with a hint of excitement.

"Yeah, I still dabble a little. I was never really serious," he was saying when the boat lunged forward with a strong jar as if they had hit a stump, but both knew that there weren't any stumps.

"Damn it!" Dusty hollered from the wheelhouse.

They both looked at each other, reading each other's mind: *Will we need a tow?*

As they slowly idled back into the marina, Dusty muttered to himself. "I bet I didn't tighten something—no big deal."

As they eased up to the dock, a large figure stood waiting for them.

"You need to burn this lug," Jimmy said as Dusty eased the trawler into reverse to keep from ramming the dock.

"It's made me a good living and will continue. To what do we owe the pleasure?" he asked Jimmy.

"You don't. I saw LeJeune's truck. My boss wants to meet with you about this dolphin crap!"

"Tell him I'll call and make time," Spencer said, tying up Dusty's boat.

"So this is who you're hanging with?" Jimmy asked Toni.

"Yes," she answered. Jimmy huffed through his nostrils and walked toward the marina store.

"Don't trust that SOB," Dusty whispered as he walked past Spencer.

Chapter 16

In 1622, with orders from King Phillip and the urgency of recovering the five sunken ships that held the fortune needed for Spain to survive the Thirty Years' War, Captain Gaspar De Vargas was called to action. Of the twenty-eight ships that tried to return to Spain from Havana, only twenty-three survived. King Phillip had consulted astronomers to determine the best date to sail from Havana to Spain, and the date was set for September 4. Little did they know that on the 5th of September, a hurricane would wreck five of their treasure ships.

Within a few days after the storm passed, Vargas set sail with five ships that were mid-sized, but fast. They made it to the Florida Keys and quickly began their search for the *Atocha*, one of the ships carrying most of the treasure. The lost fleet was scattered over fifty miles from Dry Tortugas to where the *Atocha* went down. One of the crew members spotted the mizzenmast rising out of the water, placing the Atocha in fifty-five feet of water, just past the depths of free divers. After seizing only two small iron swivel cannons from the deck, Captain Vargas aimed his ships west in search of the *Margarita*.

In the process of searching for the *Margarita*, Vargas found the *Rosario* and a few survivors and started his salvage. It was now early October, and Vargas found himself searching for cover with another hurricane bearing down on them. After riding out the hurricane and almost losing his ships, he finished the salvage of the *Rosario* and sailed back to Havana for more tools to make another attempt on the *Atocha*. On his return for the *Atocha*, though, Vargas was surprised to find that the hurricane had buried her, and after dragging the bottom for several days, he came up empty handed.

In February, the Marquis joined the salvage crew, and for seven months they searched the area, finding only a few silver ingots. In late August, the efforts were abandoned, and Vargas returned to Spain, but before leaving, the Captain hired Nicholas de Cardona to map the searched area. Once finished, Nicholas sailed to Havana with the intention of a secret meeting with Vargas in three months.

On a November evening in the outskirts of Havana, Cardona and Vargas met in a low-lit tavern to talk over something King Phillip had mentioned to only a few people, including the Marquis. During the seven months that the Marquis had joined the salvage crew, he and Vargas spent an evening drinking their problems away with rum. In a drunken stupor, the Marquis told Vargas that there were three ships from the New Spanish Fleet that had not left the port in Veracruz, Mexico, during the same time the treasure ships sank. The treasure they waited on was too large for the three ships to carry, so they built a barge to sail the treasure back to Spain. It too was sunk in the hurricane somewhere in the bays off the coast of the new world.

In his later years of life, Gaspar Vargas didn't think he would be suited for the search for the treasure barge. He enlisted his son to go with Cardona and find the treasure. The two of them and crews for two ships scavenged the bays near a large river that emptied into the gulf. After five years and the deaths of many crew members, they called off their search and Vargas's son sailed back to Spain, with Cardona heading to the west coast of the new world.

In 1631, with rumors of Cardona back in the bays searching for the sunken barge, Gaspar de Vargas set sail to confront his one-time partner. In late September, the two ships met head on, deep in the bays of the new world. A gun fight broke out, followed by cannons and mass chaos, both sides taking extensive damage and loss of life. Vargas, not trained in battle and in bad health, raised a white flag and asked to meet on land. Once the crews met face to face, the Cardona crew expected total surrender from Vargas, but instead Vargas's crew opened fire and killed most of Cardona's men.

Vargas spared the lives of Cardona and a few sailors, but blew his ship out of the water and took something of great value—a bamboo map with oblong holes cut throughout the parchment.

"Vargas! You are nothing but a pirate!" The words rang loudly from Cardona, and for the first time Vargas agreed, starting his long reign as a Spanish pirate. But little did Vargas know that the old silver coin that Cardona still held was the key to the map he now had in his possession.

During a night when all of the Vargas crew were drunk on rum, someone snuck aboard their ship and stole the map. Rumors had it that a drunk sailor saw someone slip over the edge with a leather-bound case.

Lee DuCote

Almost 400 years later, the very same leather-bound case sat in a dry box tucked deep into a compartment of a 42' center-console boat named *Waterproof.*

Chapter 17

The boat drifted up to the dock and Spencer stood on the bow with a rope in hand. Stepping off onto the weather-beaten wood, he securely tied his boat, which dwarfed the others along the dock.

"What can we do for you?" a bearded man asked.

"I am here visiting someone; what do I owe you to dock here?"

"You buying anything?" the man asked.

"Fuel before I leave," Spencer answered.

"It'll be here when you get back. Welcome to Lafitte," the man replied and walked toward another boat.

An old truck eased by on the white shell road as Spencer emerged from the Marina store, white dust forming and hovering in the air. Spencer waved to clear the dust in front of his face and walked up the road toward the Lafitte post office.

As the last stop on Louisiana Hwy 45, Lafitte is a small fishing community for both the commercial industry and the weekend warriors. It also held answers for Spencer.

While walking by the waterway, known as Bayou Barataria, Spencer read the names off the back of the shrimp boats that lined the docks. He chuckled at the name *Ain't Got None* and thought he felt that way at times.

95

He had been to Lafitte a few times with his dad, who wanted to keep his son interested in writing about pirates. The town Jean Lafitte was just up the road a few miles, named after the notorious pirate Jean Lafitte after he and his brother helped Andrew Jackson defend the city of New Orleans in the War of 1812. For their aid to Jackson, they were given full pardon for their piracy. Spencer remembered the day that he and his dad spent all day traveling from Lafitte to Grand Terre following the footsteps of the pirates.

Hanging from an oak tree, an old wooden sign read "Bayou Barataria, home of prosperity." The sign didn't bear much truth to it, considering that Barataria meant dishonesty at sea, but many local fishermen made an honest living fishing for oysters, shrimp, crab, and other finned fish.

Spencer wondered if the old store would still be intact from the hurricanes that had passed through the area since his childhood. Coming around a street corner, though, he spotted the store, and to his surprise it was still open; he could tell that it had been fairly recently updated with a new metal roof. As he walked in, the bell on the door alerted the store owner someone had entered. *Does every store in the south have a bell?* he wondered.

"How ya doing?" an older lady said, sitting behind the counter.

"Just fine," Spencer replied, pulling a bottle of coke from one of the coolers.

"You fishing?" she asked with a thick Cajun accent. Spencer didn't know how to answer the question, but he definitely wasn't going to give the truth about searching for a voodoo woman's house. "I'm fueling up down the street at the marina."

"And you walked up here for a coke? The marina out of them?" she asked as he paid for his drink.

"No, I just needed to stretch my legs," he replied, trying to avoid any more questions.

"Whew, it's too hot to just stroll," she said. Spencer just smiled and walked out.

He quickly downed his drink and placed the glass bottle in a rack of other empty bottles; he wasn't interested in the lady seeing him head away opposite from the marina.

The rock and shell road was lined with oak trees that draped over, giving him shade from the sun. Approaching the house that Toni described, he remembered his dad warning him about Lebreaux and begging him not to pursue her; his dad knew his curiosity was much greater than other boys his age.

The house was small, two-story, and wood-framed with a porch that wrapped around two sides of the home. The white louvered shutters that remained hung by a screw, with most of the louvers already on the ground. Weeds and brush hid much of the bottom floor, but a clear path wound through the grass to the porch, and Spencer thought it was probably made by curious teenagers. As he stepped up on the porch, the boards squeaked with every step, and a dirt dauber buzzed his head a few times in warning.

Watching the bug fly off, he heard a faint whisper and quickly looked around to see if someone was behind him, but found nobody. He pushed on the half-opened door and stepped in, finding the rooms filled with graffiti on the walls and a few pieces of old furniture littered here and there. The whisper came again—he couldn't make out the words, but could hear a thick French-Cajun accent. "OK, who's there?"

he asked, but heard no response. *Must be the wind*, he thought.

By the looks of it, the house had been abandoned for a long time, and most of the rooms were empty and covered in dust. He carefully climbed the stairs, pressing on each step with his foot in hopes that it held his weight. The upstairs had only one bedroom, and remnants of candle wax pooled in the floor. *Goofy teenagers, this is the last place they need to do a séance or play with a Ouija board. Huh—the upstairs is smaller than it appears outside*, he thought. He pushed on a wall—it didn't look like a load-bearing wall. It looked like it had been added. He examined the wall and couldn't find anything, so he worked his way down to the wall directly below it.

He noticed the trim along the walls didn't look intact, and feeling the baseboards, he found a quarter-inch gap from the floor. A hall tree stood in an unusual place, so he pushed it to the side and stepped back, looking at the wall. Then, as Spencer placed both hands on the wall and put his weight into it, the wall swung open.

Stepping inside, he found a small, narrow set of stairs leading up, each board creaking with Spencer's weight. Reaching the top, he found himself on the other side of the wall, and by the looks of it, he was the first to have found this hidden passage. The small room contained a few chairs and books stacked on top of each other, and everything was covered in thick dust and cobwebs. Four old leather trunks were pushed against the false wall, and the other side of the room held three dresser drawers. He opened the drawers to find letters and more books. Opening one of the trunks, he

found an old letter on a thick yellow paper, the writing in
calligraphy.

He started to read what he could. Most of the letter
was in French, and the parts he could make out included "My
dearest Lebreaux" and "sailing the seas." He gathered it was
a love letter to Lebreaux. He pulled out another letter, one he
could read. Chills crawled up his spine as he read Lebreaux's
words, talking about her love, a pirate who sailed with Jean
Lafitte. It was *déjà vu*; the words he was reading were his
own thoughts verbatim—including the scenes he had written
about as a kid and the dreams he'd had about Lebreaux since
his childhood.

He pulled out another letter, and again, it told a story
that he had dreamed about years before. As the hair on the
back of his neck began to settle down, he heard the whisper
again, but this time he made out what it was saying:
"Together with de girl." Spooked, he closed the trunk, put
everything back as he found it—including the hidden wall—
and headed outside to collect his thoughts and slow his pulse.
Walking out the door, he met a figure in the bright sun and
jumped back in fear.

"This is private property," an old man said.

"Yes, I know. I'm sorry—I was just in town and
wanted to stop by. I knew Lebreaux in my childhood,"
Spencer answered.

The man stared at him, making Spencer feel
uncomfortable. He knew that the locals didn't take to people
who just made their own way.

"You the boy from Buras?" the old man asked.

Spencer stood confused at how he would know that.
"Yes, sir."

"Lebreaux said you would be coming. Where's the girl?"

"Girl? Lebreaux told you I would be coming?"

"Bring the girl back and you'll get your answers."

"What answers?" Spencer asked. He stepped off the porch toward the old man and dropped his phone; after picking it up, though, he looked back to find the old man gone. *This is too weird!*

Chapter 18

Spencer idled his boat into the marina after a thirty-minute boat ride from Lafitte. His mind was still buzzing with the events that day. He noticed Dusty on the back of his trawler with the engine cover off, so he drifted behind Dusty's boat. "Did you figure it out?" he hollered across the water.

"Yeah, I left a few bolts loose on the idle control. I got it fixed, just putting it back together. Where have you been?" Sweat poured off Dusty's forehead.

"Let me tie up and I'll walk down," Spencer replied.

Once his boat was securely tied, he left his equipment and walked to Dusty's boat; Dusty never felt the boat take a dip when Spencer stepped on.

"I had to run up to Lafitte today."

"Oh yeah? What for?" Dusty asked.

"Work stuff. You need a hand?" Spencer changed subjects.

"Nah, I'm about done."

After a few minutes Dusty had the cover back over the engine and walked in the wheelhouse to fire it up.

"Purrs like a kitten," he said walking back out. "Untie and we'll run it out again. Unless you're busy," Dusty said.

Lee DuCote

Spencer hesitated, knowing his equipment was exposed to anyone walking the docks. "Yeah, I can go," he answered.

He was always intrigued with the quick change of weather on the bay. When he came in, the water was choppy, and now it was smooth as glass. Spencer sat inside the wheelhouse with Dusty, the open windows allowing plenty of air to circulate through. By the sound of the engine and the gratified expression on Dusty's face, Spencer knew the engine was fixed. He also knew Dusty's poker face; when he would rub his beard in a downward motion, he was happy.

"So Lafitte for work?" Dusty questioned him again.

Spencer changed his story. "Well...I have always written novels about pirates and voodoo. I was up there taking pictures, mental pictures, of Lebreaux Papillion's house."

"I read one of your books ... I think the second one," Dusty said, surprising Spencer.

"Really? What did you think?" he asked.

"It was good. Strange that you wrote about that old voodoo woman, but cool how you made her a pirate for the 1800s," Dusty answered.

Not far from the marina, Dusty turned the old luger back toward the docks. "Now all I have to do is wash her down and we'll be ready for September."

"Hey, I don't know for certain, but Hackberry Bay might be closed again," Spencer said knowing that Dusty farmed close to the area.

"I thought so. We're good. I got a good farm this year." His accent seemed to thicken when he was talking about oysters.

"Now more important things, you in for a cold one at the Oyster Bar?" Dusty asked.

"Well, yes," Spencer laughed.

After pulling into his stall and after Spencer helped him tie up his boat, he walked down to his. Stepping in, he noticed one of his bags had been moved, and looking around, he saw another bag was open and his equipment was moved out of place. *What the hell?* he thought. Nobody messed with other people's things on the docks—it was just an understood courtesy.

"Everything OK?" Dusty asked.

"I think so. Someone went through all my equipment, but it seems to be here," he said, looking through his laptop bag.

"Well if everything is there, I'll see you at the bar."

"OK," Spencer replied, locking up his compartments and grabbing his duffle bags. Walking off the dock, Spencer thought he heard a familiar outboard motor in the water, but when he turned, he saw nothing in the marina or in the bay. The sound grew even more faint as a cool northern wind blew through the docks. *That is so creepy!* he thought, walking to his truck.

The Oyster Bar was filling up with local fishermen and oil and gas hands who worked the area. Dusty and Spencer walked in together and joined a group of oystermen near the pool tables.

"LeJeune, you look more like your daddy every day," commented an old man sitting down with a beer in hand.

"You mean like his mom," Jimmy interjected in a loud voice. Everyone at the table froze for a moment to see Spencer's reaction.

"I'll take that has a compliment," he said, taking a swig out of his beer.

"Hey, didn't LeJeune knock one out on you the other day?" the old man said.

"Even a blind pig can find an acorn every now and then," Jimmy spouted off and walked toward the bar.

"Come on, I'll shoot you a game," Spencer said to Dusty, pointing at one of the pool tables. Dusty happily accepted—he occasionally played in a few tournaments and never turned down a game.

"Winner buys next round," Spencer said.

Smiling, Dusty replied, "Rack 'em."

After Spencer losing the first three games and the two bottles of beer sitting untouched by Dusty, a loud voice came from behind.

Slapping two quarters on the side of the table, "I got winner!" Jimmy yelled.

Spencer shot him a "Go to hell" look and said, "Take your quarters—we're playing here."

"Well, excuse me, I didn't know a man couldn't play at this table. I guess I'll find some men who want to play," Jimmy said.

"So you're looking for men?" Dusty said. Everyone at the tables broke out into a loud laughter.

"You can go to hell!" Jimmy pointed at Dusty. It didn't faze him, which made Jimmy even madder. He pushed Dusty, sending him back against the table. Dusty stood back up, but before either man could say anything, Jimmy felt a pool stick pressing against his jugular vein.

Jimmy turned to see who was holding the other end of the weapon, blue chalk painting his throat from the end of the stick.

"Push him again and you'll leave here on a stretcher!" Spencer growled. He had been intimidated by the bully in school, but things had changed.

"LeJeune ... " Jimmy started to say.

"I said leave!" Spencer snapped, interrupting him and forcing the pool stick farther in his neck. Everyone at the tables was quiet and waiting to see what was next, but to their surprise, Jimmy turned toward the bar. Nobody was for certain if he was going to walk away or turn and fight, but with Toni now standing in his path, things went as everyone expected.

Jimmy turned and threw a right hook, landing it across Spencer's cheekbone, sending him back two steps, but not down. With his head already down, Spencer rushed Jimmy, wrapping both arms around his waist and driving him to the ground. Once he felt Jimmy's body bounce on the ground, he sat up and with his left hand holding his shirt, Spencer drove his right fist into the jaw of his high school bully.

A size 14 work boot pressed into Spencer's chest threw him backwards, and Jimmy pounced toward him to find Spencer quickly on his feet and landing an upper cut to Jimmy's already sore chin. Spencer landed another two solid punches before he felt the grizzly arms of the bar owner pulling him off.

Both Spencer and Jimmy were escorted in a not-so-friendly manner to the front door. "You two need to cool it before you can come back. Now go talk to the sheriff," said the voice of the man who had a grip on Spencer.

Breaking into the dark parking lot, they were welcomed by the sheriff. "You must have been waiting on us," Spencer said, rubbing his face.

"I should have known it would be you two. Jimmy, you know you're treading on thin ice, and Spencer, well, you know better."

"Sorry, sheriff," Jimmy said, wiping the blood from his lip.

"I don't have time for you two. I'll let her handle it," he said, pointing past them to Toni, who was standing behind them.

"What the hell are you two thinking!? Jimmy, I'm tired of you strutting around here like you own the place. You're acting like the same bully we went to school with!"

Jimmy lowered his head as the words pierced deeply. Spencer was staring at Jimmy, thinking he was off the hook, but no!

"And you!" she started back.

Spencer pointed at himself, "Me?"

"Yes, you. You don't have anything to prove. I know you were bullied in school, but this isn't school, and you're more of a threat to him now than the geeky kid you once were!" She stormed off.

Threat? What threat? How am I a threat to Jimmy?

"Sorry," Spencer said, reaching out to shake Jimmy's hand, only to have him knock it out of the way.

"You're not going to march back into town and take my girl," Jimmy said, storming off.

Want to bet! Spencer thought, watching Jimmy climb into his truck and jet off down the dark streets of Buras.

Chapter 19

Seems like I was doing this twenty years ago, Spencer thought with his feet propped up in his father's recliner and a piece of meat slapped on his eye. *Man, he has a mean right hook!*

His phone rang; he didn't recognize the number. "Hello?" he answered.

"Mr. LeJeune?"

"Speaking."

"This is officer Bell with Wildlife and Fisheries. I was asked to call you. We have two dead bottlenose dolphins, and they said you would want to examine them. Is that right?"

Spencer threw the piece of meat into the sink. "Yes, I would. Where are you?"

"Right now we're at the marina, and the dolphins are just past the Big Island. If you like, I can bring you there."

Spencer could tell by his accent he was a local. "I'll be right there." He hung up the phone.

On his way, he sent a text to Toni, "Hey, sorry about last night. I am on my way to meet Wildlife and Fisheries about two dead dolphins. Do you want to meet me?"

Within seconds she replied, "Yes!"

"At the marina," he texted back.

Pulling up, he saw three Wildlife and Fisheries trucks and a black Expedition with an LSU front license plate—it seemed everyone in that part of the country supported the Tigers with some sort of gear.

Before jumping out, he grabbed his Border Patrol cap that a friend had given him last year. He recognized a few of the men who seem to be huddled by one of the officers' trucks.

"Wow, what happened to you?" One of the men asked about his eye.

"I ran into Jimmy's fist last night."

"That was you? The sheriff said there was a tussle at the Oyster Bar last night."

"Yeah, it was me," he answered, embarrassed.

"You want to ride with us?" one of the officers asked.

"Yeah, that's fine. I need to wait on someone."

Spencer couldn't hold his suspense about who the other men were and held out his hand. "I don't believe we've met. I'm Spencer LeJeune."

"Nice to meet you. I'm Stan Murphy; I'm with one of the oil and gas companies," one of the men answered.

"Attorneys, huh?" Spencer answered. He knew that company men wouldn't wear slacks to investigate dead dolphins.

"Um, yes," Murphy answered, confused as to how Spencer would know.

"Gentlemen, we are going to look at some dead fish. Is it necessary that you accompany us?" Spencer asked.

"We need to make sure you document the findings accurately," another man spoke up.

"And what do you suppose *accurately* is? I'm a marine biologist, not a doctor." Spencer was insulted, but he wasn't going to show it. He had worked with oil and gas attorneys before, and they mostly wanted to provoke him.

"Still," the man replied.

Toni's Jeep pulled into the parking lot, "There's the doctor. And gentlemen—I wouldn't piss her off." Spencer walked to meet her.

Toni stepped out in workout shorts, a tank top, and running shoes.

Wow! "I take it you weren't at the clinic," he said.

"No, I was out running. Clearing my head. Who are those men?" She pointed to the attorneys.

"Attorneys," he answered.

"I guess I need to look professional." She stepped back, reached into the backseat of her Jeep, and pulled out a pair of scrubs. She stepped into the pants and pulled her shirt over her tank top, and within seconds she was ready to meet the lawyers.

On the boat ride out, Spencer could tell she was a little cold toward him; he wanted to apologize, but knew it wasn't the time.

Once they got to the small, grassy island, the dolphins were visible. "Did you find them like this, or did someone move them?" Toni asked. The officers were confused that she was asking questions when they were told to call Spencer.

One of them looked at him for direction, "I called her," he said, letting the officer know that she was part of this.

"No, ma'am, no one has touched them."

"It's weird that they would be this far out of the water," she said. When the bow of the boat rested on the thick marsh grass, Toni stepped out, followed by Spencer.

Toni looked back at one of the attorneys writing in a pad, "Are you going to document everything I do and say?"

"Yes," he answered without looking at her.

"Well, then I suggest you get your ass out here," she snapped back at him.

He looked at the grassy area and then back at his loafers. "I'll be OK here."

She started examining the dolphins. "Look, their anterior nares have dead skin around them."

"Their what?" Spencer asked.

She smiled at him. "Didn't you pay attention in school? Their blowholes." He was glad she smiled; he was beginning to worry.

"Meaning?" he asked.

"I've seen this in dolphins that have gotten sick since the oil spill. I'm sure that's what our friends are doing here." She looked back at them in the boat.

"Do you mind speaking up?" one of the attorneys said.

"Again, you can get your—"

Spencer covered her mouth with his hand. "They look to have been sick for a while," he yelled back.

She fought to remove his hand. "They have to do their job," Spencer said to her.

"They should have done their freaking job by shutting the well down sooner!" she said.

Spencer knew she was upset with all the dead animals in the bay and the hard time the commercial fishermen faced after the spill.

After taking a few pictures, she said, "Let's go. I'll send one of my techs back out here to dispose of them."

"And don't worry—I'll copy you in my pics," she added toward the men as she stepped back into the boat.

"Mr. LeJeune, is this going to increase?" a young Wildlife and Fisheries agent asked.

"I don't know yet; we are starting another study very soon. I'll let you know soon as I know," he answered.

On the short ride back, the attorneys huddled and talked only among themselves. Toni shot glares at them all the way back.

Once the boat slowed its speed, one of them asked Spencer, "How soon can we get a report from you?"

"I'll have it within a week."

"OK, thank you." Once the boat stopped in the stall, the men stepped out and never broke stride walking to their Expedition.

"I think you scared them," Spencer said to Toni.

"You have no idea." She was still boiling.

Spencer helped her out of the boat, and as soon as he let go of her arm, she added, "Don't *ever* pull that crap again. Fighting? Really?"

Spencer just stood there in silence. She grabbed a fist full of his shirt and pulled him down to her face, and he thought she was going to chew him out, but to his surprise she laid a kiss on his cheek.

"I'll call you later," she added, and then she stormed off.

Wow! He just stood in place and watched her walk away.

☠ Chapter 20 ☠

The year was 1810 and piracy was at its peak. "Captain! Drop anchor?" a young man yelled over the main deck of the eighteenth-century ship. A tall, dominating man held his hand out, suggesting he wanted them to wait.

The young man looked back at the other privateers standing behind him and said, "We're going to miss Tortuga port." The men on the ship stood quietly as they watched the captain standing behind the wheel on the stern castle deck.

"Drop anchor!" he finally yelled toward the forecastle. The young man rolled his eyes at the other men and pulled a lever, dropping the hundred-plus-pound anchor in the shallow waters north of the new Republic of Haiti.

"Ready the tenders to go ashore!" the tall man barked as he walked down onto the main deck.

"Captain, why are we not going to Tortuga?"

"We have business in Port De Paix," he said without looking at the man.

The men quickly threw the rope ladders over the sides leading down to the ship tenders. Pushing his long embroidered coat to his side, the young captain climbed down into one of the small tenders waiting for him. Within minutes, they reached a dock bustling with merchants and other smugglers fighting for their goods and top dollar.

The four men with cloth sacks filled with stolen goods thrown over their shoulders followed the captain as they wound their way through the dark cobblestone streets of the port.

"Take the loot and trade for the very best, and when ye are done, come here." The young captain pointed at a wooden sign that hung above an open door leading into a tavern, and the men continued their trek without questioning their feared captain.

Leaning against the thick wooded bar, the captain ordered a bottle of rum, and after throwing a silver piece toward the barkeep, he found an empty table.

"What brings ye to these parts?" another man asked, pulling up a chair to the table.

"Tired of being swindled in Tortuga!" he said before taking a swig from a tin cup filled with rum.

"The streets are a little quieter here," the man smiled.

"Indeed. Ye made the way here safe?" he asked the man.

"Ay! Have ye seen him?"

"Setting sail first light toward Grand Terre."

"I'll be on ye wakes."

"Glad to have you along for the trip, old friend," the captain replied.

"Good to be," the man smiled and turned up his cup of rum.

In the shadows of the dimly lit tavern sat a petite young woman with her head down, allowing her rayless silk hair to hide her face.

The captain peered over his cup at the shadowed figure. "What's the story?" he asked his friend.

Spinning around in the old wooden chair, the man glanced in the young woman's direction. "She been mourning the death of her brother, five years. Careful, she is known to have the power of a strong loa."

"Voodoo? Not one to believe," the captain said, standing to walk toward her table.

"First light?" The man asked, grabbing the captain's arm.

"First light."

"Five years is a long time to mourn the death of a brother," the captain said, inviting himself to sit at her table.

"I have not yet found happiness," she said with her head down.

"Are ye looking?"

"Maybe."

The captain filled her cup from his bottle of rum and then refilled his own.

"Poison in de bottle," she replied, looking at her cup.

"Good poison," he smiled.

With her head cocked sideways, she peered through the locks of her hair into the eyes of the young captain, and without saying a word, she sat up in her chair. The two locked gazes as the captain focused on the twinkle of light in her eyes that reflected from the candle on the table.

"Ye eyes are green," she smiled.

"A smile might mean happiness," he replied.

"Maybe," she teased.

A scuffle broke out toward the bar, breaking their stare to watch the commotion. A burly man leaped over the bar, clubbing one of the men in the head with a bat. "This ain't Tortuga! Ye want to fight, go there!" He pushed the other man out the door. The captain turned back to enjoy the beauty of the young woman.

"Where are ye sailing?" she asked.

"Barataria."

"Trading?"

"In search of something," he said, pouring another drink.

She leaned partially over the table. "Ye shall find it in Temple, but beware—he is searching also."

The captain slowly pulled the cup down from his mouth, staring at the girl. "Lafitte knows? And how do ye know that it's in Temple?" His expression turned cold.

She smiled. "I bring ye no ill will. Only a warning."

The four men returned, walking up to the table. "Captain, we are finished."

"Very well, take the trade to the ship," he replied without breaking his glare at the beautiful young girl. The men had turned to leave when he added, "We sail in three days!"

His friend, still sitting at the table across the room, was startled. "Three days?"

Smiling at the girl, he answered, "Three days."

She returned a warm, seductive smile.

Chapter 21

Sitting at his desk, Spencer looked at the picture of himself at five years old, standing with his mother and father. He leaned back in his old wooden desk chair and thought back on what little memory he had of the time spent with his mother. He remembered her soothing voice and warm smile; she was always so cheerful, no matter what. The words she shared with him about his best friend had stuck with him for years. "She is a good friend, something that is hard to find, hang onto that," she said about Toni.

Speaking of Toni, he thought as his phone buzzed with a text from her.

"Big favor? Can you bring me to Grand Isle to pick up a puppy? Please?" She texted.

He picked up his calendar and studied his schedule, and thought to himself, *I guess so.* "OK, but you owe me!" he replied.

"Thanks, I'm outside." She sent a smiley face.

He spun in his chair and walking to the sliding glass door, looked down at Toni, who was wearing scrubs and holding two cups of coffee. He just shook his head, smiling.

"I figured you would say yes, so I brought you a cup." She held it up.

"Come on up." After reaching the top, she paused for a moment and looked out over the bay. "I forget your view," she said as a pair of Roseate Spoonbills flew over heading toward the marsh.

"Let me change, and we can be on our way," he said through the open door.

"Take your time," she replied, still gazing over the water.

"Are you sure you don't mind?" she asked as he walked out with his bag hanging from his right shoulder.

"No, I was going to run this morning, but it can wait."

"We'll go this evening," she said.

"What if I'm busy?"

"Are you?" she asked.

"No," he said with a smile.

She just smirked and walked toward her Jeep.

"Can you give me a hand?" she asked.

"With?" he responded.

"I figured we could release your friend today," she explained, lifting a cardboard pet carrier with something wrapped up inside.

"Friend?" he asked.

"I had to wrap him in a towel because he was thrashing so much—the crane." She held the box up.

"Oh, yeah! OK." He opened the door for her.

"Well, thank you, kind sir," her accent changed to a thick southern Georgia tone as a tease.

Securing the cardboard box, Toni untied the front of the boat while Spencer fired up the engines. At that early hour the bay was still glassy, the morning dew steaming off the oyster boats barely rocking gently in their stalls. Spencer

119

blocked the sunlight with his hand as he backed out and cut the wheel to head out. Behind the console was a row of three captain chairs, one of which Toni climbed into and kicked her flip flops off to rest her feet on the console. Spencer looked at her and smiled, hinting for her to take her feet off the console, but she just smiled back, clueless about his request.

"You want to let him go where I found him?" he asked.

"Yeah, that would be best," she answered.

Reaching the island, Spencer pulled up on the throttle. "You rode this far with a bird?" she asked.

"Yep," he replied.

She grabbed the box, smiling and thinking that while he had partially saved the bird to see her, the old Spencer would have put the bird out of its misery.

"Is there some sort of bird ceremony to release him?" he asked.

"Yes, stand on the bow and raise both arms and your right leg bent at the knee."

"Oh, ha ha. Like *The Karate Kid*," he smiled at her sarcasm.

"You asked."

Toni leaned over the side of the boat and gently placed the crane into shallow water, hearing for only a brief moment a slight whisper float across the water.

She looked back at Spencer, "What?"

He looked clueless. "What?" he echoed.

"Never mind," she smiled and looked back toward the open water for the source.

On their way to Grand Isle, they passed Grand Terre, the island where the famous pirate Jean Lafitte made his headquarters and the place Spencer had written about many times in his books. They found an empty stall at the marina in Grand Isle and tied up. Toni picked up the cardboard box for the puppy. Walking off the docks, they passed a group of peculiar individuals lingering somehow out of place. When Spencer looked back, it seemed the group was talking about them.

"I don't know—I feel funny about leaving the boat unguarded with those guys around," he said.

"Wait here, then. I'll only be a few minutes," she replied.

When Spencer returned to the docks, the group of guys decided to walk farther down the beach, leaving him to wonder what they were up to. He decided to spend his time cleaning some of his equipment.

While winding a few cables that he had chunked into a case, he heard a raspy old voice. "That's a big boat. Fishing?" an old man said, leaning against a pylon.

"Sometimes. I mostly do research for the oyster industry." The old man nodded his head without saying anything.

"You from around here?" Spencer asked to keep the conversation going.

"Yep," he replied. There was an awkward moment of silence.

"You were in Lafitte yesterday," the man added.

Spencer stopped winding the cords, "How did you know that?" he asked.

"Saw your boat." Spencer smiled and shook his head.

"Did you find what you were looking for?" the old man persisted.

This time, Spencer put down the cables. "What are you not telling me?" he politely asked.

The old man rubbed his chin, "This much equipment for research? You sure you're not looking for something else?"

"What would that be?" Spencer asked.

"Oh, I've known a few people to come here looking for the treasure barge." The man looked at Spencer, adding, "You have that look in your eye."

"What do you know about the treasure barge?" There was no use in hiding the fact—the old man was on to him.

"I believe you're on the right track—Lafitte is a good place to start."

Toni walked up with a yellow lab puppy in hand, clueless about their conversation. "Good start for what?" she asked.

"Y'all have a good day," the old man said, walking off.

"I didn't mean to interrupt your conversation," Toni said.

"You didn't; we were just having small talk," he said, putting his equipment back.

"Why so much equipment?" she asked, watching him pack his gear away.

"That's just what it takes now-a-days," he replied. She was growing suspicious, and seeing a logbook with the title *Hackberry Bay* made her more suspicious; she knew that area was closed to oyster fishing.

Thinking back on what she just heard from the old man, she added, "Did you go to Lafitte recently?"

"I had to go the other day to meet some oyster farmers," he played off the question.

She could tell he was hiding something, but decided to let it lie for a while.

"Are you in a hurry to get back?" he asked.

"Not really."

"I need to stop by Dusty's camp on the way back." She climbed back in the same seat and held the little puppy in her lap, his ears flapping in the wind as he stuck his nose up.

"What's at Dusty's?" she asked.

"I told him I would check on it from time to time," he said, turning the wheel north just past Grand Terre.

Chapter 22

After dropping Toni and the yellow lab at his house to pick up her Jeep, Spencer returned to the docks to get his equipment ready for the following day of work.

The marina was buzzing with fishermen coming in from their afternoon trips. As he walked past the cleaning area, he admired the reds and specs hanging on hooks for the men to take pictures. It seemed to be a good day of fishing with the excitement in the air and the beer being inhaled.

Sitting on his boat, he continued to watch as more and more fishermen brought in their catches, something he had loved to do while his dad worked on their boat. It was a different sight to see fish from the bay on the boards compared to the saltwater fish he saw on the docks of Florida. But both types of fish were good on the grill.

A breeze blew through the docks cooling down the warm air, and he thought about his recent trip to Spain and the events that led him back to Buras.

Only a few months ago and after a lengthy flight with two layovers, Spencer was back home in Florida. His trip was mysterious, to say the least, between receiving the coin Toni and he had lost during their childhood to being chased by the four Spaniards. He was beginning to add the pieces together. *The translator,* he thought. *It had to have been him. Can't trust anyone these days.* He held tightly to the soft briefcase that carried the leather-bound case and silver coin as he worked his way to baggage.

Two days after getting back to Jacksonville, Spencer was back to his usual routine at the farmers' market, buying vegetables and fruit. He was a regular and enjoyed visiting with the farmers. He had found everything he needed when he spotted a few men out of the ordinary.

With the sweltering air of the sunshine state, most people dressed in shorts except the farmers, who always wore jeans. Three men stood out dressed in black slacks and dress shirts, their dark hair and complexion resembling the men who had chased Spencer a few days ago in Vigo. He watched them out of the corner of his eye and noticed they were not buying anything; they seemed to be looking for something— or somebody. With an uneasy feeling, Spencer set his basket of fruit down and slipped behind a booth unnoticed.

As Spencer observed from a distance, the three men made their way through the market, clearly looking for someone. One of them looked his way, not seeing him, but Spencer saw *his* face, the same face he saw looking down the hall of the Galicia Museum of the Sea in Vigo, Spain. *Who are these men? They followed me to the US? They followed me to the farmers' market?* Thoughts continued running through his head and then his mind jumped to the main thought: *They probably know where I live!*

Sneaking out to the parking lot, he spotted another man standing near his truck, *Crap! You've got to be kidding me!* Spencer stood back and thought of what he could do to distract the man long enough for him to get his truck. As he contemplated his plan, he saw the man answer his phone and begin moving in Spencer's direction at a quick pace. Spencer was standing in the parking lot with nowhere to hide other than ducking behind a car, and with the man quickly approaching, he didn't have much time.

The man wasn't looking directly at him, but making up ground quickly, almost in a jog. Spencer ducked his head and pretended to struggle at opening the trunk to a red sedan while the man quickly walked by him talking on his phone, not recognizing Spencer. He watched the man disappear into the market and then sprinted to his truck and headed home. On the ride, thoughts continued to run through his head. *Maybe they're not looking for me—he did walk past me. Maybe they are not after me to harm me, but need me for something?*

Pulling up, he decided to park around the corner from his house at his friend's home. Fumbling with the keys, he unlocked the door to have his question answered—the house was trashed! Tables and bookcases were turned over and everything was on the floor; they were definitely looking for something. *The map and the coin!*

He was attempting to straighten up when a voice sent chills up his spine—a man was standing in the room behind him.

"We know you have Nicholas Cardona's map. It belongs to the Vargas family and has for many years now. Hand it over," the man demanded.

"Why didn't you ask before you trashed my house?" Spencer asked.

"Hand it over and we will not kill you!"

Kill me? This has gone to a whole new level. Who's to say they won't kill me when I do? "It's not here," Spencer answered. The man stood in silence, staring at him.

"Who are you?" The question had puzzled Spencer from the beginning.

The man nodded out of politeness. "We work for the Vargas Family."

Spencer immediately remembered the name from the Archives in Seville Spain. "As in the Vargas who the King sent to find the treasure fleet in 1622?" he asked.

"Yes! I am not here for a history lesson. Hand over the map!" The man's voice grew angry.

"Again, it's not here. It will take me a day to get it," Spencer shot back.

The man studied Spencer for a short moment before responding, "Very well, bring it to the downtown Marriot before 5 p.m. tomorrow. If you don't, then we will hunt you down!"

Spencer didn't doubt his words. The man shouted at the other men, who were now standing outside, to climb in their car, and the four of them sped off in a black Mercedes. After flipping back over his couch, Spencer sat with his feet propped on the coffee table that remained on its side. Gathering his thoughts, he glanced down at his watch. *It's 12:32 p.m. I don't have much time.*

He packed all the personal belongings he could, straightened up as best he could, and headed to the boat docks to retrieve boat. After loading the Yellowfin, he ducked into the marina office to visit with the owner. He asked the owner if anyone were to ask about him, to tell them he went to the Florida Keys for research. Stopping back by his house, he gave the same message to his neighbors, hoping that it would buy him some time when the men came looking for him.

Lastly, he opened one of the compartments on the boat and reached under the lid, making sure the leather case was still securely fastened. It was.

After stopping to fill up his truck, he started the drive back to his birthplace—Buras, Louisiana.

Chapter 23

"LeJeune! You daydreaming?" A voice shook Spencer out of the past and into the present.

"Hey Dusty," he said, looking up.

"Heard you had some important work today. Escorting a puppy?" Dusty said.

"Yeah, it's tough work." Spencer stepped out of his boat and onto the dock while Dusty chuckled under his breath.

"We're having a Booray game at my camp this evening. You interested?" Dusty offered.

Spencer thought for a moment. "Yeah, sounds good. I haven't gambled in a while."

"See you at 8 p.m.! Bring beer ... no puppies." Dusty walked off, still chuckling.

He gathered up his equipment and walked toward his truck, noticing that the conversations from the fishermen were beginning to settle down, with most of them heading toward the Oyster Bar to share their stories all over again with cold beer and hot crawfish.

Spencer headed to Gentry's Store to pick up the much-needed liquid supplies for the card game; it had been a long time since he played Booray, but he was confident he still remembered.

Walking in, he was greeted by Mr. Gentry. "Boating puppies around, huh?" he said, grinning.

"I see Toni has come by here, too," Spencer replied.

"Yep, glad to see you two friends again," Mr. Gentry said, holding a broom. It was a position that Spencer remembered him in since he was a kid, always sweeping.

"Big card game tonight?" he asked, popping open a paper bag.

"Yes sir," Spencer handed him a twenty. He helped Mr. Gentry place the twelve pack of beer in the sack and watched him open the antique brass cash register to get change. "Not much has changed in here," Spencer said, looking at the cash register.

"Are you kidding me? I have AC now," Mr. Gentry said.

"Well that's true." Spencer smiled.

Back at his house, the steam caused limited visibility as Spencer stepped out of the shower and picked up the buzzing phone to find a message from Toni: "Have fun at the game tonight," it read. *Good grief! Everyone knows everything around here.* He dried off and stepped into a pair of jeans as he looked into the mirror. *There's one secret they'll never learn.* He picked up the silver coin and tucked it deep in his right front pocket.

Arriving back at the docks, he noticed Dusty's trawler was gone; instead he was greeted by the owner of the marina. "I was told to send this with you," the man said, handing Spencer a brown paper bag. Inside were fresh fish wrapped in cellophane for grilling.

Evening was setting in, with the sky turning orange and the birds heading inland to roost. Spencer motored slowly out of the marina while watching a flock of pelicans fly overhead.

After a smooth ride to Dusty's camp, Spencer was surprised at the number of boats tied to the old dock, and pulling into the marshy grass, he found just enough space to park his big boat. It looked out of place here too and overshadowed the others.

Dusty walked out of the screen door. "Did you get a sack from the marina?" he called out to Spencer.

Spencer held it up while walking up the dock toward him. "Thanks. I forgot it when I left," Dusty responded. They walked in to find the camp full of men, some of whom Spencer recognized and others he didn't.

Once Dusty had the fish grilled, Spencer joined the others who had already settled at the table.

"Wow! This fish is great," he said with a full mouth.

"One of the guides today gave us an ice chest full. There's nothing like fresh-grilled reds." Spencer nodded his head in agreement.

As he threw his paper plate into the trash bag, the camp shook with a clap of thunder. "This might be an all-nighter," Dusty said, looking out the window at the lightning from an approaching storm. The men broke off into three groups, and with the shuffling of cards, the popping of beer cans, and the air filling with cigar smoke, Booray began.

Spencer was sitting at a table on the porch. The open air quickly cooled as the rain began falling from the storm, lighting striking deep in the marsh, sending another clap of thunder. An older man pulled back one of the chairs and greeted everyone as he sat. He looked at Spencer, and said, "Small world." It was the same man that had spoken with

Spencer at the docks in Grand Isle, the same man that knew Spencer was looking for the treasure. *Too small!* he thought.

After several hours of playing, the storm subsided, and Spencer walked outside to relieve himself off the pier.

Walking back up the steps, he was startled by the flash of a match lighting a cigar. "Don't worry, I'm not one to talk," the old man said to Spencer.

"Thank you. I'm not interested in letting everyone know I'm searching for the treasure. Especially if I fail," he replied.

"Oh, I wouldn't say you'll fail. You might just not find what you're looking for."

Isn't that failing? Spencer thought.

"What did you mean that I was starting off right in Lafitte?" Spencer asked.

"Starting at Lebreaux's house would be a good start," the old man replied.

"If you know about Lebreaux and the treasure, why aren't you looking for it?" Spencer cut to the chase, keeping his voice down.

"I'm too old to be searching for treasure. You know, many people think Lebreaux is a voodoo spirit." He took a long drag off his cigar. "It's rumored that she was the lover of a buccaneer who sailed with Jean Lafitte."

"Jean Lafitte? That was 200 years ago," Spencer interrupted.

"Time doesn't mean anything to a spirit. It was said that she lived in Haiti with her brother, Jean-Francois, a rebel slave trying to achieve his freedom. This buccaneer, I don't remember his name, took her aboard his ship, and together they helped Lafitte in piracy before turning on him."

Spencer listened quietly as the old man continued with his story, not knowing that he was repeating Spencer's dreams since his childhood. The letters that he had found in Lebreaux's house were starting to become clearer, and chills prickled his skin.

"Well, that's what I know. And I will not say anything about you. Good luck in your hunt," the old man said as he stood to walk back inside.

"Oh, one last thing. These storms over the years have buried anything out there deeper in the mud. Your barge might be fifteen to twenty feet under mud."

Spencer stood with him. "Thank you, and thank you for not saying anything ... and the stories." He shook the man's hand.

"Well, they're just that ... stories."

No, they're more! Spencer thought.

He watched the old man disappear into the camp, then turned and walked back out to the end of the dock. The moonlight was peeking through the clouds as the storm marched north with the faint sound of thunder. He stepped down into his boat and sat leaning against the side looking at his watch; it was 2:30 a.m. The lights from the camp house reflected off the water with the occasional shout from someone inside who was either winning or losing.

Spencer was trying to wrap his head around the fact that the dreams he had, for the most part, were true. *What is Lebreaux trying to tell me? Is there more to the treasure?* He wrestled with his thoughts until Toni entered his mind.

Lee DuCote

☠ Chapter 24 ☠

On the stern castle deck of an eighteenth-century pirate ship, stood a tall and dark-complexioned man. His black hair, looped earrings, long frock coat, and the cutlass hanging from his sash signified his status as a pirate. He barked orders to the men below on the quarter deck, who didn't question him and scurried to and fro to carry out his plan. The night was clear and bright as they sailed through the dark waters aimed toward a small island in the distance.

"Prepare the ship's tender!" he yelled toward the main deck as he walked down the weather-beaten steps. Then he disappeared into the mate's quarters toward the captain's cabin.

"Are ye sure he won't be of anger?" asked a small black woman lying on the bed. Her long dark hair curled over her shoulders as she stood to greet the man.

"He will not," the man said, running the back of his hand lightly over her face.

"Something tells me to trust you," she replied as his lips touched hers.

"We'll be anchoring soon, so get ready." He walked toward the door and stopped. "Stay with me, and I'll make all your dreams come true." He smiled, revealing his stained teeth.

"I'll follow you to da ends of da earth," she whispered as the door shut behind him.

As the tender rested on the sandy beach, the crew and the young lady climbed out in ankle-deep water, making their way to the structures on the island called Grand Terre.

"What if he want to sell me?" she asked the young man.

"You have much to offer, and I will fight for you."

They entered a dark room lit with candles and reeking with the aroma of dead fish and rum. Making their way to a table under a black iron lantern, she stood behind the young man.

"Ay! How did she sail?" a man with short hair and a long, thin mustache asked.

"Smooth and fast," the young captain answered.

The short-haired man peered around the young captain's frock coat at the young woman. "Who do we have here? Slave?"

"No, she's with me."

"What are ye going to do with a woman on board?" he asked, confused.

"She has much to offer. See for yourself." He pushed the woman closer to the table.

"What do ye have to offer?" he questioned, squinting his eyes. She stood motionless and afraid, not saying a word. "Well?" his voice rose.

She held her hand out. "What do you have on you?" she asked, her voice soft and shaking.

The man leaned back against the wooden chair and grinned. "Haitian! I know a few things about Haitian women, like voodoo. I have been known to break bread with a Cecile

Fatiman." He studied her for a short moment. "Do you know the name?"

The young girl stood quiet, for the name was well known. Cecile was a voodoo priestess and the most powerful mambo in her homeland, and the young woman's skin crawled with fear at hearing the name. The man smiled and then reached into his coat pocket, revealing a silver coin.

"Here," he handed her an old silver coin.

Placing it in her right palm, she formed a fist and closed her eyes. Standing as if in a trance, she moved slightly back and forth, humming a low tone, her hand jerking violently as she held the coin tight. The man chuckled, starting to believe she was wasting his time, but then her eyes shot open.

"Ye seek the barge," she whispered for him to hear.

His grin disappeared as he craned his head forward. "What can ye tell me?"

"It's here, in da bay."

"Where?!" his voice deepened and his eyebrows rose.

She closed her eyes, and her facial muscles twitched as she tried to recall. "I don't see it."

The man folded his arms and sat quiet for a moment. "I've told no one about this," he finally said. "You will help me!"

She looked at the young captain who had a concerned look on his face. "How?" he began to ask, but the man held up his hand to hush. The young captain drew back.

"She'll be protected," the mustached man assured him. "Now, take what you have to Temple and sell it," the man added.

She wrapped her arm around the young captain's arm, not wanting to be separated. "Stay here. I will come back for you," he assured her.

"Sit!" The mustached man ordered her, pointing at a chair across the wooden table. She sat watching the man who she had come to love walk through the darkness of the tavern and out into the air of Barataria Bay. Then she looked back at the man across the table.

"Now, I know I don't have much time here before the government forces us off this island and out of the bays. I want to find the treasure barge before then." He placed a glass in front of her and filled it with rum, spilling some on the wooden table. "To the treasure," he said, raising his glass and downing the rum.

"You are a captain?" she asked softly.

He smiled, "Ay! Captain Jean Lafitte, and what, pray tell, is *your* name?"

She looked down at the ground, then back at him with a devilish grin. "I am Lebreaux Papillon."

Chapter 25

"LeJeune!" A voice shook Spencer from his sleep. He could feel his boat rocking back and forth from Dusty's foot on the bow.

"Dang. I must have dozed off," he said, rubbing his head. The sky was light with the sun peeking just over the horizon.

"Light weight," Dusty laughed. Spencer wasn't hungover, but was disoriented from waking from such a deep sleep. "Well, come back in, we're cooking breakfast."

Spencer followed Dusty back into the camp house, where he found most of the men awake with their coffee taking the place of the beer they held just a few hours ago. After breakfast, most of the men left, leaving their all-night card game in their wakes.

Spencer helped Dusty clean up as the last few left. "Who was the old man last night?" he asked Dusty.

"I don't know—they were *all* old men," he laughed.

"No, the gray-haired man who sat at my table?"

Dusty looked at him oddly. "You must have had more than I thought; there wasn't anyone here with gray hair."

Spencer knew he hadn't drank too much, nor was he going crazy. He untied his boat and backed out from the pier, and turning the wheel, he waved to Dusty as he sailed out, heading toward the marina. Thinking about the old man, he felt his phone buzz in his pocket with a message from his friend in Florida about the piece of wood and nails found a few days ago.

"Did the professor at LSU have anything for you?" the message read. Spencer went to answer the text, but dropped the phone, and trying to pick it up and drive at the same time, he managed to change the text to Toni's number without knowing it.

He replied, "Not yet. I will call him today, and if no answer I'll just head to LSU and find out."

"Ok? I'll go with you." The returned message read.

Spencer looked at his phone, not understanding, then realized he had sent the message to the wrong person. "Haha, sorry wrong person," he typed.

"Why are you going to LSU?" she texted without giving him a chance to send it to his friend in Florida.

"Research," he answered.

"What kind of research?"

"Boy, you're nosey this morning," he replied.

"Yep. Lunch?" she asked.

"Ok, I'll call in a few."

After pulling into the marina, he walked to his truck and opened the door, allowing the heat that had already accumulated during the morning to escape. He cranked the truck and turned the AC on high, and setting his phone down, he noticed a missed text from Toni. Instead of replying, he pressed the call button, and she answered.

"So, we are going to Baton Rouge today?" she said.

Spencer thought a moment about how he could take her without telling her the real reason he was going. "Can you be ready in an hour?" he asked.

"Yep, pick me up at the clinic."

"OK," he answered.

Toni was getting something out of her jeep when Spencer pulled into the parking lot; she smiled and held up one finger asking for a minute, then disappeared back inside.

He had just changed stations on his satellite radio when the passenger door flung open and Toni climbed in. "Ready," she said. He turned to look behind him, and before he could get backed up, he heard the station change as Toni reset it. Both wearing aviator sunglasses and now listening to Toni's station, they jetted off toward Baton Rouge, home of the LSU Tigers.

On the way they talked about her parents, his parents, school, and the coming football season. Toni was an avid LSU fan and never missed a game, either going or watching on TV. It was a three-hour drive, which gave them plenty of time for her to explain the team stats for LSU and Spencer time to egg her on about Florida beating them during the season.

Once on campus, Toni began telling him directions to get to different places, including the metallurgy department, but to her surprise he drove right to the building.

"You've been here before?" she asked.

"Once," he replied. They walked toward the building, and she continued to ramble on about the live oaks that lived throughout the campus.

Walking in, they were greeted by a student. "Can I help you?" she asked.

"I am here to see Professor Collins about a piece of wood with antique nails," Spencer replied.

"Oh yes, we've had a lot of discussion on that. Wait here, and I'll get him."

"What are you doing with a piece of wood and nails?" Toni asked before the door could shut behind the student.

Fearing that it might have not been the best idea to bring her, Spencer replied, "It was caught in a fishing net and seemed strange. I brought it in to see where it came from and the oil residue that was on it."

Why bring it to LSU? Weird, she thought, but remained silent.

An older man walked through the doors with the student. "Mr. LeJeune?" he asked.

"Yes sir."

"Glad to meet you, and sorry I wasn't able to meet with you when you dropped off the piece. Come on back, interesting stuff." They followed the professor back to a lab, where there was a plastic tub on a table with the piece of wood submerged in it.

"The wood is native to Central America and wouldn't be strange to find, but the nails," the professor pulled the wood out and pointed to the nails, "they are handmade—"

"Dating them back pre-1600s," Spencer interrupted him.

"Correct. You've been doing your homework." Toni raised an eyebrow toward Spencer, but he just smiled back.

"This particular nail form was popular for ship building. We researched it back to other nails used in Mexico. Is that the answer you were looking for?" he asked Spencer.

"Yes, sir. Thank you for your help," Spencer said while shaking the man's hand.

"Anytime—let me know if I can help any further, and tell our Florida friend hello for me."

"I will," Spencer answered.

Walking out of the building, Toni asked, confused, "You drove three hours for two minutes of something you already know?"

"Yes, but I wanted it confirmed."

"What does that have to do with biology?" she asked, already figuring out the answer.

"Just an old hobby," he responded briefly, discouraging any more questions. She took the hint, but still had other thoughts already stirring.

"Where can we eat lunch?" he asked once back inside the truck.

"I have the best place. Turn here." She pointed to their left, leading him to park in front of a small restaurant that was packed with college students. "Best burger in town," she said, closing the truck door behind her.

After ordering, he asked, "Are you in a hurry to get home?"

"No, whatcha got planned?" she smiled.

"Let's stop in New Orleans."

"Sounds good."

Within a few hours of eating and driving, they found themselves in downtown New Orleans near the French Quarter. Spencer found a parking garage that his truck fit in, and they headed straight to Café De Monde for beignets. They sat outside under the canopy with the ceiling fans blowing, eating their powdered sugar beignets.

"This is so good," Toni said, trying not to engulf hers.

Looking at an advertisement sign across the street, Spencer asked, "Have you ever gone on a ghost tour here?"

"No."

"Let's go on one," he said.

She shook her head chewing a big bite, "OK."

As night fell, the city became alive with jazz music and people, and Spencer and Toni made their way to a corner to meet their guide for the ghost tour. Other people joined them on the busy corner, among them a lady dressed in an old Victorian dress, her facial skin pale with make-up, and her voice so low it was hard for everyone to hear. Their tour began.

During the tour, they were led down different parts of the French Quarter and heard many different stories. But it was a story told in front of an old building on the 900 block of Bourbon Street that shook both Spencer and Toni.

The young lady told the story of Lafitte's Blacksmith Shop Bar, the oldest bar in the United States, dating back to the early 1700s. She explained that Jean Lafitte and his brother used the blacksmith shop as a front for their smuggling operation, with many other privateers bringing stolen goods from ships and vessels sailing the Gulf of Mexico. The crowd inside broke out into a yell after someone bought the house a round. Most of the tour walked up to the bar to join the crowd in their enjoyment of the paid drinks, but Spencer and Toni stood on the street with their tour guide.

"People say they have seen Jean Lafitte himself drinking at a table in the corner by himself, always with the same iron fleur-de-lis lamp."

"Lamp?" Spencer asked.

"Silly me—a lantern, not a lamp," the tour guide replied. Toni looked up at Spencer, wondering about his thoughts.

"A mysterious female ghost has been seen many times here, a Haitian woman. She sometimes appears in a mirror on the second floor. The bartenders swear they have heard her whisper a certain phrase."

"What's the phrase?" Toni asked.

"*The mark is on the* Potosi. Doesn't make any sense, so I think the bartenders are just making it up to generate business. I better gather everyone for the next stop," she added, walking up to the building.

"I have chills," Toni said, pointing at her arms.

"Yeah, that was creepy," Spencer agreed. Both of their memories had shot straight back to their childhood encounter with the voodoo woman ... and the phrase she told them before she vanished.

Following the group, Spencer felt Toni's arm wrap around his. "You scared?" he asked.

"Cold," she replied innocently, as a faint shadow in the second-story window watched them walk away.

Chapter 26

The ride home was quiet and rather quick, with no traffic on the roads. Spencer looked over at Toni from time to time to see if she was sleeping.

Coming over the bridge into Empire, Louisiana, Toni asked, "Do you think the woman that was in the story was Lebreaux?"

Spencer realized she was quietly thinking about their ghost tour story. "Sure sounds like it to me," he replied.

He pulled up to the clinic just after 11 p.m. "Thanks for the evening," Toni said, opening her door.

Spencer got out and walked around his truck. *Handshake or hug?* he wondered.

She slipped into the seat of her jeep with one leg still dangling out. He leaned in to hug her and caught her off guard, so she gave him a one-arm hug with a pat on the back. "Let's talk tomorrow," she said, leaving him confused.

"Sounds good." He gave her a smile and wave and climbed back in his truck.

Holy crap, that was embarrassing! I should have just said goodnight—I look like an idiot, he thought.

Back at home, Spencer sat in his recliner with the TV off, rolling the old oblong silver coin in his right hand. *The mark is on the* Potosi! *What does that mean?* The question had baffled him for years, and now with the coin both in his dream and in a local ghost story, it was even more confusing.

He had looked up "Potosi" many times on the Internet, and results had always led him back to a town in Bolivia. The town sat at the foot of Cerro Rico, known as the richest mountain in the world. The Spanish had mined silver there for hundreds of years. He knew that many Spanish fleets had received their silver from the area by mule and llama trains that traveled the long distance to Vera Cruz, Mexico.

Walking over to his computer, he pulled up the information on Potosi, reading through the same material he had many times before. This time, he focused more on the coin than the area, mulling words over in his mind: *8 reales coin. Pieces of 8. All the same coin.* He continued to read through the site, noticing the assertion that "the mint Casa de la Moneda is in Potosi." Tired, he followed the screen with his finger, studying more on the mint. He learned that an old saying from Spain had evolved from Potosi: "To be worth a Potosi means to be worth something," he said out loud. Looking down at the coin that rested beside the keyboard, he added, "Um, maybe I should just go see where you were stamped."

He pulled up flight information on flights from New Orleans to Santa Cruz, Bolivia, then researched driving to Potosi from there. *A full day in travel, not too bad.* He stretched his arms over his head and yawned. A knock at the door startled him.

Turning from his computer, he saw Toni standing on the other side of the sliding glass doors. Making eye contact, she waved and made an exasperated expression. Looking at the clock beside the door, he motioned her to come in.

"You're up late," he said.

"I wasn't ready to head home yet."

He snatched the coin from the desk and walked to the kitchen. "You want something to drink?" he asked.

"I'm fine." She plopped down on the couch and threw her feet up on the coffee table.

They talked about their experience on the ghost tour and reminisced about their childhood encounter with Lebreaux. Deep into their conversation, Spencer started drifting back to his middle school days and early high school. He thought back about being the center of many jokes and the constant bullying from Jimmy. Spencer had been taught a valuable lesson by his father: "Forgive, forget, and move on!" He heard the words many times and for the most part had lived by them, *Even though it felt good to knock that ball out of the park the other night. And it felt even better to punch Jimmy in the head!*

A question from the couch pulled him out of his daydream. "Why did you wait till the week you were leaving to tell me?" Toni asked. She was lying on the couch with her head resting on a pillow, facing him.

"Well, those were some hurtful years. I just didn't feel like I owed anyone a goodbye."

"Including me?" she asked.

"Toni, we never talked, we went different ways. You were dating Jimmy, the very guy who made my life miserable."

She rolled over to her back and stared at the ceiling, "Teenage years make you do some dumb things," she said. Spencer shook his head in agreement.

"Why are you being so nice now?" he asked.

Still looking at the ceiling, she responded. "I feel like I have run off all my friends. After I broke up with Jimmy, things got weird. I was glad to be done with him, but I went into a depression for a while. I dated some in college, but I was missing something. Then I met Clint." She looked at Spencer, adding, "You probably don't know about him?"

"Dusty told me," he replied.

"Oh." *Why were he and Dusty talking about me and Clint?* "Anyway, I fell in love with Clint, and things were great for a few years. I thought we would get married, but he chased after that stupid music dream ... and well, he was more in love with his dream than me."

What does this have to do with me now? Spencer wondered.

"Spencer, you were the one true friend I had. You were always someone I trusted. I know I screwed that up wanting to be popular, but I didn't mean to hurt you. I'm sorry," she said, looking back up at the ceiling. Spencer noticed a single tear roll down her face before she wiped it away.

"Is that why you came over here? To apologize about the past?" he asked, leaning closer to her.

"No, not really." She sat up on the couch looking at the clock.

"Wow, it's 2 a.m.? I better go. I have to work tomorrow."

Walking her down the stairs and to her jeep, he said, "High school was a long time ago, I don't care about those years."

"I'm not one to relive those years either; I just wish things had been different between us." She climbed in the jeep.

"Things happen for a reason," he said.

"Maybe." She turned over the key and cranked her jeep.

"Get some sleep and I'll text you tomorrow. Thanks for a fun day. I needed it," she added.

Spencer rested both arms on the roll bar, "Yeah, I had a lot of fun too."

"Good night," she smiled.

"Drive safe," he stuttered, as she backed out and drove off.

"You still didn't answer my question," he said, watching the taillights of her jeep disappear around the corner.

☠ Chapter 27 ☠

"Welcome to the Temple," an old grungy man said, tying the tender to the pier.

"Make sure she's here when I get back!" the young captain replied, flipping a piece of eight to him.

The old man nodded and scurried to tie the back of the tender. Moving quickly through the crowded pier and pushing other pirates and smugglers out of the way, one of the oarsmen asked, "Captain, what's ye hurry?"

"Let's get this loot traded and be on our way!" he answered, pushing a drunken sailor out of his way.

Walking through the tables and tents set up by the traders, the young captain noticed more people from nearby New Orleans than normal.

"What's with all the commoners here?" he asked one of the traders.

"They're here mainly for weapons—they fear a war is coming," the trader replied in a raspy voice.

"British!" the captain frowned.

A fight broke out a few tables down, and with the wisdom the captain and the crew had of Temple, they slowly backed behind the tables. Minutes later, gunfire rained down the aisles, white smoke filling the air from the black-powder guns. The gun fight lasted only seconds, and shortly after, things went back to normal—a normal day at Temple.

Something tells me that I shouldn't have left her with him, the captain was thinking. *He's just another conniving privateer. But her beauty is spellbinding and irresistible. I will cut his throat from ear to ear if he hurts her.*

"Captain, there is word that a man with spices is in the next aisle. We are going over there," one of the crewmembers whispered in the captain's ear. He nodded with approval, knowing the high price the spices would bring in the islands.

He began to turn from the table when a bright necklace caught his eye. It was silver with a fleur-de-lis medallion, and the medallion, no bigger than a coin, held a bright green emerald in the center.

"The necklace! What do ye want?" he asked the trader.

"Three pieces," the man quickly replied.

Then the captain saw the folded-up bamboo parchment with a leather lace tying it together, and somehow it stirred his curiosity. "What is this?" he asked.

"Just some old map—it has holes cut out. Worthless. I'll give it to you with the necklace," the trader responded, sensing a sale in the making.

"Done!" The captain handed him three coins and snatched the items.

Walking to catch up with his men, he unrolled the bamboo map to find the cut out holes and the signature at the bottom: Nicholas Cardona.

"We traded everything for all the man's spices," one of the captain's crew reported. We will fetch a great price for these."

"Very well. Back to the tender!" he ordered the crew.

Again, the man who had asked earlier turned back to another crew member to wonder quietly, "Why is the captain in such a hurry?"

"He's worried about Lafitte taking the girl," came the reply.

Once the tenders were lifted out of the water and pulled onto the deck of the ship, the captain barked orders to pull anchor and set course to Grand Terre. The young captain paced his quarters as the ship, with little wind, crawled through the quiet waters of Barataria Bay.

A knock came at his cabin door. "Yes?"

The door slowly swung open, "Captain, we are having trouble sailing in the dark, can—"

The timid buccaneer was interrupted, "Grand Terre!" the captain shouted and slammed the door. *Even God will not be able to save him if he lays one hand on her*, the thought again as he sat down at a table looking at a painting of a compass rose hanging on the wall.

Another loud knock startled the captain, who had slipped off to sleep sitting at the table. "Yes?" he snapped again.

"We are almost there, Captain. Grand Terre is visible." The same voice said through a closed door.

"Very well," he yelled back, and slipping his hat on, he emerged onto the upper deck to inspect their arrival. His eye's widened and hands formed into a fist as he realized a ship was missing—Jean Lafitte's ship. He knew Lafitte would not have left her behind, but ordered the tenders into the water to go ashore to make sure.

Bursting into the dark tavern with wet, sandy boots, he scanned the room to find only a few drunken sailors.

"Where is he?" he barked at the bar keep.

"They set sail this morning," the bartender's voice shook.

"Where!"

"He didn't say."

"The girl?"

"She was with him," the bartender admitted, backing up in fear of the captain, but took a breath of relief when the captain sat at one of the tables with his men looking on.

After a few moments in silence, he looked back at the barkeeper with a demand: "Paper, ink, and a bottle of rum!"

"Coming right up." The barkeep fumbled with the paper and ink while the captain moved a lantern from a nearby table.

"That backstabbing freebooter!" he said, pouring a cup of rum. He then leaned over the old, yellowish paper and began to write. His men quietly made their way to the bar and ordered their own bottles, trying not to look at the captain.

After half the bottle had disappeared, the captain folded the letter and handed it to the barkeeper. "If they should return, you will give this to her!" he ordered.

"I will," the trembling barkeeper replied.

The captain snatched his bottle and walked to the door. "We sail at first light," he said before descending into the night air of Barataria Bay with the bamboo map inside his coat.

Chapter 28

Mr. Gentry was at his normal duties sweeping the wooden floors of his store. The store hadn't changed much since it was constructed in the early 1900s with the exception of a few rebuilds due to storms. Even the surge from Katrina had a hard time trying to destroy the old building. With brick walls and a tin roof, Mr. Gentry would tell folks that the floods only preserved the old wooden floors. The only thing that had disappeared from the store was the old soda fountain and oak bar, and he blamed video games for that declining business. "Kids want to stay home and play those dang TV games," he would say.

Retrieving the dustpan that he kept behind the counter, he heard the bell on the door. Looking up while sweeping dirt into the dustpan, he greeted the four men that entered with an "Afternoon." It was obvious to Mr. Gentry that the four men were not local, and he wondered if they were even from this country. He watched the men walk throughout the store, looking at the shelves with food, drinks, a few tools, and other small items. They were dressed in dark slacks and dress shirts, and all four men were dark complexioned with dark hair.

"Can I help y'all find anything?" Mr. Gentry asked from behind the counter with a concerned tone.

"No. We are just looking," one of the men replied without looking up. They eventually came together in front of the coolers, and Mr. Gentry heard them laughing about something and heard them speaking in Spanish. One man reached in the cooler and pulled out four tall glass bottles of soda, and Mr. Gentry noticed that they were the Mexican cokes he carried. Many people enjoyed the Mexican cokes over American. "Real sugar! None of that manufactured crap!" Mr. Gentry said.

They approached the counter, one of them smiling at Mr. Gentry as though trying to befriend him, but it wasn't working.

"This is good, no?" he asked.

"Most people like 'em," Mr. Gentry said, punching the buttons of the brass cash register. "$8.26."

The guy standing in front of him spoke to the man behind him in a language Mr. Gentry didn't understand. The man frowned and retrieved a $20 from his pocket and handed it to him.

"You keep the change," he told Mr. Gentry.

"I'll put it in here." Mr. Gentry placed the change in a donation jar on the counter for a local baseball team. Three of the four men walked out, leaving the one that had handed the money for the cokes.

"You wouldn't know where to find Spencer LeJeune?" he asked Mr. Gentry.

Most people who asked questions would normally get more information than they asked for, and if asking about someone, they always got an answer unless they mispronounced someone's last name—then Mr. Gentry always quizzed them before giving any information. In this case, not only did this dark-complexioned man mispronounce Spencer's name, and badly, but he acted a little too peculiar for the old man.

"Can't say I know him," he said, shaking his head.

The Spaniard studied him for a moment, "Really? I understand he lives here."

"I can't say I have ever met a Spencer LeJeune," Mr. Gentry said, repeating the last name exactly the way he heard it; that way he didn't feel too bad about lying.

"OK," the man said with a funny look on his face as he turned to walk out.

"If I do run into this Spencer fellow, who can I say is looking for him?" he asked the Spaniard.

"Don't worry about it; I'll find him," the grim-looking man said, walking out.

Mr. Gentry walked around the counter and watched through the door as the four men climbed into a black Mercedes and drove in the direction of the marina. He then quickly ran back behind the counter and reached down, picking up an old rotary phone and placing it on the counter. He dialed seven numbers. "Bob? Yeah, hey, four strange men just left here looking for LeJeune … No. Spencer. I told them I didn't know him, so get word to him they are looking for him. Seems trouble." He hung up the phone.

Bob, the marina owner, walked out toward the docks when he noticed the black car come to a rest in the parking lot. He slowed down his walk for the men to have time to approach him, and he saw why Mr. Gentry was concerned.

Not many people came dressed up to the marina unless they were with the oil companies.

"Would you know where we might find the owner?" one of them said, pointing to the marina store.

"You found him," Bob replied.

The man smiled. "I understand Spencer LeJeune has a boat here. Would you know where I can find him?"

Bob looked over at the empty stall that housed Spencer's boat. "Can't say I know Spencer LeJeune," Bob said, repeating the same words the Spaniard had heard from the old man at the store.

His expression turned to frustration upon hearing Bob's answer. "You don't have any LeJeune here?"

Bob shook his head. "No."

The man turned back to the car disgruntled, pointing in the air and twirling his finger, motioning them to crank up the car. The car tires spun on the white shell rock as the visitors jetted out of the parking lot. "These small-town people are protecting him!" the man said to his driver.

"Gentry! Hey, you were right, those men just left here. Spanish, maybe?" Bob said into the receiver of his phone.

"Yeah, I think so too. If you see Spencer before I do, let him know. What do you think they want him for?" he asked.

"I don't know," Mr. Gentry said. Hanging up the phone again, he looked over at the book rack with three copies of Spencer's first book, *Pirates and Voodoo,* that had a thin layer of dust on them. "I wonder … " Mr. Gentry said to himself.

Chapter 29

With little to no wind on the water, the temperatures had reached a sweltering 98 degrees as Spencer sat sweating under his canopy, assembling a new piece of equipment he had acquired from his friend in Florida. The hint from the old man at Dusty's camp gave him an idea on his search. He had been running side-scan sonar for both research with work and searching for the barge, but the sonar covered only the surface of the bay floor. He needed something that would allow him to look farther into the mud, so he was rigging up his friend's multi-cam echo sonar, hoping that it would give him the depth he needed.

Plugging the cables into the monitor that sat on his console, he trolled toward the grassy island where he had snagged the fishing net with the old piece of wood. After a few passes, he stopped to adjust the screen for better clarity. He thought back to the day he and his dad started running sonar in search for the *Griego* and how much time it took, allowing them to have many heart-to-heart talks.

It seemed like yesterday Spencer and his father were out in the Atlantic searching for the ship and how he could forget the memory of his father breaking the surface with a small rusted cannon baring the name *The Griego*.

The events that followed over the next five weeks would seem to Spencer to come from a story book as he became one of the crew aboard the *Miss Furry*, the main expedition ship for the recovery of *the Griego* and her treasure. He worked side by side with his father, and at the end of their five weeks they were greatly rewarded in their effort.

That experience began their love of chasing lost treasure, and together they spent immeasurable time researching different ships that had vanished off the Florida coast. It was after Spencer had graduated with his masters and was in the work force that Steve was given the most valuable information about their next ship. A friend had heard that an elderly lady had passed away and her children were having an estate sale. The lady had been married to an old treasure hunter who had passed away years earlier, and maybe her estate would have something of interest to them.

Spencer and Steve went to the estate sale, and the only thing they found of interest was a leather trunk. Steve bought it in hopes of restoring it and using it as a furniture piece in their beachside cottage. Carrying the trunk back to his truck, Spencer made the comment that it seemed heavy, and opening it on the tailgate, they found research for a Spanish ship called *the Compostela*. Steve, being an honest man, took the information back to the sellers, who only smiled and told him it now belonged to him.

Once home, Steve found a letter addressed to the old man from a family in Spain. The envelope carried a family crest, and after research, Steve found that the crest represented royalty. Though the paper sustained water damage, most of the words could still be made out. The letter explained that a pirate in 1810 discovered the location of a Spanish treasure in the bays of the New World, close to a river that ran into the sea. It was rumored that the captain and his female companion outwitted the infamous Jean Lafitte. The rest of the letter was unreadable with the exception of the name of the pirate's ship, *the Compostela*.

Spencer slowed his boat to a drift as he closely watched the monitor and the printout it was producing. He set up and spun the boat around for another pass when the reflection off a boat in the distance caught his eye. He studied the boat before moving back over the area; it seemed to be drifting and was not in an area known for red fish. It was smaller than an oyster boat, so Spencer pulled out his binoculars and took a closer look. *One person, no fishing rod in hand. I can't tell if they are ... they're looking at me!*

He put down the binoculars and slowly turned his wheel away from the spot, speeding up and aiming his boat north. Ducking behind another small grassy island, he pulled up and killed his engines. Listening, he could hear a boat coming closer and then silence. *Did they kill their engines too?*

Not interested in finding out who it was that close to the area, he cranked up his engines and fired out from behind the isle. The other boat was close, and as Spencer jetted in the opposite direction, the boat wasted no time in pursuing. *There's no chance in hell they'll catch me,* he thought, pushing down on the throttle and opening up all four 350s. Soon the boat faded into the distance, but Spencer didn't let up until he entered the marina. A few fishermen looked at him like he was crazy, flying into the marina at such a high speed.

He was pulling the last bag of equipment out of his boat when he saw the other boat enter the marina. It wasted no time winding its way through the docks and coming to a drift behind his.

Spencer reached for a Billy club he kept onboard and stormed to the back of his boat. "What the hell do you think you're doing?" he yelled at the person in the boat.

"Don't use that language with *me*, and what the hell are *you* doing?" Toni pulled her cap and sunglasses off.

"Toni!?"

"Yeah!"

He was stunned. "Why are you chasing me?"

"Spencer LeJeune! You be truthful with me! Are you chasing that damn treasure?" Her voice echoed across the marina.

"Shhh." He waved his hands for her to lower her voice.

"Don't *shhh* me!" Her boat, which belonged to her father, was only a couple of feet from the back of his. Spencer leaped into her boat, but being the tomboy she was, Toni pushed forward and put her finger in his face, demanding an answer. He shoved his way to the wheel and throttled toward the open bay, leaving his gear on the dock and trying to keep her calm and quiet before everyone in Buras, Louisiana, knew about the treasure.

Once on the open water, he killed the engines to face a 5'4" steaming brunette who had her arms folded in front of her and her right foot tapping the fiberglass floor. "Well!?" she demanded.

"Yes, I am! Happy?" he said, letting his guard down.

"So that's the only reason you returned?"

"No!" He snapped back. He paced to the back of the boat and then turned. "Sit!"

"*Excuse me?*" she answered.

"Sit!" His voice rose. She was a little surprised at his demand and sat.

For the next hour, Spencer spilled everything, from finding *The Griego*, to going to Spain, to the old man, Lebreaux's house—well, almost everything.

She squinted her eyes at him. "Do you expect me to believe that?"

"Believe what you want. You asked, and there it is," he answered.

Toni gazed over the bay, letting the wind blow her hair back. After a minute of silence, she looked back at Spencer with a more settled tone. "Spencer, when I saw you in the park the other day, I was so excited to see you, see you as an adult. As a kid you were obsessed with finding these make-believe treasures, even to the point you didn't care about Lebreaux's death."

"That's not true!" he shot back.

"I loved being around the Spencer who wasn't fixated on make-believe treasure and legends."

"I'm not asking anything from you," he said.

"Spencer, you came back, and I was so excited to have my friend back, someone I really needed," she paused. "Clint became obsessed with his music career until I meant nothing to him. I can see that this is going to happen again."

"Toni, I didn't—"

"Just take me in," she interrupted him.

He shook his head. "OK." They eased into the marina and docked, and Spencer stepped out of her father's boat, turning to her. "You say, 'make-believe treasure.' Then how do you explain this?" He held out the silver coin.

Toni walked closer. "You had it the whole time?" she asked in disbelief.

"No, it was given to me in Spain."

She looked down for a moment, feeling the tears beginning to build up in her eyes. "Just go, Spencer."

He studied her for a short second, thinking *I had a bad feeling about letting her in on this*. "Would you just please not tell anyone?" he asked.

Without looking at him, she agreed as she walked away. "You know I won't."

Chapter 30

"Jimmy, you need help with that?" the parts store owner asked Jimmy as he was studying the instructions for oil additive.

"No! I can read," he answered.

The owner shook his head and went back to reading his computer screen and putting together a parts list for a local mechanic shop. The parts store was no more than a warehouse with parts, lots of fans, and an old yellow dog that rarely got up from her dusty bed in the corner. Much like Gentry's store, the parts store had brick walls and a tin roof that had been replaced dozens of times. Jimmy grabbed two quarts of oil and his additive and made his way to the counter.

The door slammed shut with the force of the fans blowing inside, and four men walked toward the counter. Jimmy looked over his shoulder at the men, grinned, and gave a head gesture, then turned back to pay.

"That'll be $22.50," the owner said.

"You can put it on my ticket," Jimmy replied, gathering his oil and turning to walk out. "Kinda hot to be wearing long sleeves," he said to the four men as he walked past them. They didn't pay the comment any attention.

One of the men asked the owner, "Do you know where we could find Spencer LeJeune?"

The owner had received the same phone call yesterday from Mr. Gentry, who called all the business owners in town to spread the word.

"No, never heard of him," he replied.

The Spaniard gave a discouraged smirk, "Very well." Jimmy, who was standing at the door, overheard the question and was baffled about why the owner wouldn't give any information.

They had begun to walk out when Jimmy said, "You mean LeJeune," pronouncing the last name correctly.

"Jimmy! I need you a minute to show me something on this car in the back," the owner called, trying to run interference. Jimmy just gave him a dirty look.

"Yes, you know this man?" the Spaniard asked with an interested look.

"Yeah, I know him. He lives in the blue house on stilts just past the post office," Jimmy said, throwing his thumb over his shoulder in the direction of Spencer's house. "Whatcha want with him?" he asked.

"It doesn't concern you," the man replied and motioned for the others to follow him.

"Excuse me! Doesn't concern me?" Jimmy was shocked at the rudeness. As the door slammed behind them, Jimmy looked back at the owner, "Who were those assholes?"

"I don't know, but I wish you wouldn't have told them that."

Jimmy looked back out through the glass door at the men. "I might not get along with LeJeune, but ain't nobody gonna talk to me like that." He walked outside and stepped in front of their car. "Bud, I don't know who the hell you think you are, but around here you show people respect when they do you a favor!" he said, pointing at the man in the passenger seat.

Rolling his window down, the stranger responded, "As you can tell, I'm not from around here, and … how do you say in English … don't really give a shit!" The car shot forward, causing Jimmy to leap to the side to avoid getting run over.

"I don't think so!" Jimmy climbed in his truck and raced after the black Mercedes. Braking at a stop sign, Jimmy slid to a stop beside them, jumped out, and approached the passenger-side window. "You got some things to learn around here!" he yelled.

The tinted window rolled down to expose a pistol in the Spaniard's hand. "I'm tired of talking with you," the man said, pointing the gun at Jimmy. In most cases, Jimmy would have told him where he could shove the gun, but that was mostly for bluffs. This one, he knew, wasn't a bluff, so he backed off.

The car sped off, leaving Jimmy in a cloud of dust.

Spencer, who had been eating breakfast at the café, pulled out on the road as the black Mercedes zipped past him. "Dang! In a hurry?" he said, looking at the black car. *That car looks familiar,* he thought, turning to follow them. Rounding the corner, Spencer saw the black car parked in front of his house with the four men running up his stairs. *Well it didn't take long for them to find me.*

He watched as the men walked through the sliding glass front door. Spencer never locked anything; most people in Buras never locked their doors. "Still looking for the map," he said out loud, thinking he had better move it.

Just then, Jimmy's truck slid to a stop beside Spencer's, and before Spencer could say anything, Jimmy was out and standing at Spencer's window.

"Those guys seem to be pretty serious. Just pulled a gun on me," Jimmy said.

"Yeah, they're bad news," Spencer replied with little emotion.

"What the hell do they want with you?" Jimmy asked.

"I'm not sure. I think they have me mistaken for someone else," he said, avoiding the question.

"I'll make a call and grab my shotgun," Jimmy said, stepping away.

"No, it's best they just leave."

Before Jimmy could make a call, two of the men reappeared on the balcony, and seeing Jimmy and his truck, they yelled back into Spencer's house for the others. The one man who had been asking all the questions glanced down the sandy street toward the two trucks. Spencer locked eyes with the man, who yelled something in Spanish, and the four of them ran down the steps.

"I'll hold them—you get out of here," Jimmy yelled, walking back to his truck. Not one to argue at a time like this, Spencer slammed his own truck into reverse.

Jimmy stepped in front of the charging Mercedes with a sawed-off Remington 870 shotgun, holding it waist high. As the car quickly approached, he saw the driver's window open with the same pistol aimed at him, and this time he saw the fire come from the end of the barrel. Three more shots rang out before he had time to dive behind his truck. Jumping to his feet, he fired back with three quick shots that only peppered the car as it quickly gained speed.

Spencer's truck fishtailed around a corner as he blew through town with the car quickly gaining on him. *Toni!* he suddenly wondered. *Do they think Toni is involved?* The red truck flung rocks across the front of the parts store as they sped by, and with every turn the loose gear in the back shifted, causing Spencer to keep an eye on his equipment.

Spencer jetted by the entrance to the city park and blew through the stop sign before realizing he was outrunning the Mercedes. After a few more turns, the black car broke the chase, leaving Spencer wondering, *What are they doing now?*

He got an uneasy feeling and headed toward the clinic. Seeing Toni's jeep parked on the side, he pulled around the back. Bursting in the back door, he was greeted with a surprised audience of veterinary assistants.

"Where is Toni?" he gasped, almost out of breath.

They pointed to the next room.

Exploding through the door and into the surgical area, he found Toni prepping a German shepherd for surgery with another assistant.

"Spencer!" she yelled at his surprise entrance.

"Listen, there's no time to explain. You have to come with me."

"I'm about to be in surgery. What's the matter?" she asked concerned.

"Just come with me," he insisted.

She turned to her assistant. "Finish prepping, and I'll be right back." She walked Spencer out of the room,

Lee DuCote

lowering her surgical mask, and asked, "What's gotten into you?"

"There are some guys after me, and I'm afraid they might think you're involved."

"Involved with what?"

Knowing her answer, he didn't want to tell her: "The treasure."

"You need to leave!" she turned to walk back in.

Spencer grabbed her arm and spun her around to face him, "Toni, this isn't make-believe, they're dangerous."

"I can handle myself." she walked back into the clinic.

Frustrated Spencer jogged back to his truck and thought for a moment about his next move: *Dusty's camp house!* Within minutes, he was at the marina and firing up *Waterproof.*

Chapter 31

Spencer stepped out onto the camp dock and placed his foot against the bow of his boat, preventing it from ramming against the splintered old pier. Wrapping the last line around the pylon, he jumped back down into the boat and opened one of the compartments, pulling out a waterproof case with the map tucked inside. *I need to find a better hiding place for this,* he thought. Standing in the boat, he stooped down and glanced under the camp house dock. *That will work.* In the thigh-deep water, he waded under the pier, concealing the case between two joists.

The camp house creaked with the marsh winds blowing through the saw grass and pushing against the wooden siding. Spencer let the screen door slam behind him as he entered the kitchen and pulled out his cell phone.

"I hope you don't mind, but I need a place to lay low, be OK to use your camp?" he texted Dusty.

A few minutes later, Dusty replied with, "You already having girl troubles?"

"No, I'll fill you in later. Can you get my number to Jimmy and tell him to call me?"

"OK. You really MUST be in trouble. Lol."

A few minutes later, Spencer's phone rang. "LeJeune! You mind telling me why I'm shooting at foreigners?" Jimmy asked.

"I didn't mean to drag you into this," Spencer answered guiltily.

"What's it all about?"

"They are part of a Spanish crime family. They think I have something of theirs, which I don't. I'm hiding out trying to figure out what to do next. I really can't go to the authorities," Spencer said, hoping that would satisfy Jimmy's curiosity.

"Hell, I wouldn't go to the police either. We Cajuns can handle it ourselves. You let me know what I need to do."

"OK, I'll call you back this evening."

"Take care!" Jimmy said in a light voice.

Spencer chuckled, "I will." He couldn't believe they were actually getting along on something. Spencer wasn't sure if it was because Jimmy finally wanted to put the past behind him or if he just liked the shootout. Either way, he was glad Jimmy was on his side for a change.

"Hello?" Dusty answered his phone in a thick Cajun accent.

"Hey, do you have a few minutes?" Toni asked.

"Sure."

"Meet me at the diner." He hung up and turned his truck around, aiming toward the only diner in town. Pulling up, he saw Toni's green jeep already parked in the front and her sitting at a table near the window.

"What's up, kiddo?" he cheerfully asked as he walked in.

"I'm hoping you can give me some advice."

He sat down in time for the waitress to walk up to take their order. After ordering fries and a drink, he turned back to Toni, "What kind of advice can I give you about Spencer?" he asked.

"Is it that obvious?" She rolled her eyes.

The waitress returned with their drinks, and Dusty peeled open a straw and took a sip of his water. "Talk to me," he said with a smile.

"You know how I felt toward Clint. Crap, everyone in town knew how I felt. He was so obsessed with his music career that he didn't have time for me."

"Sweetie, he wasn't faithful. You know that," Dusty said.

Toni rubbed her forehead, not wanting to hear the truth again. "Yes, I know."

"I'm sorry, keep going," Dusty said.

"When I heard Spencer was coming back, I was so excited, it felt like my best friend was returning, and I knew with both of us grown up, things would be different ... well, they're not."

"How so?" Dusty asked.

Toni carefully thought through what she was going to say next. "He just seems to be worried about his work and other things, kinda like an obsession."

173

"And you want him all to yourself?" Dusty asked.

"No, you make it sound like I'm in love with him."

"Kiddo, you are."

She thought for a second, then said, "We're just friends."

"OK, then what's the problem?"

"I'm such an idiot." She lowered her head, remembering her actions with Spencer in the marsh.

"No, you're not an idiot. You were hurt by Clint; I get that. Spencer isn't Clint—we're talking about your buddy from childhood." He sat back, adding, "Crap, Toni, what's your rush? Let your friendship grow into whatever it grows into. Can you imagine if all couples were friends first?"

"Has he said anything to you?" she asked.

The waitress returned with Dusty's fries and set them on the table, looking over them out the window and saying, "There goes that same black Mercedes. Either a bunch of kids are running the roads daddy's new car or they're looking for someone." She laid the check on the table and left. Dusty and Toni paid no attention to the car.

"He's talked a little," Dusty paused. "Toni, you've known Spencer a long time, and you just said that you're grown up now. Why don't you tell him how you feel?"

"I'm not sure how I feel," she said, stealing one of his fries.

"You wouldn't be here asking me questions if you weren't."

"I don't want to run him off. He already thinks I'm crazy for acting as friendly as I have been."

"We're Cajuns, of course we're crazy."

Spencer's actions on bursting in her clinic were still bothering her, and she wanted to say something to Dusty, but wasn't sure what to say.

She reached over and stole a few more fries from his plate. "So who can I fix you up with?" She smiled, trying to change the subject.

"I'm good," he replied. Just then the door swung open, causing a breeze to blow across the table and send their napkins to the floor. Toni reached down and picked them up to find Jimmy standing in front of her.

"Spencer talk to you guys?" he asked both of them.

"No, just wanted me to pass you his number," Dusty said.

Toni looked at Jimmy. "What about?"

"I better not say, then," Jimmy replied and turned to walk back out.

"Jimmy, what are you two up to? Who's chasing him?" she asked.

He spun with a smile, "He did tell you!"

Dusty looked at them like they were crazy. "Is he in trouble?" Dusty asked.

"I don't think so, but those Spanish guys sure want him."

Toni walked closer to the window and looked down the street. "What? Where is he?" she asked.

"At my camp house," Dusty answered.

"Can you bring me there?" she asked.

"I guess," Dusty answered as he stood up.

"I'll distract them while you guys head out," Jimmy exclaimed.

"You're enjoying this too much," she said to Jimmy. He smiled and walked out to his truck.

Toni followed Dusty to the marina, and driving by Spencer's house, they saw the black Mercedes parked out front. With the tinted windows, Toni couldn't see if anyone was in the car, but she began to get nervous. *What has he gotten himself into? Can the treasure really exist?*

"Dusty is bringing me out there," she texted Spencer.

"Are you OK?" he replied.

"Yes, we are fine. This is starting to scare me. Be there in 30."

Spencer was standing at the end of the dock when Toni's father's boat rounded the corner of a small island with Dusty driving. *She must be nervous if she's not driving,* he thought.

Dusty pulled up on the throttles and drifted into the dock. "You guys OK?" Spencer asked.

"Yeah, I don't believe those guys know who we are," Dusty replied. "What's this all about?" he asked.

"They think I have something of theirs."

"And since you don't, you're hiding at my camp house?" Dusty asked.

"I'm trying to think through my next move."

"Well, I'm not one to pry. If you need me, you know where to find me."

Toni stepped out of the boat and pushed Dusty back off, leaving him drifting a few feet from the dock.

"Thanks, Dusty," she replied.

"Don't wait," he answered her. Spencer raised an eyebrow, wondering what they were talking about.

"We need to talk," she said, walking past him toward the camp house.

☠ *Chapter 32* ☠

The day was hot with a thick humidity that created a haze over the deep blue sky above Grand Terre. Sea gulls flapped with little effort to skim over the calm waters in search for their next meal. A few gulls parted the way as a small tender slid onto the beach of the scarcely populated island. Two men and a young women stepped out into the ankle-deep water, the woman pulling her dress up to keep it from getting wet. She followed the men to the buildings, looking back in search of another ship.

"He's gone. And if I know him, he's more concerned with piracy than women. You, on the other hand, have a job," the taller and thinner man said, looking back at her.

They burst in the bar doors. "Aye, Captain Lafitte!" the barkeep said with an audacious smile.

"Rum!" Lafitte bellowed. He and the other man sat at a table, with Lebreaux standing off in the distance while the barkeep set a bottle and two cups down.

"Temple was good?" he asked Lafitte.

"We had better things to do than trade at Temple this trip." Lafitte poured the two cups and belted one of them down.

The barkeep didn't ask any more questions; he knew to mind his own business.

"I have something for you," he whispered to Lebreaux walking back around the bar.

She cocked her head sideways and warily studied him for a moment. He walked back around the old wooden bar with a cup of water and the note hidden out of sight. Presenting her the water with his left hand, he forced the letter with his right hand into hers unnoticed. She never broke eye contact with him, wondering why he was helping her; being a woman of color, she received little respect in the New World.

She downed the water, then excused herself to the hot air and bright sun. She walked toward the beach, grasping the letter in hopes that it would be from her lover. Once out of sight from the buildings, she unfolded the letter and instantly began crying, seeing her name written by the one who loved her.

She cupped her mouth with her hand and desperately fought against the tears that were flowing down her flawless complexion. She wiped her eyes with the hem of her dress and then carefully wiped the letter dry. She had been well educated by her mother and had read to many of her friends and other slaves in Saint Dominque before the rebellion freed them. Now she found herself enslaved by a famous pirate and reading a letter from the man she had fallen in love with at first sight.

After spending several minutes sobbing, she composed herself, folded the letter, tucked it under her dress, and made her way back to the tavern. Entering, she recognized that Lafitte and the strange man had finished one bottle and were well on their way to a drunken stupor.

"There's my voodoo queen," Lafitte said, holding up his cup.

She ignored him, and walking up to the barkeep, whispered, "Do you have paper?"

He nodded, but didn't attempt to retrieve it with the stranger stumbling his way to the bar. "Don't ignore Lafitte, you Haitian whore!" he smiled, delivering a back-handed blow to her face that sent her across the floor.

"That's not necessary!" The barkeep ran from around the bar and bent over to help Lebreaux.

He felt the boot of the man in his backside shoving him over her. "Let her lay," he ordered.

The barkeep pushed himself off her and stared into her frightened eyes. "Here," he whispered, shoving the paper and ink well into her hand.

He stood and dusted himself off, then turned to the stranger, who landed his fist into the jaw of the barkeep, sending him back down to the floor. "She needs no help. Now go do your job!"

The man turned and stumbled back to the table with Lafitte. Lebreaux ran out the door with paper in hand and nowhere to go.

The following morning, Lebreaux felt a mist of sand spray across her face from the boot of a hung-over pirate, "Get up! Lafitte says we are sailing north." He turned and walked toward the small tender resting on the beach.

Lebreaux had fled the tavern after the man backhanded her and found herself sleeping on the beach. She rose to her feet and dusted the sand from her dress, then looked at the tender and back at the tavern.

She took a chance and ran to the tavern, and the stranger saw her flee. "Captain?" he bellowed.

"Where she going to go? Leave her alone—I've seen enough of your abuse," Lafitte replied.

She ran inside the tavern with the door still open from the night before. The barkeep was sweeping the floors.

"Here, please give dis to him," she asked as she handed him her letter.

"You write?" he asked.

She nodded and then handed him the paper and ink, only for him to reject it. "Keep it. Write to him every day; write down everything. Give it to any privateer in these waters and tell them it's for me. They will deliver it without question. I will see that he gets it. Be careful of the man with Lafitte," he replied.

She gave a warm smile, saying, "I am not afraid."

"Go!" He nodded toward the door.

"What took you so long?" Lafitte asked as she walked up. "Business," she replied, giving him a cunning look that distracted from her bruised cheek. He smiled and pushed off the beach.

Chapter 33

"I'm sorry for busting in on you at the clinic," Spencer explained. "I'm worried these guys will find out about you and me."

"First, who *are* these guys? And second, we need to talk about us. But first." She put her hands on her hip with an attitude, something Spencer was used to.

"Sit down and I'll explain."

He plopped down beside her on the old leather couch. "I'm sorry. I didn't want to bring you into something like this."

"Well, it does prove you're not the only one chasing this legend," she answered.

He propped his feet on the coffee table made of pallet wood and stretched his arms over his head, taking a deep breath. He looked at the old pictures that were neatly framed and nailed to the wooden walls of the camp house, some black and white, while others seemed newer. Many of the pictures were of Dusty's family and their oyster boats that lined the piers of Buras, but one stuck out more than the rest. It was a picture of Dusty in his early twenties and Spencer's dad; they were standing in front of the marina store with Dusty wearing the same attire, white shirt and cut-off blue jeans. Spencer smiled at the notion that his father was remembered as a hero of sorts to many people.

He took out the coin and handed it to her. "This one was given to me in Spain last month."

"By whom?" she asked.

"I'll explain that later; first, let me explain Vargas." He went into the story of his trip to Spain on the hunt for the manifest of the *Compostela* and his trip to Seville and Vigo. Toni felt herself slipping back to her childhood emotions where treasure hunting had the alluring feel of adventure that she craved. Once Spencer explained his house in Florida being ransacked, he stood, saying, "I'll be right back." He walked through the kitchen and out to the dock to retrieve the waterproof case.

He had the case open before the screen door could slam behind him and placed the old bamboo map on the makeshift coffee table. "Here is what I was given." Toni's eyes widened and lit up; as children they had always played with imaginary maps, but their games were over. Now it was real.

"Spencer?" she said in a soft voice.

"It's real," he replied. She studied the old map, running her fingers around the cut-out holes and tracing over the signature of Nicholas Cardona.

She looked back at him. "Do you know where it is?"

"I don't—I haven't figured out the map yet."

"What are you going to do?" she asked.

He took a deep breath, then said, "Please, let the question be 'What are *we* going to do?'"

A smile formed across her face. "We?"

"We started this, and I wouldn't want anything more than for *us* to find it."

She looked back down at the map with a grin, whispering, "Adventures."

"So, the coin?" She held it in her hand.

"Do you remember what Lebreaux told us in the marsh that day?" he quizzed her.

"Something about the *Potosi*," she replied. It shocked him that she would remember.

"I think we need to start there," he said.

"What is Potosi?" she asked.

"In all the research I've done," he answered, "I can only come up with a city in Bolivia, where the Spanish got their silver in the sixteenth and seventeenth centuries."

She shook her head with the same grin and looked back at him. "Research?" She remembered his computer screen from the other day.

"Yeah. I really think the only way to understand what the mark, Potosi, and the coin have in common is …" He pulled out his phone.

"So, we need a computer for research?" she asked, confused.

"No, we are going to Potosi, Bolivia. That is, if you can leave for a few days."

She gave him a funny look. "We're just going to hop on a plane and head to South America?"

"Yep." He held up his phone, showing two tickets from New Orleans to Santa Cruz, Bolivia.

"And we're paying for this how?" she asked.

"Don't worry." He smiled, then looked back up at her. "You in?"

She smiled and agreed. "I'm in." He purchased two tickets leaving the following day.

"We have time to talk about this, but right now, I'm starving. How about supper?"

"Ok," she replied. *But you don't want to talk about us?* she wondered.

"I'm going to try catching something," he said, heading out the screen door.

Spencer was fishing off the pier, thinking about how they were going to get through town with Vargas's men searching for them, when he hooked a spec. He filled the live well on his boat with water and the fish, and went back to the end of the pier and cast back out, and on his fifth cast he hooked another. *Who would have guessed it—supper!*

Once the fish were grilled, he heated up a can of green beans and set two plates on the table. "I can get used to this," Toni said, sitting back in her chair. Spencer smiled; cooking fish on the grill was something he could do blindfolded. His father had taught him many ways to cook fish, but grilling was their favorite.

As they played Booray into the night, Toni kept wondering why he hadn't brought up their relationship and began to worry that it was something he was avoiding, but eventually the late hours and the stress of the day won out.

"I'm sinking quickly," Toni said, leaning back on the couch, and before she knew it she was asleep.

A loud clap of thunder shook the camp house, and both Spencer and Toni shot up from their deep sleep.

"Holy crap, that scared me," Toni said.

Spencer was holding Dusty's sawed-off shotgun. "Me too," he agreed. They settled back down on the couch, and he kicked his feet up as Toni leaned back on him.

"Who would have thought we'd be here," she said.

"I don't know; hopefully it will settle down by the time we get into town," he replied, thinking she was talking about Dusty's camp. She quietly smiled.

The music from Spencer's phone helped drown out the rain that was pelting down on the tin roof as they cuddled back up on the couch and watched the light from the candles dance on the old wooden walls of the camp. Closing her eyes and taking a deep breath, Toni exhaled slowly, soaking in the moment and feeling Spencer's warm body against hers.

Chapter 34

The next morning they snuck into town and went to Spencer's house to remove anything of value and pack, and then they made a quick stop by Toni's and headed to New Orleans undetected by Vargas's men. Catching the first flight to Atlanta, they spent five hours on a layover, then boarded a 747 headed to Brazil, then Bolivia. Landing at Viru Viru International Airport in Santa Cruz, Bolivia, Toni stood from her seat, feeling dizzy from the fifteen-hour flight.

With his backpack on and phone in hand, Spencer looked back, realizing Toni didn't look like she was feeling well, and he grabbed her hand. "You OK?"

"Yeah, just never flown that long." She smiled.

They made their way to baggage claim, where he bought her a bottle of water. "Drink, it will help."

"We are catching a small plane to Potosi," he said, throwing one of the bags over his right shoulder. "Can you carry that?" he asked.

"Yeah, I got it. Plane again? I thought we were driving?" she asked, following him to an information desk.

"Too far," he smiled back. Thankfully, the lady at the information desk spoke enough English to direct them to the private flights, and Toni walked beside him, wondering what their trip was costing. He was reading something on his phone as he weaved through the crowd to their plane.

"Spencer," Toni called out over the noisy terminal.

He stopped and looked back. "You OK? You're not sick?" he asked.

"No, hungry," she said, setting her bag on the floor.

He smiled back. "We'll have a meal on our plane," he added and turned to trek forward again.

Walking out on the tarmac, they were greeted by a uniformed young lady who spoke limited English. "Mr. LeJeune?" she asked.

"Hi, we made it," he answered.

"Please board—I'll get your bags. Hola," she smiled at Toni.

Following Spencer, Toni stepped into the King Air 350i; the interior of the plane was lined with dark lacquer mahogany and the smell of new leather seats. Another young lady greeted them. "Hola, your meal is ready. Can I get you a drink?"

Spencer looked back at Toni for her answer. "Water, please," she requested.

"Two," he smiled. They sat on the leather couch that was adjacent to a mahogany table and a set of chairs. The flight attendant handed each of them a plate with a small slice of seared tuna steak laid over a bed of pasta.

"This looks amazing," Toni commented, leaning over to Spencer. "Who is paying for all this?"

"Relax and enjoy the flight," he replied, placing his hand on her knee. She didn't flinch.

Once they felt the wheels clear the runway, the captain came over the speaker system. "Good day, Mr.

LeJeune, we have clear skies, and our arrival time to Potosi is less than five hours. Hope you enjoy your flight." Hearing "five hours," Toni handed her empty plate to the attendant, closed her eyes, and quickly drifted to sleep. Spencer propped her feet up on the couch, covered her with a blanket, and sat at the table studying a map of Potosi.

"Madame?" Toni felt a light touch on her shoulder. She opened her eyes to see a uniformed flight attendant. "We are on our final approach." She smiled at Toni.

She looked around but didn't see Spencer. "Where's Spencer?"

"He is with the captain." The attendant pointed to the open cockpit door.

Overhearing their conversation, Spencer walked out. "Hey, you seem to have slept well."

"You bothering the pilot?" she smiled.

"He gave me some great info on an old man who works at the mint." She leaned over and grabbed a couple of carrot sticks that were neatly assorted on a bronze tray.

The King Air made a pass over Potosi, giving Spencer and Toni their first glance at the once-largest city in the Americas, and Cerro Rico, the richest mountain in the world, containing silver and other precious metals. A short time after touching down on the runway, they descended the steps from the plane and were greeted by a man standing in front of a cab. "Welcome to Captain Nicolas Rojas Airport and Potosi, Bolivia." He smiled, then collected their bags. Toni thought he was being a little over friendly, but then realized he'd seen Spencer tip the pilot and flight attendants.

They climbed in the back of the cab. "Hotel La Casona," Spencer said.

"Si," the driver answered, driving out of the airport.

"I take it you've planned everything," Toni observed, cutting her eyes at Spencer, part curious and part uneasy.

"Making it up as I go along," he answered smoothly.

"You're not fooling anyone," she smiled, looking back out her window at Cerro Rico in the distance.

"The pilot said he had an old friend that worked at Casa de la Moneda and he would help us."

"What?" Toni asked, clueless.

"The mint … where the coin was made."

"You didn't tell him—"

"No, they think I'm a history professor," he interrupted her. "A man named Francisco de Toledo had the mint, Casa de la Moneda, built in 1572 so that the silver they mined from the mountain could be processed into coins and bars for shipping, and it's still in existence today, as a museum."

"You *sound* like a history professor," she said.

"Internet. Anyway, hopefully this Pablo Lasuer can give us some information on whatever the mark means." Spencer tapped the driver. "Café?" He motioned drinking.

"Si, Cherry's. Calle Padilla," the driver answered.

"Gracias," Spencer said, looking at his map. "Good, right around from our hotel."

"What is?"

"Coffee shop."

Toni leaned in close to the cab window, admiring the structure of the old buildings that quickly passed as the driver sped through Potosi. Most of the buildings had stucco siding, while others were made with brick. Red clay tiles covered 90 percent of the roof tops, and many of the buildings had second-story balconies that overlooked the cobblestone streets. The streets were extremely narrow, with barely enough room to allow their cab to pass other cars, and with the sidewalks so thin, many of the doors opened onto the streets, worrying Toni that someone at any moment was going to step out in front of them.

The driver brought the cab to a stop outside a yellow-golden stucco building with balconies that lined the second story. "Hostal La Casona," the driver said.

"This is us," Spencer said, stepping out. After paying the driver, the two of them walked into a lobby painted the same bright yellow as the outside. "LeJeune," Spencer said to the old lady sitting behind the counter. She smiled and took his credit card, and as she was running the card, Spencer asked her, "Exchange?" He pointed to the American money he had in hand.

"Que puedo hacer desde aqui." She waved for him to hand over what he had, and she exchanged the bills into bolivianos and handed him a key.

Walking to their room, they passed through a large courtyard with a fountain in the center that was lightly spraying water over the sides, misting the brick floor with water. The area was covered with a glass cathedral roof, and several picnic tables were scattered across the brick floor for places to eat. Opening their room, Toni walked into a wooden floor with yellow curtains that matched the rest of the hotel.

The room was small, but quaint. "One bed?" she asked. Spencer stopped with bags in hand and looked at her, not sure if she was offended. "I can go see if they have a room with two. Or I can sleep on the floor."

She smiled. "You're not going to sleep on the floor." She threw her bag down and walked into the bathroom.

"I'm starving, and I hear they have great food here," Spencer said, throwing his duffle bag in the corner.

"The way you've navigated your way around, it's like you've been here before."

"Internet," he replied.

Stepping outside from their hotel hungry and tired, Spencer didn't care if people thought of him as a tourist with map in hand. "Padilla is this way."

They walked around a corner, Toni with some difficulty. "I am so tired, I can't breathe," she said, grabbing her chest.

"Potosi is one of the highest cities in the world, 13,420 feet above sea level."

"No wonder!" she gasped.

They pressed on and turned down Padilla, a pedestrian street running on the east side of the 6 August square with lamp posts running down the center to block any cars trying to drive down it. In the backdrop of the street was Cerro Rico, the mountain that made Potosi the city it once was. They found a single wooden door with a small sign that hung above, *Cherry's*. The aroma of vegetarian pizza filled the small shop as the two of them stepped up to order.

Chapter 35

"Drink lots of water. It helps with the altitude," Spencer told Toni.

"Plum juice?" she asked, smiling and pointing at the menu above the counter.

"That might help with more than altitude," he laughed.

After finishing their pizza and Spencer's coffee—Toni thought it was a weird combination—they walked toward Casa de la Moneda. Cutting through the plaza 6 August square and walking under a long set of white arches, the two south Louisianans found themselves in the main square, plaza 10 November.

"We saw a lot of arches coming into town, but why so many?" Toni asked.

"I read that the arches are where the border of the town used to be. Also, they were used to separate the Indian settlements from the Spanish ones. Potosi is a very interesting city with just as much history as the old world."

"You sound like a professor again," she smiled.

"Hey, it's the Statue of Liberty," she said, pointing down a cobblestone path. The statue wasn't over twenty-five feet in height and ten feet in diameter at the base. The path was lined with wrought iron arches that blocked people from stepping onto the grass, and lamps and other lighting features peppered the area to provide plenty of light at night.

"There it is, Casa de la Moneda," Spencer said, pointing to a large building adjacent to the square. The front of the mint was covered in ornate detail; large columns nestled into the wall on both sides of a large arch that led inside the mint to a giant courtyard.

A lady met them as they entered. "The mint will be closing soon." She smiled, trying to distract them from going any farther.

"I am looking for Pablo Lasuer. I was told he was here," Spencer said. She smiled and replied, "Come with me," waving them forward.

Walking toward another set of doors, both Spencer and Toni stared at a giant face sculpture that was mounted above one of the archways.

"Madame, what is that?" Toni asked.

"Mascaron," the lady answered. "It's a mystery of who it is; it appeared in 1865 and has since become a symbol of the mint. Pablo is this way." She again waved them to keep up. They stumbled on a step as they walked trying to look at everything. The lady led them down a long hallway with a wooden ceiling, brick arch columns, and golden framed art on both sides of the hallway. The larger art hung higher at an angle for tourists to view, while smaller pieces lined the walls in no particular order.

Swinging open a door, she led them into a room with large wooden tools and machinery from the early seventeenth century for pressing the silver and making coins. "Señor Lasuer," she spoke to a feeble old man who was sweeping behind one of the presses; he reminded both of them of Mr. Gentry.

"Si?"

"Que les gustaria hablar con usted."

"Si?" He pointed at the two Americans who stood behind the lady.

"Do you speak English?" Spencer asked, hoping he would.

"Yes," he replied.

"I was told you could tell us about this coin," Spencer explained as he presented the coin.

The man smiled. "This is a good piece. It's OK," he said to the lady, who turned and walked out.

Walking to reach more light, the old man held the coin up and examined it closely. "Where did you find this?" he asked.

"It was given to us when we were children."

He pointed to Toni and then to Spencer. "Siblings?"

Toni smiled, "No, sir."

He smiled back and then turned his attention to Spencer. "What do you what to know?"

Spencer hesitated to tell him about the phrase Lebreaux told them, but volunteered it anyway. "We were told that there was a mark on the *Potosi*. Do you know what that means?"

The old man lowered the coin and studied Spencer for a long pause, and Spencer looked back at Toni for her reaction. "Indeed, it was stamped here, probably 1620." He looked at the two of them again, "You're treasure hunters?" Spencer didn't know how to answer the question; they had come so far and didn't want to lose their only help by being something he didn't like.

"I'm an author, and yes, I have been part of a treasure hunt."

"Which one?" the man asked.

"*The Griego*," he answered.

"Si, it was found not long ago."

"Yes, sir." Spencer felt he was losing his lead on the coin.

"The mark is the cross," the man explained.

"You're sure?" Spencer's question surprised Toni; she too thought they were going to lose their lead.

"I am a fifth-generation *numismatico* from Potosi. Would you like to know what fleet it was placed with?"

Spencer didn't really know what he wanted to know, he was so bent on finding out what the mark meant, but being told it was the cross didn't help much either. "I would like to learn," he answered the man.

It was the right answer, as the man smiled. "Come with me," and he led them down a narrow stairwell to a room that was obviously not meant for tourists.

The room was damp, and with the moist stains on the brick walls, it was clear they were underground. Wooden rafters held lights with wires exposed, so if it were not for the condensation, the room might have been a fire hazard. The old man sat behind a wooden desk and peered through the stacks of paper at the two Americans, saying, "Please sit." He pulled a large magnifying glass from the top drawer, and Spencer and Toni sat on a long wooden box on the opposite side of the desk.

"In 1622 there were two large fleets from Spain—the more famous Tierra Firme Fleet and the New Spain Fleet. The Tierra Firme Fleet stopped at Cartagena and Portobello to load their treasure. The New Spain fleet stopped at Vera Cruz to load many precious goods from the Orient." Toni was resting her head in her hands as she sat with her legs crossed on the box, resembling a child at story time. The man could tell he wasn't teaching Spencer anything he didn't know and turned his story to the coin. "This coin is from a gang that was sent to Vera Cruz by mule train; I know this because it was this gang that made the fleet late rendezvousing with the other Spanish fleet."

"Gang?" Toni asked.

The man smiled, "A *gang* is a group of coins. Legend has it that the gang was so late that three ships stayed as the others sailed for Havana to meet up with the Tierra Firme Fleet. The gang was so large that the sailors of the three ships built a barge to sail it back to Spain. Not the brightest idea, can you imagine how slow sailing would be pulling a barge?" Spencer sat up, thinking, *That's what I'm looking for!*

"Do you know the name of the three ships?" Spencer asked.

"No, it's just a legend."

"But if it were real?" Spencer pressed.

"If it were real, they would have kept a record of it. Most records are kept in The Archives of the Indies in Seville, Spain." The man looked at his watch. "It's getting late. If you would like to come back tomorrow, I can give you a personal tour of the mint."

"So the mark is the cross. Could it mean anything else?" Spencer asked.

"Not to my knowledge," he smiled.

"Thank you for your time," Toni spoke up.

Spencer caught her hint to be polite to the man, "Yes, thank you. You have answered our question," he added.

The man escorted them to the archway where they had entered the mint. It was closed with a large wooden gate painted green, but he opened a small door cut into the gate. "Please come back when we can have more time together," he added, "and don't lose that coin—it's very valuable."

"We won't. Gracias." They walked out into the busy streets of Potosi.

Chapter 36

Spencer and Toni made their way back through the
plaza with the buzzing of people celebrating a small festival.
The excitement carried through the air, making it electric.
Dusk was falling on the city of Potosi, and the aroma of
different cuisines from the many restaurants filled the
historical district.

"Wow, I don't know what smells so good, but I'm
hungry again," Toni said.

Spencer stopped a local who was celebrating, asking
him, "Beun restaurant?"

The partygoer pointed in the directions of Padilla
Street. "Phisqa Warmis!" he exclaimed.

"Calle Padilla?"

"No, Calle Sucre!" The man replied and turned to
continue dancing with other people in the street.

Spencer and Toni wove through the small pedestrian
streets, thinking that the nightlife resembled New Orleans in
the French Market during the weekend. They came to a
coral-color stucco building with double French doors that led
inside; a neon sign hanging on the wall read *Phisqa Warmis*.
The smell of the grill increased their appetite, and as they
entered the lobby, a young girl waved them to a table for two.
The table was set in a room with more cathedral glass

ceilings, and Toni, looking around them, noticed that one of the plates resembled Natchitoches meat pies, a fried delicacy from home.

"Wine?" Spencer asked Toni.

"Sure—I doubt they have Coors light."

"Would you rather have a beer?"

"Yeah," she answered.

The waiter walked up with a cheerful "Hola," and before he could ask them anything, Spencer interrupted him with "Beer?"

"Si, dos?" the waiter smiled.

"Si," Spencer answered. He situated his backpack under his feet and looked back at Toni, who was rolling her head around in a circle stretching her neck.

"Are you tired?" he asked.

She smiled, "Yeah, been a long two days. I wish we could stay longer and enjoy the city." The waiter returned with two Potosina Pilsener beers.

After they ordered, the lights in the room dimmed with a young boy walking from table to table lighting the lanterns that served as centerpieces. Toni thought the cold beer tasted good even though she was so tired. She watched Spencer as he took out the map and studied it, and she began thinking about the last few days. *How did I get here? I had a normal life until this geeky kid returns as a ... well, grown man! He loves traveling and adventure, and my life can't compete with that. My life is in Buras at the clinic.* She took another sip from the locally brewed beer. *But how much fun it would be to travel with him ...*

Spencer sensed her staring at him. "What?" he smiled.

It caught her off guard. "Nothing. Just thinking."

"About?" he quizzed her.

"Your life seems so adventurous. Mine is so dull."

"Dull? You're here, aren't you?" he replied.

"True, but what happens if you don't find the treasure?" she asked.

"I'll just keep looking."

"But at some point, you'll have to give it up."

"Give up? I don't plan on giving up on a dream." He wondered where she was going with all this. The waiter returned with two dishes, placing a steak dinner in front of Spencer and a bowl of quinoa soup and side of empanaditas in front of Toni.

"These would give Natchitoches a run for their money," she held up one of the empanaditas after taking a bite.

Finishing the last sip of beer, Spencer paid the waiter, and the two of them strolled out into the street. They both agreed that the travel had caught up to them, so they made their way through the busy streets back to their hotel. She walked close to him, pushing and teasing him to put his arm around her, which he finally did. Once back at the hotel, though, Spencer's nerves began playing a game with him. *One bed?*

Entering the room, Toni stopped and turned to face him; it was an awkward moment. They stood so close to each other, and to break the awkwardness she punched him in the arm.

"I'm going to brush my teeth," she said, disappearing into the small bathroom. After a minute, she came out to look through her bag, and then he closed the door to the bathroom and brushed his teeth.

He stopped and stared in the mirror. *Why am I so nervous? Just go out there and tell her how you feel.* He opened the bathroom door to walk out, his heart beating rapidly and his hands beginning to sweat. Toni was lying on her side on the bed in a night shirt, her hair flung over the pillow.

She looked beautiful.

She looked peaceful.

She looked … asleep.

Glancing at the floor and then back at the space beside Toni, Spencer thought, *I'm not sleeping on the floor!*

Changing into shorts, he quietly climbed in the other side. He thought about the coin and the mark, and how it played into them finding the treasure. He thought about Mr. Gentry, Dusty, and Jimmy and if they were all right with Vargas's men on the prowl for him. He didn't want anyone to get hurt, and for the most part didn't want anyone included—he was so close to finding the treasure. Thoughts continued to race through his head until he found himself in a dream.

The following morning he awoke to Toni curled up and cuddling against his chest; his arm had found its way around her during the night. He didn't want to disturb her, but the sudden urge to go to the bathroom hit him, so he gently replaced his arm with a pillow for her to rest her head on and tip-toed into the bathroom.

After he was done, he opened the door quietly to walk out, and Toni met him in the doorway pushing her way through. "Move it!" she said, shutting the door behind her.

He put on his jeans and was holding a shirt when she came out.

She jumped back in bed and pulled the sheets over her. "It's cold," she said.

"I'll go down and find some coffee," he said, pulling his shirt over his head.

Down in the atrium and nestled in a corner, Spencer found a coffee station with local coffee, so he poured two cups and headed back up. Opening the door, he almost dropped the coffee at a sudden outburst from Toni.

"Holy crap! I remembered my dream while you were gone!" she exclaimed.

"What's that?" he asked, handing her a cup and setting his on a table. "We were in the restaurant where we ate last night, and the little boy was lighting the lanterns. When he came to our table, he exchanged our lantern with an old black iron lantern with a fleur-de-lis on the side and the silver coin hanging off the black iron ring on top." Spencer listened intently, recalling his similar dream, the lantern at Jean Lafitte's table.

"Lebreaux sat down with us; she looked the same as the day she took us out into the bay with her. She said something about letters and you've been there before. Honestly, I didn't understand what she was talking about. Do you?" she asked.

"I don't know," Spencer replied. "Cool dream, but we need to get ready; our plane leaves in two hours," he said, thinking about the letters in the room he found at Lebreaux's house.

Packing, Toni thought back to her dream and the part she didn't share with Spencer—the part where Lebreaux told her they were meant to be together.

Chapter 37

On the way to the airport their cab wound through the mountains as Toni watched Cerro Rico disappear out their back window. Pulling through the gates of Captain Nicolas Rojas Airport, she could see their plane waiting for them on the tarmac. Stopping just shy of the King Air 350i, they pulled their bags from the trunk, paid the driver, and found the same flight attendant waiting for them at the foot of the steps.

"Good morning. I hope you had a pleasant stay," she said.

"A quick one," Toni smiled back.

Once airborne, Toni resumed the same position on the couch that she had coming into Potosi and fell asleep. As Spencer sat at the table reading a book he had bought at the Atlanta airport, something struck him about the map that was given to him in Spain. *Vargas wants the map and the coin. What do they have to do with the barge? What do they do together? The entire Gulf of Mexico is on the map and Barataria Bay. Why such a large map for one spot in the bay? I need to look at that map again.*

Once on the ground at Viru Viru International Airport, the two of them checked in at the front desk and waited to board their long flight back to the States.

"I'll be right back," Spencer told Toni and walked up to the gate counter. Toni watched him talk with the lady and hand her a credit card.

"What was that about?" she asked as he returned to their seats.

"Upgraded to first class."

She stared at him with a raised eyebrow. "Not to be nosey, but where is all this money coming from?"

He smiled at her, answering briefly, "Science."

She kept quiet, but wasn't buying into his humor. *Marine biologists don't make that kinda money. What is he not telling me? Is there more to the story with the Spaniards who are after him?*

There wasn't any questioning once she boarded and saw the amount of room her first class seat had. A flight attendant gave them each a bottle of water, and as she leaned back and took a deep breath, Spencer put his hand on her knee. She looked down at his hand; it felt safe, wanted, loved … she grabbed the back of his hand and locked her fingers through his, feeling him grip her hand in return.

"Thanks for including me on this," she said.

"We did start this together," he replied.

And something tells me that together we'll find the treasure. She thought back to the conversation with Lebreaux in her dream.

Spencer held onto her hand, thinking, *I hope this isn't just a friendly gesture.*

Once back in the states, Spencer's phone buzzed with several messages and a few missed calls. One of the messages was from Dusty, and instead of texting back, Spencer called him.

"Hey, it's Spencer. How are things in Buras?" He paused as Dusty caught him up on something.

Toni nudged him, noticing the concerned look on his face. "What? What's he saying?"

He put his finger up. "Hang on."

He continued listening with Toni standing in front of him with folded arms and tapping her foot.

He hung up. "Seems our friends paid Mr. Gentry a visit and got kinda forceful with him."

"Is he all right?" Her eyes widened.

"Yeah, not physical. He confessed where we went."

Toni drew back in shock. "Really?"

"Yep, Jacksonville, Florida." He smiled.

They landed in New Orleans, and the thought crossed Spencer's mind that if Vargas had men staked out at the airport looking for them, it wouldn't be hard to find out what flight he was on. After they retrieved their bags, they cautiously headed toward his truck. Walking through the parking garage, Toni spotted a black Mercedes aimed in their direction.

It was on them before they realized it. "Spencer!" Toni's voice shook, and Spencer grabbed her arm and readied himself for an escape through the parked cars. Relief overwhelmed them as the car drove past with an elderly man behind the wheel. "Get me home," Toni said.

"Can we make a stop on the way home?" Spencer asked.

"Ok, where?"

"Lafitte," he replied.

Her eyes light up. "Lebreaux's house!" she exclaimed.

Spencer could tell the stop was fine from the excitement in her voice. The thoughts of her life being boring were quickly leaving, and Spencer's words to her back in Potosi over supper, "You're here, aren't you," continued playing over and over in her head. *I'm really doing this!*

Spencer parked his truck on the side of the street just outside of the old white two-story house. "It's so old. How has it survived this long?" she asked, stepping out of the truck. Her father had brought her by the house when she was a kid, but her memory had escaped her, not remembering the front porch. "I always thought the porch wrapped around the house," she commented as they approached the house.

"Can we just go in?" she asked.

"I think it will be all right." Once inside, he let her snoop around and see the rooms, and after coming back down stairs, he walked to the wall.

"Ready for this?" Before she could answer, he pushed the hall tree out of the way, then smiling at her, he pressed against the wall, causing it to open.

Toni's mouth fell open. "How in the world did you figure that out?"

"I don't know, the walls just looked out of place." He stepped aside and motioned for her to head up the narrow stairwell.

Toni stood in amazement at all of Lebreaux's personal belongings. She began to rummage through the room, and thumbing through small black and white pictures, she founds a tin picture of Lebreaux and the buccaneer. "Spencer! Is this the guy from your dreams?" Her voice escalated.

Chills ran up Spencer's spine at seeing the tall young man from his dream. "That's him," Spencer said.

"The same guy in your books?"

"That's him. Crazy."

"There is something I haven't been telling you about my dreams," Toni paused. "Lebreaux has constantly told me that the two of us need to be together to find the treasure. I didn't tell you because I didn't want that to mislead you. I'm not sure what she means by that."

"Do you remember her telling us that on the bay when we were kids?" he asked.

"I do. She said more, do you remember?"

Spencer thought for a moment, "What?"

"That together we would find the treasure," she said, remembering Lebreaux holding their hands in hers.

"I do remember that." He spaced out for a short moment, wondering what she meant by *mislead* him. "Here are the letters," he said.

Toni thumbed through them, shaking her head, "I can't believe this. This is what I dreamed about," she explained.

"We need to get back—I want to look at the map again," he said, standing.

"We can't leave all this. Someone will find it." She held the letters up.

"It's not ours to take," he replied.

"I believe she would have liked for you two to have them," a voice came from the stairwell.

Spencer spun around and Toni jumped to her feet. "You scared us," Spencer said after a few seconds, recognizing the man from the last time he was there.

"I'm sorry, not my intentions. You brought the girl back," he replied.

Toni stepped behind Spencer. "What is he talking about?"

"Well, do you have the answers?" Spencer asked, remembering the old man told him to return with Toni for the answers.

"What you're looking for is here," the man replied, handing them an old envelope. "I translated what I could," he added.

Taking the envelope, Toni asked, "Can we take the letters too?"

"They belong to you; everything here belongs to you," the man replied.

"We'll come back for it. It's been safe for twenty years, so it should be OK a few more days," Spencer said.

He looked back toward the man to thank him, but again he was gone. "OK, that was creepy," Toni commented, seeing that the man had vanished.

☠ *Chapter* 38 ☠

The hot, humid air subsided with a steady downpour on the small island of Grand Terre. "Captain, his ship isn't here. I say let's head to Tortuga where we can pick up a few more sailors and then look for more Spanish ships." The dark, leather-skinned man standing at the wheel was trying to be practical with his advice.

The young captain gazed at him from the corner of his green eyes, but said only "Keep quiet and drop anchor!" Within a few minutes, the captain and four other men rowed themselves to the shore of Grand Terre. Upon landing on the beach, the captain didn't wait for the others and stepped out in full stride to the weather-beaten tavern.

The doors were open, the old dilapidated shutters on both sides flapping in the wind and the rain. The captain shook the water from his hat and coat and wandered to the bar. "Have you seen her?" he demanded.

The barkeep scanned the room for lingering eyes and then reached below the bar, presenting the captain with the letter she had left. "She was here a week ago," he whispered.

The captain looked down at two letters. "She wrote two?"

"I gave her instructions to send any letters with privateers and I would see that you got them." The captain grinned at the barkeep's willingness. "I'll do the same for you," he added.

"Where were they heading next?" the captain asked.

The barkeep scanned the room again and then leaned over the bar. "New Orleans, the blacksmith shop," he said under his breath.

One of the shutters on the front doorframe slammed shut, and the lantern on the bar flickered with a gust of wind blowing through. *With this wind, sailing north would be no problem.* "Do you have more paper?" he asked. The barkeep smiled, handing him paper and the ink jar.

After writing a letter, he gave it to the barkeep and walked swiftly out of the tavern and toward the tender. "Back to the ship," he barked to his men who were shooting dice outside the tavern.

The rain began pelting them harder as they rowed back to the ship, causing them to shield their faces. The captain never budged, focusing on the ship and his thoughts.

"Pull anchor and set course for New Orleans!" he yelled, stepping onto the main deck.

"New Orleans?" one of the men asked. Before he got his answer, he smiled and rejoiced with the other men, excited to go to a large city. For the men, the visit to New Orleans meant whores, bars, and cheaper rum, plus a night or two in a real bed. For the captain, it meant reuniting with the girl he had fallen in love with at first sight.

With the small storm pushing against the sails, the ship made quick time through Barataria Bay and up the smaller canals leading to the river before dropping anchor and rowing the rest of the way to New Orleans. The ship would have to remain out of sight, meaning they would have further to row, but with the excitement of the crew, the distance didn't matter. Before long, the crew and captain stepped onto the brick streets of New Orleans and into the night life.

In a two-story house on the corner of a brick and stone intersection, Lebreaux huddled to stay warm near a fireplace located in the center of the ground floor. The house was known as a blacksmith shop among the residential homes that lined the streets. Since the US had recently purchased New Orleans, the population was on an upswing. The blacksmith shop was operated by the Lafitte brothers and was the perfect front for selling their smuggled goods. "We will gather what supplies we need, then head back out to sea tomorrow. Ye need to show me something new about the Spanish treasure," Lafitte insisted, holding up Lebreaux's face with one finger under her chin.

"Or we'll cut you from ear to ear," the other man said, holding a knife to her throat.

Lafitte gave him a stony gaze and pushed his blade down with one finger. "Careful, matey!" he cautioned. "Ye might find that blade in ye own throat."

Lebreaux climbed the stairs to the second story and sat on a bed facing a full-length mirror. "I am nobody's slave," she said, reaching in her pocket and taking out a piece of chalk she had acquired earlier in the day. Moving the mirror back against the wall, she drew a circle on the wooden floor with the chalk. Kneeling in the circle and facing the mirror, she began whispering a chant, summoning a spirit to free her. She had been part of a ceremony in her homeland where the African slaves turned rebels summoned a spirit for their freedom. After sacrificing a black pig to the loa, the blood was drunk and a pact with the devil was made. A week later, over 1,500 plantations were burned and over 1,000 slaveholders murdered; the pact had freed the slaves, and soon after, Haiti was born.

Now, kneeling on the floor, Lebreaux proceeded to make the same pact to free her from the captive state she was in. Her mother, who had educated her, had warned her not to call upon the spirits unless needed. There was always a price to pay. Opening her eyes and gazing into the mirror, she could see the ghostly figure of someone standing behind her. *It's working,* she thought for a moment, and then a loud commotion sounded from below her. She could hear yelling and shouting, but couldn't make out the words. She quickly stood, noticing the ghostly figure gone from the mirror.

Stumbling down the short and narrow steps, she saw Lafitte standing in the room, pointing his finger at someone behind the fireplace. Stepping out on the ground floor, she peered around the brick fireplace to find the young captain.

Without hesitation she ran to his side and wrapped her arms around him. "You came!"

"Do you really think I'm going to let you take her before I find this treasure?" Lafitte said, still pointing at the young captain.

The captain drew his flintlock pistol, saying firmly, "You don't have a choice." Lebreaux slipped behind the young captain as he backed up toward the open door.

"You're not leaving," the other man replied, pulling his pistol. The men stood poised waiting for the first twitch to fire. Lebreaux lowered her head toward the fireplace, and with her pupils dilating, she peered into the fire, saying in a low raspy voice, "I summon thee." Immediately fire shot out of the fireplace on both sides, blinding everyone in the room, including the young captain. As the men held their arms in front of their faces to block the heat, she grabbed the young captain and fled into the dark night of New Orleans.

As the fire settled back down in the chimney, the stranger holstered his pistol. "Grab ye guns, we have a voodoo woman to kill," he ordered.

"Let 'em go," Lafitte replied.

"I don't think so!" the man snapped back at him. "I'm not letting that wench get away!"

"They are not going to get away. Sit down," Lafitte ordered everyone, and they quickly obeyed his order.

"Lafitte, my family has searched for that treasure for years, and I'm not going to let some young privateer steal it from me," the man insisted heatedly.

"Sit down, Vargas. Let them do the hard work," he replied in a nonchalant manner as he turned back to the bottle of rum he had left resting on an anvil.

Chapter 39

With their anxiety level high, Spencer and Toni drove to Buras, hoping for a quiet and normal day. Since the narrow town was located between Barataria Bay and the Mississippi River, back roads didn't exist, and sneaking into town wasn't an option.

"Spencer, I'm scared," Toni said as they crossed the city limits into Buras.

"It'll be OK," Spencer answered, hoping his words were true.

He pulled behind Mr. Gentry's store, and together they snuck around and through the front door. "No need to be sneaking around. I sent those boys on a wild goose chase to Florida," Mr. Gentry said from behind the paper he was reading.

Now how did he know it was us, Toni thought.

"I wish you would have told them the truth; I don't want anything to happen to you," Spencer said.

"Hell, son, you think four Spaniards are going to bother me in my own town?"

Well, you've got a point, Spencer thought.

"What the hell do these men want with you? You owe them money? I got money if that's the case," Mr. Gentry said.

216

"No, thank you, though. They think I have something that belongs to them, and until I figure it out, I'm not turning it over," Spencer replied.

Even if it means someone getting hurt or worse, Toni thought, looking at him with a funny expression. It was the first time she saw the determination in Spencer, and it worried her that he might be so determined to find the treasure that he would put others in harm's way.

"I need to head to the clinic and check on things," she commented, and Spencer nodded OK.

"Don't let them push you around," Spencer told Mr. Gentry.

He just smiled and lifted an old .45 Colt revolver up. "I can handle myself."

Pushing the screen door open, Spencer noticed that one of his three books was gone; he started to turn and ask, but felt Toni's urgency to get to the clinic.

"I'll drop you off, and then I'm going to move my truck, trailer, and boat to the south-end pier," he said, pulling up to the clinic.

She looked at him funny. "I'm helping you!" she exclaimed.

"Toni, this is getting serious, and if they still don't know you're involved, I'd like to keep it that way."

"Spencer LeJeune! You're not going to carry me halfway around the world, then dump me off. You stay your ass here until I get back!" She slammed the door before he had a chance to say anything.

"There's the girl I grew up with," he laughed to himself.

Spencer sat in his truck looking over his shoulder every minute or two. He was nervous and felt vulnerable sitting in the opening. *I've let this go too far,* he was thinking, *and even if I do give them the map and coin, will they let us be?*

The door to the clinic swung open, and Toni walked out with Tucker on her shoulder. "Do you mind if we run by my house?" she asked.

"No, are we taking him?"

"No, one of the girls is coming by to pick him up and sit with him." She climbed in with the raccoon perched on her shoulders. Spencer reached over to pet him, but Tucker bowed up and growled. "Don't be mean," Toni said and pulled him into her lap.

After leaving her house, they stopped by Spencer's house, and walking up to the front sliding door, he noticed it was cracked open. "Someone's been here," he said, cautiously walking in. There was food left out on the counter and a few empty beer cans near his couch.

"What? Did they just eat and leave?" Nothing else was bothered, and after cleaning up, he grabbed more clothes and headed back down the stairs. "This seems weird. It's almost too quiet around here," Spencer commented, shutting his truck door. He looked over his arm that was resting on Toni's headrest as he backed out. "I need to fuel up and then we'll grab my boat and move everything."

"Where are we staying?" She asked.

"Are you OK with Dusty's camp?" he asked.

"Yeah, it's OK," she answered.

Spencer stood by his truck watching the fuel pump count off the dollars; he felt uneasy and caught himself looking around, but not carefully enough. With Toni looking at the radio stations and Spencer glued in on the enormous amount of dollars clicking off on the pump, he felt a solid object press against his back.

"Don't move," a voice whispered in his ear. The hair on the back of his neck stood up, and his thoughts went into protection mode for Toni: What move could he make? He figured, with the gas pump in hand, maybe *that* would be his move, to spray down his assailant and get away from there.

Just as he started to move the nozzle out of his truck, the voice started laughing. *Wait,* Spencer thought. *That's not a Spanish accent. Sounds like....*

"Man, you should see your expression," Jimmy pointed at him, laughing.

"I never thought I'd say it, but am I glad it's you!" Spencer said, relieved.

"I haven't seen those foreigners since the day before yesterday. I camped out at your place hoping they'd come back."

That explained the mess. "Thank you. I'm worried about Mr. Gentry," Spencer said.

"Aw, don't worry about that old man .... What's the plan?" he said, looking more serious.

"Jimmy, I don't want to bring you into—"

"Aw, shut-up. I'm in!" he interrupted Spencer.

"We're staying at Dusty's camp tonight to make our plan, so I'll call you first thing in the morning," Spencer said, replacing the nozzle on the pump.

Jimmy looked over Spencer at Toni. "Well, you've kept her safe this long," he replied.

Spencer wasn't sure what that meant, nor did he ask.

"If I see them, I'll call you," Jimmy slammed his hand on Spencer's shoulder. *Man,* Spencer thought, *I'm glad he's on my side.* Jimmy started to walk off, but turned back to Spencer. "This isn't about that legendary treasure … that Spanish barge, if my memory is correct?" he stunned Spencer.

"It's about something they think is theirs," Spencer answered, trying not to get into the conversation about the treasure.

"Well, if you think you're right, then I got your back."

Pulling out, Jimmy paused in front of Spencer's truck, holding up the book missing from Gentry's store. "Damn good book!" he hollered.

"He reads?" Toni asked sarcastically.

"Be nice," Spencer said.

She looked at him oddly, adding, "There's a switch."

Smiling, Spencer answered with "I'll bring you to the marina, and you bring my boat around to the south end pier."

She smiled, "OK!"

Pulling up to the south end pier, Spencer found Dusty's truck parked near the dock. "How did you know I'd be here?" he had to ask.

"Please. I know you, LeJeune. Just like your daddy, being precautionary."

"Toni told you," Spencer answered.

Dusty smiled, "Yeah. I already replenished the food at the camp. You should be good for a few days."

"You didn't have to do that," Spencer said as he saw his 42' center-console come flying down the bay.

"Man, she must have that thing aired out," Dusty observed, looking in her direction.

"Yep."

After Spencer stepped down into the boat, Dusty added, as he pushed the boat back out from the dock, "I have everything here, so don't worry."

"I'll call you in the morning and let you know what the plan is," Spencer said, trying to take over the wheel.

Toni gave him a funny look and insisted, "I got this."

Chapter 40

The ride out to Dusty's camp house was peaceful and warm, the smooth water allowing Spencer's boat to glide across a tranquil surface. Spencer watched as Toni steered around a few small islands, her hairflowing behind her in the wind and her expression content.

"Why me?" Spencer asked.

She cut her hazel eyes at him. "I don't know. Why you?" she joked back, not fully understanding his question.

"Why do you trust me like you do?" he asked.

The question confused her. "You're my best friend," she answered.

He shook his head, hoping that his expression didn't give his true feelings away.

Where's he going with this? she thought, watching Dusty's camp house getting closer. He let the conversation subside.

Tying his boat up to the dock, he could barely hold his anxiety about retrieving the map. He started to jump in as Toni was making her way to the camp, but something stopped him; maybe she didn't need to know where the map was hidden. He followed her into the camp house. The pantry was restocked, and two fresh bottles of Dusty's homemade wine were on the table with a note. "Enjoy, but not too much!" the note read. Spencer wadded up the note and stuck it into his shorts before she could see it. *Dusty's sense of humor.*

"I guess he was expecting us," Toni said from the living room. Spencer rounded the corner to find fresh flowers and an unlit candle on the makeshift coffee table.

"I guess," he laughed, holding on to the note in his pocket.

"Think you can catch us some fish again?" she said with a spark.

"Well, let me go see," he said, glad to have a chance to retrieve the map without her seeing. He pulled the same rod he had used before from his boat and casted out, but after the third time he looked back to make sure the coast was clear. Not seeing Toni, he jumped in the thigh-deep water and waded under the pier, and reaching between the beams he pulled out the waterproof pouch. Putting it between the small of his back and his shorts, he casted for another ten minutes with no bites. *Not tonight.*

"What, no fish?" Toni asked before the screen door could shut.

"Sorry, they weren't cooperating."

"We'll figure something out," she said pulling out a can of beans and a roll of summer sausage.

"We can run to Grand Isle in the morning for cold stuff," he said, grabbing one of the bottles of wine and two Mason jars.

"You want to sit out front?" he asked.

"Sure."

The front porch to the camp house was small, with two rocking chairs and a two-rail railing that lined the porch.

Spencer poured a mason jar half full of wine and handed it to Toni, who sat on the ground with her back against the railing, facing the sun. "It's beautiful out here. I can't imagine growing up anywhere else." As the words came out, she caught herself, remembering Spencer not growing up there during his teen years.

"Florida was cool. A lot more people, but there were peaceful times, too," he answered.

"Where do you see yourself in a few years? I mean, if you find this treasure, will you stay or move on?" she asked.

He smiled. "You mean *when* I find the treasure. I don't know, I love it here, but there are other places I'd like to see. I can imagine buying a sail boat and sailing the islands of the Caribbean."

I could handle that, Toni thought to herself.

"What about you?" he asked.

"I don't know—this is home. I feel safe here, plus I love working at the clinic. I don't know if I can see myself anywhere else."

A gentle breeze picked up and blew through the saw grass that lined the small island the camp house rested on. The bay was coming to life with different species of birds heading to roost for the night; a flock of pelicans glided over, not paying Spencer and Toni any attention. "I can't imagine not being able to see that." Toni said, pointing at them.

Spencer agreed and was curious to know where the questions were coming from and their intentions.

"I can't believe Jimmy bought one of my books; I think they've been there since I left."

"How many have you written?" she asked, knowing the answer.

"I'm on my sixth right now."

There was a long pause. "The first five were good," she said, breaking the silence as she took a sip.

"I don't know about good, just fun to write. Wait, you read them?" he asked.

"I bought my first one when we were sophomores in high school."

Spencer thought back to the day when one of the books was uncounted for. "From Gentry's?"

Were you selling them somewhere else?" she giggled.

"No, hmm." He took a sip of his wine.

She took a deep breath. "They're really good stories; I love Lebreaux in them."

"Thanks," he said.

Toni took a slow sip from her Mason jar. "Your dreams led you to write the story *Pirates and Voodoo*, right?" She didn't give him time to answer. "I mean writing them so young and considering the depth of the books, it's like you would have to have been there to know." She paused for an answer.

"I guess it's just from reading a lot of pirate books too," he said.

"Where do you think they are?" she asked.

"Vargas's men?"

"Yes."

"Probably still on the wild goose chase from Mr. Gentry," he answered.

"What are we going to do?"

He looked out as dusk started to fall on the marsh, "I don't want to drag anyone else into this mess. If I can just have a few more days, then maybe we can pinpoint the exact location and give them the map after we've taken the treasure."

Toni stood up and arched her back while stretching, Spencer eyeing her while she brought her arms over her head. She walked up to his chair and placed her hand on the side of his face, her touch soft and alluring. "Let's find this treasure and then we'll figure out the future." She smiled and disappeared inside.

He sat staring out over the water until the reflection of the stars and water couldn't be separated by vision. *I have to find this treasure soon*—he looked back at Toni in the kitchen—*so I can get on with the next phase of my life.*

Chapter 41

Spencer reclined back in his chair on the porch and faded off in a deep sleep dreaming of a foggy, windless night and the sounds of a wooden ship creaking as it quietly pushed through the waters of South Louisiana. With only a few lanterns lit, the helmsman squinted his eyes trying to pierce through the thick white mist. He mistrusted the navigator, who was sleeping against the rail, and had questioned his decision. A tall man dressed with a frock coat and sword on his side entered the stern castle. "Wake up, you fool!" he kicked the navigator.

"Sir, we are thicked in. I say drop anchor before we run her on shore," the navigator's voice shaking with his advice.

"Keep her on heading," the tall man barked and disappeared back into the captain's chambers.

"Do ye think he'll come after us?" a soft voice asked from the shadows of the room.

"He will." The man threw his hat onto the table. Sitting, he began studying a map he had rolled out onto the old wooden table.

Small soft hands ran over his shoulders onto his chest. "I owe ye my life," she whispered into his ear. He didn't answer. She made her way around him and sat in his lap while running her fingers in circles on his chest. Looking into her eyes, he saw not only the loyalty, but the mystery of the Haitian woman.

"We will be together forever," he teased back. "But first, I have to figure out this map!" his voice raised.

She rose to her feet and placing both hands on the table, studied the map with him. The map was thick and made out of small strains of bamboo, with several holes strategically placed throughout the map. The man sat back in his chair and pulled out the silver coin from his coat pocket. "What does this have to do with anything?" he said, staring at the coin.

The young Haitian woman looked at the map and then back at him. *I know!* she smiled.

She suddenly stood up straight and stared into the dark corner of the room as if startled by someone. She tilted her head and walked delicately toward the figure lingering in the shadows. Stopping a few feet from the figure, she straightened up and motioned for it to come forward. The man was still studying the map, unaware and oblivious to what was happening behind him.

"Boy! Come here," she said. Spencer walked forward. In this dream, Spencer found himself the ten-year-old boy he was when Lebreaux went missing. "You and da girl, together?" she questioned.

"I don't know," he sheepishly answered.

"Give me ye hand." Spencer turned his right palm over and volunteered it to her, and running her finger through the palm of the young boy's hand, she smiled.

Spencer peeked around her at the man sitting at the table. "What's he looking at?"

"Come see," she waved him forward. Spencer could feel the boat gently rocking back and forth and the lanterns swaying with each pitch. The man didn't notice Spencer in the room as if he were a ghost.

"That's the map I have!" Spencer said in an excited ten-year-old voice. She nodded her head. Spencer looked down at the map and noticed the difference, "It doesn't have as many holes as it does now. Why?" She slightly turned her head and gazed at him, and he felt her hinting to him, but what?

Lebreaux put her arm around him and led him out onto the quarterdeck as if they were invisible to everyone else. "Boy, we find tings at great cost. And when it comes your time, you will have to make a decision—da treasure or da girl."

"Why?" he asked.

"Soon you will have da answers. But for now ye have to go." She led him down the stairs, and stepping onto the main deck, he felt himself waking up. Before his eyes left the ship, he saw the bell with the ship's name embossed on the rim. "What? This ship is named the—" He woke up.

"You OK?" Toni asked with her hand on Spencer's shoulder. Blinking his eyes, he realized he was still sitting outside on the porch of Dusty's camp house.

"Yeah, what time is it?" he asked.

"Just after 3 a.m., come inside." She led him back through the screen door. He stood up and stretched his arms, a warm breeze blowing past him from the bay. "Da girl or da treasure!" a faint whisper said in the breeze. He looked out across the water, thinking, *Did I just hear that?*

Toni climbed back in her blanket on the couch and smiled at him as he walked in. "Come cuddle with me." Her voice held a hint of his ten-year-old friend. He crawled onto the couch and wrapped up in the blanket with her. She pulled against his chest, drawing herself close to him, took a deep breath, and faded back to sleep.

How can I ever get past this buddy stage? he thought as he held her close and dozed off.

Waking with a crick in his neck and to the flicker of the only candle lit in the room, Spencer struggled to untangle himself from the blanket without waking Toni. Stumbling into the kitchen, he opened a fresh bag of coffee, the aroma quickly filling the small kitchen. Spencer sat at the table with the mismatched chairs waiting for the coffee to brew. He glanced out the screen door at the light beginning to break into the bay.

Thinking back to his dream, he tried to wrap his head around the remark Lebreaux gave him, the girl or the treasure. *What does that mean? Am I going to have to give up the treasure for Toni?* Rubbing his head, the sight of the map broke into his thoughts, and he realized in his dream it had only half the holes it had now. *If Cardona made the map years before Lebreaux, then how and why did the other holes get cut into the map? The bell?* His thoughts changed. *What was the name of the ship? I saw it ... what was the name?*

He heard Toni wrestling in her sleep, so pouring a cup, he walked back into the living room to find her moaning something in her sleep. He set his cup down and gently sat on the edge of the leather couch. "No!" Toni shouted, still asleep. Spencer chuckled at her outburst. "But why?" she asked. Spencer was trying not to laugh out loud. "Lebreaux, don't go." The words pierced Spencer: *Lebreaux? She's dreaming about Lebreaux?*

Suddenly Toni shot up from her dream, scaring Spencer, who was still sitting on the edge of the couch. "You OK?" he asked.

"The map! Get the map!" she exclaimed.

"Why? What's the matter?" he asked.

"Just get it."

Without questioning more, he walked outside, again retrieved the map from under the pier, and walked back in. He sat back on the couch with her and unrolled the bamboo map. "Look!" she pointed at the holes located over the Gulf of Mexico. "These are newer than the others."

"How can you tell that?" he asked.

"In my dream, Lebreaux showed me."

Spencer cocked his head, "Lebreaux? You dreamed about the map?"

"Yes."

"Where you in a ship with a man sitting at a table?" Spencer asked.

Toni's expression turned from excitement to bewilderment, "How do you know that?"

"I dreamed it too."

The two of them sat back on the couch and quietly gathered their thoughts. Spencer thought back on the room, the man, table, lantern, the rocking of the ship. *So strange we're now dreaming the same thing.*

"Toni?" Spencer suddenly stirred.

"Yeah?"

"How long has that lantern been there?" He pointed at a black iron lantern decorated with a fleur-de-lis sitting on the coffee table.

Chapter 42

"What a weird night," Toni said, blowing the stream from her cup. She sat in the chair that Spencer had fallen asleep in the night before.

Spencer walked out holding the lantern. "Did Dusty have this here the whole time? I wonder if I've seen it before and that's why it's in my dreams."

"We need to ride into town. I need to check on a few things," she said.

"Yep, I want to look up the Cardona family," he added.

"How's everything in town?" Spencer texted Dusty.

A few minutes later, Dusty replied, "Quiet. How are the love birds?"

Spencer hid the screen from Toni, replying with "Friends! We are coming in to Gentry's store."

"I'll leave my truck at the south end pier for you," Dusty texted back.

"It sounds quiet in town," Spencer commented to Toni. "You ready?"

"Yep, give me a second." She washed out her cup and straightened the kitchen. A short time later, as Spencer fired up the four 350s on the back of *Waterproof*, Toni walked down the wooden steps leading to the pier with the map in hand. "Do we want to take this?"

Spencer took the map. "No," he replied, hopping down into the thigh-deep water and disappearing under the pier.

"I take it that's the safe place?" Toni asked, stepping in the boat.

"I hope so," he said from under the dock while stuffing the case with the map in the beams.

Untying the front of the boat, he felt it backing out from the pier, and looking back he saw Toni standing at the wheel while glancing back. *Already taken over my boat.*

"You ready?" she asked. But before she got an answer from him, she throttled down, forcing the boat to shoot out of the water onto a plane and jet east toward Buras.

"We're not trying to break a record," he shouted above the engines and wind. He got only a smile as a reply.

Coasting into the south pier, they saw Dusty's truck parked near the dock. With a sense of urgency, they wasted no time in making their way to the truck and heading toward Gentry's. Spencer parked out front. "No need to hide this truck," he said, walking in with Toni.

"Hi, Mr. Gentry, can we use your computer again?" Toni asked.

He nodded toward the back room. "Yep."

They sat together in front of the old monitor and pulled up the name Nicholas de Cardona on the Internet. Very little came up that they didn't already know, with the exception that he was from Seville, Spain. They read through a few sites. "Nothing is said about him and Vargas working together. Just that Vargas had him make a map of the area where the Tierra Firme ships sank," Spencer said, glued to the monitor.

Toni sat back in a deep thought, "Didn't Pablo from Potosi say that the Archives of the Indies was in Seville?" she asked. Spencer was surprised that not only was she listening, but remembered that from their conversation with the old man.

"Yes, it holds much of the trade information from the Americas to Spain during the sixteenth and seventeenth century. Weird that it is also the same place the Cardona family lived." Spencer dug into the history and contents of the Archive of the Indies.

"Seville was where I went to look for the manifest of the *Compostela*, but I didn't find what I was looking for and ended up in Virgo," Spencer told Toni as he scrolled through a site. He placed his finger on the screen and followed the text. "There is a lot here, maybe too much."

Toni leaned in and looked at the site, noticing a symbol. "There!" She pointed at a compass rose.

"What?" He asked.

"I've dreamed about that very symbol."

He looked back at her. "A compass rose?"

"It was framed on the wall of the captain's quarters," she said.

Spencer pushed back from the desk and stood up. Pacing the room, he thought back on his dreams. *I never saw a compass rose.* "You want to go to Spain?" he asked, knowing her answer when she looked up from the computer screen smiling.

Spencer texted Dusty. "I need my truck. We are heading to New Orleans for a few days."

"Be right there," Dusty replied.

Spencer sat back down and pulled up the flights to Seville Spain. "Spencer, those prices are too high!" Toni said, seeing the cost.

"It will be worth it," Spencer replied, booking their tickets.

"Good morning, Mr. Gentry," Dusty said, walking in.

"How ya doing, sport?" Mr. Gentry replied.

"Ready for oyster season. Those kids here?"

"In the back glued to that computer," he replied, never breaking from the newspaper he was reading.

"New Orleans? My place not good enough?" Dusty said, walking in the back room.

"Yes, your place is good enough," Toni smiled.

"Bud, you get all this worked out?" Dusty asked Spencer, referring to the Spaniards.

"I believe so, and we'll have it figured out in the next few days," Spencer answered.

"All right, make sure y'all stay safe," Dusty replied, handing Spencer his keys.

"I'll text you tonight," he told Dusty.

As they walked out together, "You three sure make for a lot of excitement around here," Mr. Gentry said.

"Never a dull moment," Spencer replied. Out front, they said their goodbyes to Dusty and made their way to the back, where he had left Spencer's truck.

"Can we stop by my place and let me grab a few things and check on Tucker?" Toni asked.

"Yeah, but we need to be quick—I'm still uneasy about being out in the open," he replied.

The following day, a black Mercedes sped through New Orleans heading for Buras. Once it reached the city limits, the car pulled up to Spencer's house, and the four men walked up the steps leading to the sliding glass door. The door was open, and the men entered, not speaking a word. After two of the men quickly searched the small house, "No one is here," one of the men said. "He's been here—too much is moved around since we were here last."

"The old man's store!" another man replied.

The car slid to a stop in front of Gentry's store, and the men entered the empty store to find Mr. Gentry sitting behind the counter.

"Did you find him?" Mr. Gentry asked in a sarcastic tone.

"I don't believe Mr. LeJeune was ever in Florida, and I believe you know where he is," the man replied with a snarl.

"I might, and there's no way in hell I'll tell you." The other men walked through the store searching for anything, when one man found in the back room that Mr. Gentry had never closed down the screen to his computer with the display confirming Spencer's tickets to Seville.

"He bought two tickets to Seville and flew out last night!" the man yelled as he walked out of the back room.

"Go back there again and you'll not come back!" Mr. Gentry growled, a .45 revolver appearing in his hand from behind the newspaper.

"Easy, old man; we don't want you." The man in front of him held his hands up.

"Come back through that door again, and I'll blow all four of you to hell. You got me?" Mr. Gentry growled.

"We got you," the man smiled as he disappeared with the others through the screen door.

Chapter 43

Feeling the plane beginning to descend, Toni sat up from their business class seating; she had gotten little sleep with the thought of going to Spain, a childhood dream. She reached over her blanket and tapped Spencer. "We're close to landing."

He rolled over, muttering, "Let me know when we've landed."

"Wake up," she punched him.

"I'm up."

The flight attendant announced their arrival in Seville, Spain, just after the wheels touched the ground. The flight was half full, and debarking took only a few minutes. Spencer pulled his backpack straps over his shoulders while looking at the signs. "Baggage is this way," he tugged on Toni. Once they found baggage claim, Toni slipped into the bathroom, and coming back out, she found Spencer with their bags.

"That was fast."

"Small airport," he replied.

Walking out under the large awning that ran the length of the building, they hailed a cab. "Hotel Alfonso," Spencer told the driver. He smiled, loaded their bags, and sped out from underneath the awning into the bright sun and the 92 degree weather.

Within minutes, they were driving through town with Toni pinned to the window. "Wow, this is nice," she was chattering with excitement, "much different from Bolivia." She was still struggling with the thought of being in three countries and on the opposite side of the world all within a week.

A stadium came into sight as the cab driver took the long way to the hotel. "Sanchez Pizjaun," he called out and pointed out the window toward the stadium.

"I take it that's their soccer field?" Toni said to Spencer.

Spencer was charmed at the sight of it. "Looks like Death Valley," he observed, referring to LSU's football stadium.

As they pulled up in front of the hotel, Toni's eyes grew large. "You don't believe in staying at Motel 6, do you?" she commented, looking at the hotel lined with palm trees facing the tram tracks.

"I saw this place the last time I was here," he said, climbing out and tipping the driver. A bellman snatched their bags, and they followed him inside like a newlywed couple.

"So are we getting one bed again?" she teased him.

"I'll get two," he replied.

"I don't mind snuggling," she smiled.

I'm not interested in just snuggling, Spencer thought.

After checking in and throwing their bags in their room—with two beds—they headed out toward the Archive of the Indies.

"I can't believe how beautiful everything is here," Toni commented, looking at the University of Seville that neighbored the hotel. Across the street, buildings lined the tram tracks with coffee shops, restaurants, taverns, and shopping.

Spencer pulled out his phone and opened his maps to make sure of the directions. "This way," he pulled her arm.

"We have to come back when we have more time," she said as he pulled her along.

Turning up a side street, Toni was surprised to find a Starbucks. Past the familiar coffee shop, they passed a small deli and restaurant with umbrella tables sticking out in the street. Once through the narrow alleyways they came out at Alcazar, the Royal Palace.

"Holy cow!" Toni looked up at the walls that protected the palace and gardens.

"Yep, but look at this," she heard Spencer reply. Turning to her left, she found the Cathedral of Seville standing before them. Speechless, she just stood in place, hypnotized with the beauty of the third largest cathedral in the world and the sixteenth-century architecture that stood with boldness.

"Well come on, we're on a tight time frame," Spencer once again grabbed her arm and pulled her out of her trance. They turned another corner and found themselves facing the Archive of the Indies. The large, two-story square building with a courtyard in the center was dwarfed by the Cathedral across the street. Built in 1584, the Archive of the Indies houses over nine kilometers of shelving and well over 80 million pages of the most important and valuable archival

documents from the sixteenth century illustrating the history
of the Spanish Empire in the Americas.

"I hope we find what we're looking for," Spencer
said, walking beside the building.

"Are we just going to walk in and ask information on
Nicholas Cardona and the map?" she asked.

"I don't know what we're going to ask."

They walked up to the small opening for the front
door with *Archivo General De Indias* written above the
doorway in iron letters. Passing through the opening, they
were met by a guard on the other side of a giant iron gate.
Once inside, Toni was mesmerized by the fine details of the
arched ceiling and marbles floors. They made their way
through the hallways and came to letters dating back to
Christopher Columbus. "Look at this letter," Toni grabbed
Spencer's arm in amazement.

Immersed in the ornate interior of the Archive and
overwhelmed with how to begin their search, they were
rescued from their confusion when a young man approached
them. "Puedo ayudarle?" he asked.

Both Spencer and Toni looked at each other. "I'm
sorry, we don't speak Spanish," Spencer replied.

The young man smiled. "May I help you?"

"Do we look *that* lost?" Spencer said with a smile.

"You look … confounded," the attendant replied.

"We are looking for information on a man named
Nicholas Cardona from the 1620s."

The young man turned and began to walk off, and
Spencer looked at Toni in confusion, wondering if they had
said something wrong. Within a few steps the young man
turned and smiled, waving them on. They continued through

the marble hallway and past the portraits of many early pioneers, coming to a halt in front of a painting of a man that portrayed him not only as a nobleman, but a man of great authority. The young man pointed to the plaque centered on the bottom of the golden frame: *Nicholas de Cardona.*

"What would you like to know?" the young man asked.

"Actually, we are wondering if there is any information on a map he created for the 1622 Spanish fleet," Spencer asked.

Nodding, the young man replied, "Si, it would be in the Spanish Archives Portal; there is a computer room here. It's open to the public—I'll show you." He held his arm out for them to follow.

"Would you know of any living Cardona family members?" Toni asked, walking behind Spencer.

"Si, there is one. He is a large supporter of the Archives of the Indies. Hence the portrait of his ancestor," their guide smiled.

"Would you know how to contact him?" she asked.

"He lives just north of Seville."

The young man stopped at an open door. "There are people here who can further assist you. Good luck on your search." Spencer and Toni walked in to what looked like the sort of computer lab one would find at a university.

A lady approached them, "En que puedo ayudarle?"

"We are looking for a map made in 1622," Spencer started.

The lady smiled. "Have a seat and I'll help you. You don't read Spanish, do you?" she asked.

"No."

She nodded with a grin. "We are not busy, so tell me exactly what you are looking for."

After a few minutes of searching, Cardona's map was on the screen. "We already know most of this—I say let's go to Cardona's house," Toni whispered in Spencer's ear. Agreeing, Spencer studied the screen for a moment not to be rude and then thanked the lady. Walking out, they passed by Cardona's portrait again, and Toni stopped Spencer. "Look," she whispered, pointing to another portrait hung across the hall. Spencer turned to see Gaspar Vargas portrayed in oil paints—staring at him.

Chapter 44

Leaving the Archives, Spencer and Toni walked back toward their hotel, and Spencer pulled out his phone to check the map of their area. "I'm starving, burgers?" he asked.

"Sure," she answered.

Weaving back through the same small streets and alleyways toward Hotel Alfonso the two of them never noticed the two men in black suits following. "Boston Burgers is just past the hotel," Spencer explained, leading Toni.

As they made their way along the sidewalk, a four-car tram quietly passed, the sound of a bell signifying the next stop. Toni looked back at the people exiting the gray tram with red strips and spotted the two men, but thought nothing of it. With the afternoon sun settling behind the row of buildings, they sat at a table outside under an umbrella and ordered burgers, fries, and much-needed water. Spencer pulled out his phone and looked for Cardona families in Seville, but the only listing was Rocio Cardona. "This should be easy," he told Toni. "This guy is pretty popular here in Seville." After a few more searches, he pinpointed the address.

Across the street, leaning against a half brick wall and iron fence leading into the university, the two men watched as Toni and Spencer ate a mid-afternoon meal. One of the men's cell phone rang. "Hola. Si … si … we are looking at them now. Si." He hung up. "He wants us to continue to follow," He told the other man.

While Spencer was paying the waiter, Toni again noticed the two men that had been standing across the street, but still didn't think anything of it. As they walked out from underneath the umbrella tables, another tram came from the opposite direction, blocking the view for the two men as Spencer and Toni boarded.

"Where did they go? Did they get on the tram?" one of the men suddenly stood up from leaning on the wall.

"They might have gone back to the Archive," the other said as they made their way to the middle of the street.

"Quickly, we can't lose them." They jogged to the end of the street.

Spencer and Toni hailed a cab once the tram stopped a few blocks from the restaurant. "Can you take us here?" Spencer showed the driver his cell phone with the address. "Si," the driver replied as Toni rolled down her window while they sped off toward the Cardona estate.

Parking outside the enormous gate and stucco fence that fortified the compound, Spencer asked the cab driver to wait. They walked up to the speaker box mounted on a pole outside the gate, and Spencer pushed the button. "Si?" a voice came back.

"We are here to see Mr. Cardona," Spencer asked, praying they understood English.

After a long pause, "Do you have an appointment?" a different voice asked.

"No, but we need to ask him about a map. We've come here from the US."

After another long pause came the response: "Go to Archives of the Indies."

"We have," Spencer said.

"I am sorry, then, I cannot help you. Mr. Cardona doesn't see people." The box went silent.

Toni pushed the button again. "We are here to see him about a map that Vargas and his ancestor Nicholas Cardona created about a Spanish barge." Spencer looked at Toni, worried about showing their hand. "I'm sorry, but we didn't come this far to be turned away," she told him. The speaker box remained silent.

Then, with a buzz the front gate began opening, "Please come to the front door," the voice instructed. Spencer waved back at the cab to continue to wait, but the driver waved back and drove off.

"Where is he going? I haven't even paid him yet." They walked up a long curving drive lined with landscape and palm trees. The surroundings were immaculate.

Reaching the top of the drive, they were greeted by two well-dressed men. "Follow us," they demanded.

"I hope we haven't messed up coming here," Spencer whispered to Toni. Led by their guides through the 12,000 square foot home, they ended up in the library.

"Mr. Cardona will be with you shortly." The men left, closing the French style doors behind them.

Suspicious, Spencer pulled on the doors, "They're locked." He quickly walked to another door. "Locked!"

He looked at Toni, who was calmly standing in the center of the room, "I'm sure there's an explanation."

"There is. They automatically lock; it is a safety precaution," an older man said, entering in the room. "I am Rocio Cardona, and you two have some information on a legendary old map?" he asked.

"Well, we were hoping you had information," Spencer said.

"Please sit," Mr. Cardona said, pointing to a brown leather couch that faced two matching chairs. The room was filled with head mounts from different animals throughout the world, along with a large collection of books. "This map, which I question even exists, has put many people in danger. There is a family here in Spain that believe the map belongs to them."

"The Vargas family," Spencer interrupted.

"Yes," Cardona paused. "My intention to bring you in was to warn you, but I see that is too late. If you have been confronted by these people, give them whatever information you have and go home!" He stood.

"I'm afraid we might be too far in," Spencer said.

Cardona smirked, "Then may God be with you—He might be the only one to save you."

He began to walk out of the room. "Wait!" Toni started to say something, but Spencer stopped her from mentioning anything about them having the map. Cardona stopped and faced her.

"What if someone did have this map?" she asked. Spencer gave her a look to keep quiet, and Cardona noticed the gesture from him.

"Even if one did have the map, they would have to have a key to go with it," Cardona answered.

"Key? Or a coin?" she said.

"A coin." He looked at her with a puzzled expression. "Do you have the map?" he asked.

"No." Spencer blurted out.

Cardona looked at him, considering his quick answer. "You don't understand how serious the Vargas family can be. It could easily be your lives you are toying with. Besides, the coin disappeared hundreds of years ago. This legendary treasure you are hunting for is thought to be long gone." Toni stepped in to say something else, but Cardona cut her off. "Heed this warning—go home. You're not safe here in Seville." He walked out, leaving the door open.

One of the men who escorted them to the library walked in. "I'll show you the door," he explained. They followed him out, walking down a long hallway draped with curtains.

"Spencer, I don't know," Toni whispered. "Maybe we should give the map to Vargas's men. This is scary."

"No, I didn't come this far to give up. We'll go back home; they can't win on our ground," he persisted.

Cardona stood on the other side of an opened doorway listening to their conversation.

Chapter 45

Cardona's personal Audi A8 dropped Spencer and Toni off at Hotel Alfonso. Spencer hadn't said much since they left Cardona's estate, leaving Toni wondering if he was going after the treasure at whatever cost. She was surprised at his persistence and lack of concern for their safety, and finally was not able to keep quiet about it any longer. "Spencer," she insisted, "I think we're getting in over our heads," she said as they walked into the lobby of the hotel.

"Everything will be OK once we get back. I'll understand if you leave the search."

"Leave?" Her voice shot up. "I am *not* leaving, but I can also see there is no winning to this." She could feel her temper rising, and Spencer put his hands up, knowing that when Toni got fired up, nothing was going to calm her down.

"OK, we're tired. Let's get some rest before our flight in the morning," he suggested.

"I'm not going to spend the rest of my day sitting in a hotel room! I'm going to go see what I can of Seville while we are still here."

Spencer wasn't interested in arguing. "Fine, what do you want to do?"

She looked at him for a brief moment. "Rent scooters!"

Scooters?

Spencer remembered seeing a rental place just around the corner from the Starbucks. *Great, now I'm going to chase her all around Seville on a scooter,* he thought, but what he said out loud was "OK." He walked back out of the busy lobby and led the way to the rental place.

After paying their rental fee, the two of them walked out with helmets in hand and jumped on the scooters they had for the next four hours. "Where to?" he asked her.

"You lead," she said in a calmer tone. Spencer didn't have a clue on the road rules for Spain, but thought, *How bad can you mess up on a scooter in Seville, Spain?* Leaving a puff of white smoke behind, they sped down a back road and crossed the tram tracks to join in the traffic heading south. With hair flapping out from under her helmet in the wind, she quickly passed him and laughingly stuck out her tongue at him. He shook his head and sped up to catch her, happy she had calmed down.

Busy chasing each other and weaving in and out of traffic, they never noticed the black town car with tinted windows keeping up with them. "Don't lose them," the man in the passenger seat demanded as he pulled out a Berretta 92FS from his shoulder holster and screwed on a silencer. "Get beside them," he told the driver. In the far lane and a car length behind the two scooters, the man rolled down the passenger window and took aim at the helmet with the long dark hair coming out from under it. *Kill the girl and the guy will surely talk.* He slowly squeezed the trigger, keeping the sights on her helmet.

Never hearing the shot from behind, Spencer and Toni took a sharp right into the Plaza de Espana. "You missed!" the driver exclaimed, not able to follow the scooters.

"Turn around!" the other man shouted, rolling his window back up.

Spencer and Toni putted through the remarkable gardens of the plaza. "I can't believe how beautiful everything is here," she shouted to Spencer, who was looking at the landscape.

"Pull over," he told her. They parked their scooters on a curb and made their way to the pavilion buildings. "What is this place?" Toni asked, amazed with the size of the buildings.

"This was the place for the 1929 world fair. Spain built this to show their industry and technological exhibits during the fair."

Toni looked at him. "Thanks, professor," she smiled. "How do you know that?" she asked.

"Internet," he replied without looking at her.

Toni headed for the fountain in the center of the pavilion, but felt Spencer snatch her arm back. "Don't say anything or make any moves. We are being followed!"

They turned and walked at a faster pace back to their scooters. Toni looked over her shoulder at the two men that were approaching. "Spencer, I saw them earlier today," she said.

"I know, I did too." Spencer looked back at the two men that were now running toward them. "Run!" he pulled on her arm. They sprinted to their scooters, and without buckling their helmets, they took off down through the plaza. Toni, confused, jetted down a walkway, giving Spencer no choice but to follow. "This isn't a street," Spencer yelled at her.

"I'll follow you," she shouted back, pointing for him to take the lead.

Spencer turned down a path that led to another street, and the black town car slid to a stop, blocking their way. A man stepped out and lowered the Berretta 92 onto Toni once again, but this time Spencer saw the shot coming. He quickly veered right with Toni following, causing the man to miss again. They sped down another walkway leading to a garden of overhead trellises, columns, and concrete benches. Zigzagging in and out of the columns and down a crooked stone path, Spencer saw an open gate leading out onto the street sending them back toward the cathedral. "Stay close," he called to Toni, who was hot on his back wheel.

Once in traffic, Spencer thought for sure they had lost Vargas's men. *They're now shooting at us? This is too much.* Hearing the screeching sound of tires, Spencer looked back and saw the black car six car lengths behind them. Their scooters made it easy to dart through traffic and escape the chase. Toni followed Spencer as he zipped around the cathedral and parked in front of Arzobispado de Seville, the Catholic Church across the street. "Ditch the scooters here," he said, hanging his helmet on the rear view mirror.

"We are on the other side of Alcazar from our hotel," Toni said as they walked at a fast pace toward the palace.

"Maybe we can cut through the gardens. That should put us back out at Boston Burgers." Walking in front of another hotel, they spotted two other men who looked out of place and obviously looking for someone.

"Do you think they're looking for us?" Toni said as they picked up their pace through the alleyway.

"I'm not taking any chances," he replied.

"They are!" Toni shouted, seeing the men running in their direction.

"We are on the wrong side of the wall for the gardens!" Spencer said. *Don't panic! Think!* He pulled out his phone and opened a map. Pinpointing their location, he pulled on Toni, "This way!"

Running and looking down at his phone slowed them down, but kept enough distance from Vargas's men. They continued ducking between buildings with Spencer's cell phone leading them toward the palace walls. Reaching a dead end, Spencer looked up and saw one of the towers on the wall. "This is the wall to the gardens!" he exclaimed.

Toni pushed against a small arched wooded door on the wall, and it opened. "Spencer!" They crawled through the small opening and into a dark room.

She quickly turned on the flashlight on her phone, lighting a long cinder-block room. "We're in the wall," Spencer said in a quieter voice.

Ducking under old wooden beams and darting around landscaping equipment, they rushed in the direction that felt right. A light formed from behind them as the men entered the same door and shouted something in Spanish toward Spencer and Toni. "Keep running!" Spencer reached back and grabbed Toni's free arm, and she held the light with her other hand, illuminating their path. Shadows of another wooden door appeared in the distance, with Spencer racing to the door, dragging his childhood crush. Reaching the arched door, he lifted up on an old iron latch and pushed forward, exposing the palace gardens. Slamming the door behind them, he pulled a wooden beam across the door, locking Vargas's men inside.

Chapter 46

Provoking a confused expression from a few Asian tourists, Spencer and Toni emerged from the sixteenth-century wall. Toni tucked her cell phone into her front pocket and reached for Spencer's hand. Their quickest way out of the gardens was to blend in with the tourists. Spencer smiled at the tourists as they passed. "It won't take them long to find another door; we need to get to the hotel," Spencer said, leading Toni toward the back of the gardens.

"Are you sure we can get out this way?" she asked.

"There's a gate on the back corner," he insisted.

They wove their way through the landscape and tourists aiming for the back corner, and soon Toni could see the wall tower Spencer was heading for. Overhearing tourists raise their voices, Toni turned to see their pursuers pushing their way through people and rushing toward them. "Spencer!" she yelled.

Spencer spun to discover the men chasing after them with guns drawn. "Run!"

Toni was almost beside Spencer as they rounded a fountain in the center of the pathway, where Toni broke to the left and Spencer to the right. As they came around the corner of a portico with a striped canvas top, they were faced with a hedge maze. "I don't think this is a good idea," Toni yelled, slowing down.

"Come on," Spencer insisted. Toni paused long enough to look back to see the men round the corner of the portico, and when she turned to Spencer, he had already entered the maze. *Left or right? Where did he go?*

"Spencer!" she screamed.

Spencer quickly figured out that the hedge maze was more of a design and easily made his way through, reaching the back. "There's the gate!" he said, turning to speak to Toni, but she wasn't in sight. "Toni!" He started back in, but feared she would emerge as he was looking for her; he hesitated for a moment, then ducked around the side of the maze. Bending down and trying to see through the hedges, he struggled to see anyone, much less Toni.

Tourists were walking and admiring the gardens, taking pictures and reading the historical plaques, all unaware of what was taking place. Two South Louisiana Cajuns were running from the most notable organized crime family in Spain, and hardly anyone noticed. Trying his best to blend into the crowd, Spencer walked around the edge of the maze. "Toni?" he called. He found a young couple looking at a brochure on the palace and asked them, "Have you seen a girl with dark hair in jeans and a blue top?"

"No English," the guy replied in a thick accent.

"Dang it!" he said, gritting his teeth. He spun in a 360, looking for anyone who resembled her, but now the thought of not seeing her was also arriving at the realization that he wasn't seeing Vargas's men either.

His phone rang. Looking down, he saw it was Toni, "Where are you?" he answered, still scanning the crowd, but the voice that replied to his question was not who he was expecting.

"If you want to see this girl again, then bring the map and coin to the bar Estrella!" Spencer froze for a moment, hoping this was a cruel joke, but he now realized how serious it was.

"I don't have it," he answered.

"Get it!"

"It's in America," he said.

After a pause at the other end of the line came the threat: "You have 48 hours until the girl dies. Go to the bar when you get it!" The line went dead.

Spencer knew the coin was safely hidden in their hotel room, but getting the map in 48 hours was going to be almost impossible. He walked to the gate tucked in the back corner of the garden to find it locked. He looked at the walls, thinking it was low enough to scale, but that didn't matter anymore—they had Toni. He walked back to the front of the gardens trying to calm his thoughts and think of what to do, but only one thing came to mind—Dusty!

"Well, hello, world traveler. How are you guys?" Dusty answered his cell phone.

"Not good," Spencer answered.

Dusty immediately picked up on his shaking voice. "What's the matter?"

"I don't have time to explain, but Toni is in trouble. I need you to go to your camp, and under the pier you'll find a waterproof case with a map inside. Can you get it to me here in Seville ASAP?" Spencer asked.

"I can. Are you OK? What else can I do?" Dusty asked.

"That's all for now. The quickest way is to UPS it overnight. I'll text you the address and I'll pick it up at the airport."

"Ok, I'll call you after I get it sent off. Spencer, are you sure I can't do anything else?"

"Maybe if you were here, but right now just send the map. I'll explain everything else later." He hung up. Spencer thought of the next thing—Cardona. *Maybe he'll help!*

With a press on the gate button Spencer could hear the buzz ringing inside the Cardona estate through the speakers.

"Can I help you?" a familiar voice asked over the speaker.

"I need to see Mr. Cardona."

"You were told there is nothing he can do. I am sorry." The speaker went silent.

"Wait! They took my friend!"

He wasn't sure if they heard him, but after a delay, the voice returned. "Come to the front." The gates opened.

Walking up the drive, he saw Cardona making his way toward him. "Is there anything you can do?" Spencer asked.

"Give them what they are looking for," Cardona answered.

"I'm having the map overnighted to me. Will they let her go?" he asked. Cardona stood silent facing him, and the stare made Spencer uncomfortable.

"You have the map?" Cardona asked.

"Yes."

"And you are sure it's the original map?"

"Yes, it's a bamboo map with twenty different oblong slots cut throughout it." Spencer could see his expression change.

"Come with me." Cardona led him inside and told one of the well-dressed men to get someone else and meet them in the library.

Pouring a glass of brandy and handing it to Spencer, Cardona explained, "It will help calm the nerves. Please sit." He walked around the couch, shutting the doors for privacy. Spencer took a gulp of the brandy, finding its woodsy taste went down smoothly.

"I have never met anyone who knew what the original map looks like," Cardona went on. "But it is useless … unless you have the coin. I wonder if the Vargas family has acquired the coin." He stopped and looked at the frame that held an old painting of a compass rose.

Spencer wasn't sure if he wanted to play all his cards, but on the way to Cardona's estate he had stopped and retrieved the coin hidden in their oversized showerhead. Spencer finished off his brandy by turning up his glass, and something caught his eye that he had not seen before. On the top shelf of the adjacent bookshelf was a bust of an African-American woman who looked all too familiar.

"Where did you get that?" he asked.

Cardona turned and looked to see what Spencer was pointing at. "Just a bust of an African woman."

"African or Haitian?" The room went silent.

"How do you know of the Haitian woman?" Cardona asked.

"Her name is Lebreaux," Spencer answered, "and I know more than you think."

Cardona set his glass down and walked to the door, calling to the men outside. As they walked in, he turned back to Spencer. "We are going to get your friend!"

Chapter 47

Toni had turned around for only a split second as Spencer dashed into the hedge maze. "Spencer!" she screamed, trying to catch up to him. Running into the maze, she dashed to her left and quickly found herself winding through what seemed to be an endless jungle. Pushing past tourists who were as lost as she was, she checked over her shoulder at every turn, expecting the men to be hot on her trail. Finally seeing the exit and part of the brick wall beyond the hedge, she swung her arms harder to gain momentum as she sprinted to the opening. A dark-complexioned man dressed in an Armani suit stepped into her path holding a 9mm pistol with silencer aimed at her.

Sliding to a stop only feet from the barrel, she sensed the other man stepping in behind her, blocking her from turning back. Thoughts of screaming ran through her head, but the cold words from the man behind her changed her mind. "Scream or run—I have no problem killing you."

Where is Spencer? Please help me! She could tell by the demeanor of the man in front of her that they didn't know where Spencer was either. They escorted her out of the gardens along the far side of the wall where they had run through. Nobody in the garden noticed her scared expression or the out-of-place trio.

Thoughts of running continued passing through her mind, but the cold barrel pressed against her side told her otherwise. Walking through the entrance to the palace, Toni thought for sure that someone would notice them and stop them for questions, but a nod from one of the guards toward Vargas's men told a different story. The same black town car stopped in front of the palace with the back door swinging open. Toni was quickly forced into the back seat and as the other two men climbed in behind her, she felt the car take off.

Her fear escalated as Toni watched the man in the front seat pass back a syringe, "What is that?" she asked. Nobody answered. "Please don't," she begged, shifting her weight away from the man now holding the syringe. The other man grabbed her arms and with his strength held her motionless as she watched the needle disappear into her thigh. At first there was a strong pinch, and as she struggled to pull her arms away, she felt her lower extremities becoming heavy and numb. Quickly her eyes became heavy, and before she could scream, Toni disappeared into darkness.

A young man who Spencer had not seen before entered the library with Cardona and Spencer. "This is Arturo," Cardona introduced them. Turning his attention to Arturo, Cardona asked, "Can you track a cell phone?"

"Yes sir," Arturo replied.

Cardona held his arm out with a curt "Lead the way," and the three men left the library and made their way through the large estate. Spencer, still feeling confused with all that was taking place, never saw the massive art collection they passed, figuring Nicholas Cardona as the center attraction of all the paintings in the corridor.

Leaving the main house and entering its west wing, Spencer followed Arturo and Cardona into an elaborate office with computer screens and monitors mounted on the walls and keyboards and consoles littering the wrap-around desk.

Arturo pulled a chair up to a keyboard that centered the monitors and turned to Spencer. "Can I have the number, please?"

Spencer thought for a moment. "I don't know it," he replied, beginning to panic.

"May I see your phone?" Arturo quickly caught on that Spencer was still not thinking clearly with Toni having been kidnapped.

"I'm sorry. I just can't seem to think," Spencer replied, realizing why he wanted his phone.

"It's OK," Arturo smiled.

Spencer felt the hand of Cardona rest on his shoulder. "I assure you that your friend is OK for now. They want the map, and she is their bargaining chip to getting it."

Bargaining chip? he thought.

Soon the screens on the wall and in front of Arturo blinked a few times and then presented a map of Seville. "The phone is turned off, but according to the history, they traveled from the palace to a building near the bullring." He turned his attention to Cardona.

"History? How can you track the history of a cell phone?" Spencer asked.

Arturo smiled again. "There are lots of things you can do with a cell phone that the public is not aware of." He turned back to Cardona, adding, "The last signal was from a building behind the Maritime Museum."

"Maritime Museum?" Spencer asked. Then it hit him. The interpreter he had hired last year was from a restaurant that was located behind the museum—Vargas's restaurant.

"Can you show video from the phone?" Cardona asked.

"I can, but first I will have to turn on the phone, and it might make a noise in doing so."

"Do it," Cardona ordered.

The young man turned back to his computer, and with a few clicks of the keys, announced, "It is powering up now." A short moment later, a live picture appeared on the screens. "Looks like it's an upstairs room," Arturo observed, pointing at the window in the background.

The picture on the screen began spinning around, and the face of a Spaniard appeared on screen. "Her phone just turned back on," the man said, oblivious to the audience watching from across town.

"Turn it off," a voice in the background demanded. The screen went blank.

"So she's above the restaurant!" Spencer exclaimed.

"Her phone is," Cardona replied.

"Keep me up to date," Cardona said to Arturo and motioned for Spencer to follow him out.

"This map you have … you are sure it's real?" Cardona asked Spencer as they walked back to the main house in a slower pace.

"Yes, I believe so."

Cardona took a deep breath. "My ancestors wanted to find the treasure more than anything; it even cost some of them their lives."

Spencer thought back to the words from Lebreaux, *The girl or the treasure.* The treasure was costing him the one thing he wanted more and with a deep breath, he added, "You can have the map and the treasure—I just want Toni."

Cardona smiled at Spencer with his willingness to give up a treasure worth millions for this girl, who was obviously more than a friend. "I understand you wanting your friend back, but I don't want the treasure, nor do I want Vargas to have the treasure. It should go to the people who need it the most."

"Who?" Spencer asked.

"That's for you to decide once we find the treasure."

With blurred vision, Toni awoke tied to an old wooden chair and gagged in the corner of an upstairs room. She tried to cry out, but the tight cloth around her head wouldn't allow her voice to carry. She fought to free her arms, but the ropes restricted her movement. Overwhelmed with her greatest fears coming true and tears beginning to run down her cheek, she realized she was helpless and at the mercy of the men that left her alone in the room—and all because of Spencer's treasure hunt.

Chapter 48

Spencer had received a text from Dusty reporting that the package was in the air and should be at the airport in Seville by 2 p.m. the next afternoon. "You must be hungry. Come to the kitchen," Cardona said, veering off from their path through the estate.

Entering the kitchen, they were greeted by a lady wearing a chef's uniform. "Mr. Cardona, would you like something?" she asked, standing at an informal attention.

"See that our friend here is fed and make sure that Josephina prepares a room for him. He will be our guest for the next few days," Cardona replied.

Returning his attention to Spencer, he explained, "She will take care of you. I have to see what my men are planning. I will be back shortly." Without waiting for an answer, Cardona disappeared out of the room.

"Please have a seat, and I will bring it to you," the lady instructed Spencer. He was impressed with the large kitchen that was mostly cobblestone walls and exposed wooden beams crossing the ceiling above him. "Tea?" the lady, asked hovering over him.

"Just water, thank you." She brought him a tall glass of water with a lime and in a few minutes, placed a plate of pork tenderloin and vegetables in front of him.

"If you would like something else, please let me know," she added with a smile, and walked back to the opposite side of the granite stone island.

Spencer began eating, but without warning his eyes began to fill with tears. It was the first time he had been able to slow down enough to realize the gravity of their situation. Not only his childhood crush—but the woman he had fallen deeply in love with during the last few weeks—was captive somewhere in Spain, and it was his fault. *I am such an idiot! I should have never got her involved in this.* "Please forgive me, Toni, and please stay alive!" he whispered through his hands propping up his head.

"Vargas's arrogance will get the best of him," Cardona said, entering the kitchen.

"Excuse me?" Spencer asked, wiping his face.

"It seems they have your friend in the same building where the cell phone signal came from."

"When are we going?" Spencer said, hiding his eyes.

"I know you are eager to get her, and I would be too, but we must be patient for her safety. They are expecting you to deliver the map in 48 hours. We will rescue her in 24 hours." He took a cup of tea the chef had prepared for him.

"Then what?" Spencer asked.

"We find the treasure!"

After hearing the rest of the plan to free Toni and get the both of them out of Spain, Spencer was at the breaking point of exhaustion. "Josephina will show you to your room," Cardona said as he and Spencer walked out of the kitchen into a large foyer, where another lady waiting patiently for them. Spencer thanked him, and as he turned in her direction, he noticed the centerpiece in the foyer. In the center of the room, resting on a circular tiled floor, was a stained wooden display with a glass top. Under the glass was an old antique iron lantern with a fleur-de-lis.

Spencer paused long enough for Cardona to catch his pale expression and blank stare at the lantern from his dreams. "Where did you get that?" Spencer pointed. Cardona looked at the lantern, then back at Spencer. "It is from one of my ancestors."

"Ancestors?" Spencer asked.

"It is from an eighteenth-century ship."

Spencer didn't reply—the day had been crazy enough.

The night was the longest Spencer had ever had. He paced his room until 2 a.m. and then walked the halls of the estate, looking at the massive art collection that lined the walls. He sat on a red velvet bench and sank his face into his hands, thinking, *What have I done?* Horrible visions flashed through his mind about what was happening to Toni.

Spencer sensed he was being watched, and looking up from his bench, he saw an elderly man at the end of the long hall. Startled, Spencer thought he must be dreaming, but the elderly man approached him. "Master Cardona explained your circumstance. I wouldn't be able to sleep either. Would you like a glass of warm milk? It might help you get some rest," the old man asked.

"Sure," Spencer replied, rising to his feet. He walked slowly behind the man toward the kitchen.

As Spencer sat at the granite island in the center of the kitchen, the old man put a mug of hot chocolate in front of Spencer.

"Hot chocolate?" Spencer looked down in the steaming cup.

"Never too old for hot chocolate. Have a good night," the man said, vanishing through the doorway. Spencer sat in the quiet room sipping on something his father used to fix him when he had trouble sleeping. He made his way to a set of leather couches that faced a stone fireplace, and before he knew it, he dozed off.

"Mr. LeJeune?" A soft hand shook Spencer's shoulder. Opening his eyes, he saw the face of the lady who had served him supper the night before. "You couldn't sleep?" she said.

Gaining his bearings, Spencer said, "No, sorry, I must have fallen asleep here."

"It's OK," she replied, walking back to the stove where Spencer could see her warming a skillet.

He walked to the counter and placed his mug in the stainless steel sink, "Here is my cup. The elderly man fixed me something to drink last night."

She looked over at him while cutting a potato. "Elderly man?" She seemed confused.

"I was in the hallway when he asked me if I would like some hot chocolate."

"Hot chocolate? I didn't think we had any. You must have been tired. The men that work for Mr. Cardona are all younger." Spencer thought for a moment, *I know he was older. I'm not going crazy.*

Cardona walked in, saying, "You might want to come to my office to hear the briefing on today's events."

Spencer turned to the lady fixing breakfast. "Thank you," he said before following Cardona. She smiled back.

Walking into another large office with one main desk in the center of the room, Spencer found a dozen men, including Arturo.

"I turned the phone back on this morning and didn't get any other pictures," Arturo said.

"Can you hear anything?" Spencer asked, hoping for the best.

"No, sorry," Arturo answered.

After hearing the instructions from Cardona and not hearing his name in the plan, Spencer asked, "Where do you want me?"

"You will be with me," Cardona responded, and turning to another man who stood out from the others, added, "We will contact you once we leave the airport."

The man turned toward the others and began barking orders in Spanish. Cardona turned to Spencer, saying, "It's going to be a long day."

Spencer agreed—the morning was the longest morning he had ever spent, and he walked several times to Arturo's office, asking if anything had changed, only to receive the same report—nothing.

Spencer found himself back on the leather couch in the kitchen drifting in and out of sleep when Cardona hurried in with a brisk "Time to go to the airport." He walked through, barely giving Spencer time to react. They rushed outside to an awaiting car and sped toward the Seville airport. "We will drop you off in the parking garage so that we are not seen," Cardona explained. "You are to retrieve the map and then quickly head toward security."

"Security?" Spencer asked.

"Ask for Roberto Deleon, and he will take you out another way in case you are being followed." Spencer nodded that he understood.

The car came to a stop on the third level of the garage, and Spencer walked briskly to the UPS counter located near baggage. A young, red-headed girl standing behind the counter smiled at Spencer as she noticed him approaching her. Five feet from the counter, a shadow stepped between him and the young lady, and Spencer walked into the man. "Going somewhere?" the man asked in a thick Cajun accent.

"Dusty! What are you doing here?" Spencer asked, surprised and relieved at the same time.

"My friends are in trouble, you didn't think I was just going to mail this?" He held up the map.

Spencer pushed it back down and quickly scanned the lobby. "Follow me." He walked toward security and did just as Cardona had told him. The security officer led the two Cajuns out a side door where Cardona's car was waiting on them.

The car door swung open. "Who is this?" Cardona asked, pointing at Dusty.

"My close friend from home," Spencer replied, stopping short of entering the car.

"Get in!" the driver yelled over the seat. The two men dove in as the car sped out of the garage.

Chapter 49

One of Vargas's men untied the gag that was tightly wrapped around Toni's head. "If you scream, I'll re-tie you, and you can starve. Understand?" he growled.

"Yes," she replied, clearing her throat. He untied her hands from behind the chair, freeing her to eat the sandwich and chips he had brought. Taking a sip from the bottle of water, she felt relieved from her cottonmouth and dried throat; it was the first time she was given any water since being tied to the chair. The man sat in another chair across the room looking at his phone and occasionally glancing back at her.

"How long are you going to keep me here?" she asked with a mouth full. The man ignored her question. "I guess I should ask someone who would know what's going on," she said, intentionally antagonizing him.

Without looking up from his phone, he replied, "If your boyfriend doesn't deliver the map by tomorrow, you won't be let go, instead buried." Toni knew that he wasn't trying to scare her—he was serious.

But the one terrifying question she had, she didn't ask: *Are you going to release me once you get the map?*

The food and water gave her the energy she needed to start planning her escape. *How can I overpower these men?*

As she was eating the next bite of her sandwich, the man glanced up at her, and her plan hit her. She reached for the bottle of water that sat on the wooden floor in front of her. "Do you have kids?" she asked, making conversation. He glanced back at her without an answer, so she took a long swallow from the bottle, awaiting his answer.

"Finish eating," he barked.

"Listen, we're here, so you might as well get used to me talking," she snapped back.

"Two. A boy and a girl," he answered, still studying something on his phone.

"So you are married?" she asked.

He took a deep breath and sighed. "Stop talking and finish your food."

"Sorry, just asking." She took another bite, slowing down her eating.

A few seconds passed. "She left me last year," he replied.

"Sorry to hear that," Toni replied.

"I'm sure you are," he answered sarcastically.

"I wouldn't say it if I didn't mean it," she fired back.

"Thank you," he answered in a softer voice.

I got you now! she thought, hearing his tone change, *a softy.*

"Your boss isn't going to let me go once Spencer turns over the map?" she asked.

"I don't know," he answered.

"Yes, you do." He just looked at her without answering, and she knew the truth by his silence.

"You have kids. I would like to have the opportunity to have kids also. Please help me," her voice turned to a begging tone.

He shook his head. "There is nothing I can do."

"You can make sure they don't kill me once this is over."

"What makes you think that?" he asked with his head still down.

"You wouldn't be here guarding me if you didn't matter to them."

"And why would I want to help you?" he asked.

She took a short pause and then with alluring eyes and a soft tone, she said, "Maybe I can give you something you haven't had in a while to make sure that I live." He sat back in his chair and studied her, and she took another sip from her bottle with her lips puckering around the opening of the water bottle. She gave a seductive smile.

"And what makes you think I haven't had it in a while?"

"You haven't had this," she replied, pulling up her shirt and exposing her flat stomach.

"And you would do this willingly?" he asked with the intoxicating idea.

"If you promise to keep me alive." She paused again, then added, "A lot can happen in 24 hours." She smiled at him again.

He stood and approached her with caution. "I can't untie you," he said.

She thought for a moment that her plan had just backfired, "OK," she answered, "but you can't have it all unless I have room." She looked down at her feet tied to the chair.

"I don't know if that would be a good idea," he said, but as Toni reached out to his thigh with her right hand rubbing the inside of his leg, he didn't hesitate to take a knee and untie her legs. Once free, she stood up with him and pressed her body close to his. He reached for her shirt to pull it off.

"Not so fast," she whispered, "I have something special in mind."

He smiled as she took a step back and grabbed his belt with both hands—and then, with all the experience of rough housing with boys she had grown up with, with all the karate training she practiced as an adult, with years of always trying to out-do the boys her whole life, it all came to one move, one blow, one punch, and with everything she had she stepped sideways and landed her fist in the man's Adam's apple. He grabbed his throat, trying to catch his breath, but nothing entered, and he quickly fell to his knees, where Toni finished him off. A crashing blow to the back of the head sent pieces of the wooden chair she had been tied in all directions, and one of Vargas's men lay unconscious on the floor.

Cardona's phone rang, "Yes," he answered. Spencer and Dusty could hear Arturo's voice on the other end, but couldn't make out what he was saying. "Keep me informed," Cardona said and hung up.

"What?" Spencer asked.

"It seems there was a loud noise in the background of Toni's phone followed by groaning."

"Dammit!" Spencer felt his blood pressure go up.

"That doesn't mean anything," Dusty said, trying to reassure him.

"It means I am going to kick someone's ass if they have hurt her," Spencer replied.

"I'm afraid it's going to take more than kicking someone's ass today," Cardona replied, pulling out a pistol and screwing a silencer to the end of it.

Spencer's phone rang. Looking at the caller, he exclaimed, "It's Toni's phone!"

Cardona looked at the screen, then quickly called Arturo, explaining, "He is receiving a call from the phone."

"The video went blank before I could make out who is using the phone," Arturo replied.

Cardona looked at Spencer. "Answer it," he instructed.

"Hello," Spencer said, prepared for Vargas or one of his men.

"Spencer!" Toni's voice whispered in the other end.

"Toni! Are you OK? We are on our way to get you!" Spencer sat up in the seat, hearing her voice.

"Please hurry! I don't know how much time I have," she replied, looking back in the room at the man tied with his hands and feet behind him and gagged, still out cold.

"We are. Can you get somewhere safe?" She ran back in the room and looked outside the window as a black town car slid to a stop on the street below.

"Spencer! They're here." She ran to the other room to find the only door locked from the outside.

"I'm trapped!" Her heart began to race.

"Hide somewhere," Spencer's tone escalated. She ran back to the window and glanced out, but this time Vargas's men saw her free and staring out the window. One of them pointed up and yelled something in Spanish, and they raced to the front door of the building. She could hear the commotion coming from downstairs, "Spencer! They're coming." She began panicking.

"Just stay on the phone with me!" Spencer's voice was shaking.

She could hear the men storming up the old wooden stairs that echoed throughout the building. A larger commotion broke out beyond the stairs, and she knew without a shadow of doubt her plan had failed.

"Spencer, please!" she begged in a panic.

"Stay on the phone," he shouted. Tears began running down her face, and with her heart beating as though it was about to come out of her chest, she stepped backwards away from the door, hearing the footsteps closing in on the other side of the door.

"Spencer … I'm sorry!"

"Sorry for what?" he asked.

"I'm sorry for not being honest with you. I'm sorry for leading you on."

"What are you talking about?" he yelled into the phone.

She paused for a moment and took a deep breath. "I don't want to be your buddy … I don't want to just be your friend … I'm sorry you're just now hearing it from me, but if this is going to be it, I want you to know the truth." She stopped with the footsteps now silent, then added, "Spencer … I love you!"

The sound of the door being kicked in echoed through the phone, and the next sound heard was Toni's cell phone bouncing off the wooden floor. Then silence.

Chapter 50

Twenty-five years earlier Toni remembered lying in the grass behind her house feeding Skip and Mac the crackers she had taken from the pantry. With tears in her eyes, she talked to the two busy ducklings as they scrambled over each other to get to the next cracker. "That boy thinks of one thing and only one thing, treasure!" She wiped her nose with the back of her hand. "I want to tell him I like him, but every time I start to, he changes the subject to treasure. He doesn't even care that Lebreaux is dead." Her emotions shifted from Spencer to Lebreaux and then back.

"Child. Why are you crying?" The voice scared Toni, who quickly jumped to her feet. She stood in silence as a woman approached her.

"Are ye OK?" The lady asked.

"Yes." Toni replied, still facing the lady.

"Are dees your birds?" she asked, trying to calm Toni.

"Yes, that's Skip and that one is Mac." She pointed to the ducks, who were still busy eating.

"And dees tears?" She wiped Toni's face with the back of her sleeve.

"I'm just upset." She didn't want to confess.

"Over da boy," the mysterious visitor added, catching Toni's attention.

The lady coaxed Toni to the back steps leading down from their porch. "You like da boy, don't you?" Her smile comforted Toni.

"Yes, but all he cares about is treasure," she began to confess.

"Boys like adventure, and they like girls who like adventure. Can you be dat girl?"

"I don't know, I want to cheer and play softball. I don't know if I have time for adventure." She picked up the ducks that had waddled over to the two of them.

"One day you will have to choose. Just make sure dat day doesn't pass before you have chosen."

She touched the end of Toni's nose, and Toni smiled. "Were you ever in love?" she asked the lady.

"Ah, yes. Long time ago." She looked toward the sky and its deep blue color.

"What happened to him?" Toni asked.

"He left, but one day we will be together again," she answered. "Child, give me your hand." Toni volunteered her hand, and the lady turned it over, running her fingernail through Toni's palm. "You see dis line?" She pointed at the crease in her hand.

"Yes," Toni replied.

"Dis is a strong love line—it goes straight to your heart." The lady pointed at Toni's heart.

"Always hold da boy with dis hand, and he will fall in love with you." She stood.

"Will I see you again?" Toni asked.

The lady smiled, "Search your dreams and der you'll find da answers. Follow da boy to da ends of da world!" She walked toward the side of the house.

"Wait!" Toni sprung up and set down her ducks, but running to the side of the house, she found herself alone. "Lebreaux?"

Now twenty-five years later, Toni found herself in the position she never imagined—kidnapped with her life in jeopardy. The door crashed open, breaking part of the doorframe, and her small hands could no longer hold on to the cell phone. Toni's heart sank as she realized this was the end. All those years of not letting Spencer know just how she felt, all those years of lying awake at night thinking what he was doing and where he was—all those years came down to this moment, to the moment the figure in the doorway would take away … or give.

She cupped her mouth, and tears rained down her face as she stood paralyzed in place. It seemed like a dream until the shadow in the doorway spoke.

"Toni!" Spencer raced to Toni, who was still unable to move, with thirty years of emotions bursting for the man she loved. She wrapped her arms around him and began sobbing so uncontrollably, Spencer could feel her heart pounding through her chest.

With soft words that vibrated through his entire body, Spencer repeated, "I love you, Toni Benoit!" Tears ran faster down her face and onto Spencer's shirt. He pulled her away, not letting go of her arms. "I've loved you my whole life. I can't imagine going through life without you. You know that—"

She grabbed both sides of his head with her hands and quickly drew his face down where her lips met his. He started to pull away and finish his sentence, but she forced him to continue their first kiss. The tears from her hazel eyes now ran down his face.

"You found me," she said, her entire body shaking as she took a breath.

"You're the treasure, Toni! I don't care about the barge," he said.

She kissed him again and within inches of his face, said, "Thank you. I've waited a long time for you to come back and even longer to tell you. But there is no way in hell I'm going to let Vargas have the barge." She wiped her face dry with the back of her hand. Then with a sinister grin and a raised eyebrow, she added, "Let's finish this!"

"OK," he replied smiling, but before Toni could answer, someone else appeared in the doorway.

"You two will have all the time in the world for making out. Let's get the hell out of here," Dusty said, peeking around the corner with pistol in hand.

"Dusty!?" Toni said with her eyes widening.

"You don't think I was going to let him come alone?" Dusty smiled.

One of Cardona's men entered the room, grimly intent. "You three get out of here," he ordered. "You might not want to see this." He pointed his pistol at the tied man lying awake on the floor.

"No!" Toni shouted. Spencer looked at her, puzzled.

283

"He is a father—let him live," she ordered.

"He'll talk," the young man replied.

"No, he won't," she replied, looking at the man. Cardona's man backed off, and the man on the floor breathed a sigh of relief as he made eye contact with Toni. As the four of them left the room, Toni looked back to catch the man's eyes; he closed both of them and nodded in gratitude.

Racing down the hall and down the old staircase, they stepped over the bodies of Vargas's men. Toni hid her from at the sight of the dead bodies that littered their way out. Once outside, Toni, Spencer, and Dusty dove into the back seat of a black BMW as it sped out into the streets of Seville. Cardona turned from the passenger seat. "Good to see you again," he smiled at Toni.

She returned the smile, "You too."

The BMW raced around the north side of the bullring and out onto the highway leading to Cardona's estate. "So how's your trip going so far?" Dusty asked, laughing.

"Just an average trip to Spain," Spencer smiled as Toni rested her head on his shoulder in relief.

Their fingers interlocked as they held hands. "I love you," she whispered.

Chapter 51

Spencer, Toni, and Dusty reclined on the couches in Cardona's kitchen after eating. Cardona had excused himself to check in with his men. "So now you know," Spencer said to Dusty, who had just heard everything explained.

"You always asked about treasure growing up, but not many kids grow up chasing treasure," Dusty said.

"Yep, and we are going to find this treasure," Spencer smiled at Toni.

She gave a halfhearted smile back. "Not at the cost of people losing their life."

"Of course not, it's not going to be easy," he replied.

"No, but with my backing and men, I would say you have a good chance of finding this treasure," Cardona said walking in.

Spencer sat quietly on the couch with Toni nestled against his arm, and he could see the wheels turning in her expression. "You OK?" he whispered.

Looking up at him, she whispered back, "Yeah, just thinking."

Spencer looked at Cardona, voicing the thought that had been intruding on his relief at Toni's rescue. "Vargas's men will never stop coming after us, will they?"

"Oh, I don't know—once you cut the head off the snake, the rest will go away," Cardona answered. He turned and asked everyone else to leave the room, and once the doors were shut behind them, Cardona turned back to Spencer, saying, "Let's look at this map." Spencer rolled out the bamboo map on the table in front of the couches.

"I know this is Barataria Bay, and here is the mouth of the Mississippi River," he said, pointing to the map. "But I don't understand these oblong cutouts throughout the map," Spencer added.

"Have you noticed that the cutouts are only over water and not land?" Dusty said, looking over Spencer's shoulder.

Spencer cocked his head and stared at the map. "No, I never paid attention."

Cardona pulled the map in his direction, explaining, "I was told by my great grandfather that the coin had something to do with this, but these holes are not round, and coins are round." Toni's eyes widened with the remark she had just heard; she had started to speak up when she felt Spencer squeeze her arm.

Dusty walked over to Cardona, "Well, that hole could be round."

"No, it's still oblong," Cardona answered.

While the two of them studied the map, Spencer leaned over to Toni's ear. "I never told him about the coin," he whispered.

She cut her eyes up at him. "He got us this far and saved me," she said. Spencer took a deep breath, knowing she was right.

Cardona was glued on the map when an oblong old tarnished silver coin landed in front of him on the bamboo map. Picking it up and studying it, he looked at Spencer. "You have it?"

"I wasn't sure what to do with it," Spencer replied.

"Where did you get this?" Cardona held up the coin.

Toni sat up with the answer: "From Lebreaux Papillion." Cardona stared at them like they were crazy.

"Lebreaux Papillion?"

Spencer nodded his head, "Yes."

"The old voodoo woman from Lafitte?" Dusty asked.

"Yes," Toni answered.

Cardona held the coin and smiled. "A Potosi coin. You see the cross here on the coin?" Everyone agreed that they saw. "Also known as a mark," he added. Then, like a missing puzzle piece, he scanned the cut-out holes on the map until the coin fit one of the holes—a hole that was in Barataria Bay. He snapped the coin down into the hole and pointed at the cross on the coin. "X marks the spot." The three Cajuns just stared at the map.

"The mark is on the *Potosi*," Spencer said out loud, repeating the words from Lebreaux. Toni smiled at him.

"I guess we're going after this treasure. We'll split it four ways," Spencer said.

"Three ways. I just want to be credited for helping find the treasure and to make sure Vargas doesn't," Cardona said. "My family's name will finally be cleared. That is worth more than the treasure to me."

Spencer looked at Dusty. "Hell, yeah!" Dusty replied.

Looking back at Toni, Spencer asked with a grin, "You ready for your adventure?"

"Sure," she smiled.

"It's getting late, and we have had a long day. Let's meet over breakfast and make our plan to get you guys out of Spain and find this treasure. Sound good?" Cardona asked. Everyone agreed. "Dusty, if you will follow me, I'll show you your room." He stood. "Spencer, you know where your room is," he added.

What about me? Toni thought.

"I'll walk you to your room," Spencer said, pulling Toni off the couch.

They walked out of the kitchen and into the foyer, where they passed the old iron lantern, "This is getting weirder by the moment," Toni said, recognizing the lantern from her dreams.

Following Cardona and Dusty, they watched them disappear around the corner. Spencer stopped in front of another room. "After you," he said. She walked in, and finding his things in the room, she turned with a smile and wrapped her arms around his shoulders. The door quietly closed behind them.

☠ Chapter 52 ☠

"Captain, we are near the rendezvous point," a young sailor called from the crow's nest. The captain didn't reply and walked toward his quarters.

As the door closed behind him, he greeted Lebreaux, who was lying across the bed. "Is your friend here?" she asked.

"Not yet."

"And you trust him?" she questioned.

"With my life. Plus his ship is much bigger, and we need all the room we can get."

She stood and sauntered toward him, "Trusting him with your life is what you will have to do. The name of his ship?" she asked.

"The *Potosi*," he replied.

"There she is!" he heard a sailor yell from the stern castle deck. The *Potosi*, an Argosy class ship, was one of the largest ships in the Caribbean waters and newly acquired from Venice, Italy. She was well built with three masts and took very little crew to sail her—something that attracted the young captain to the ship, since there would be fewer men to share the treasure with. Drifting up alongside the *Potosi*, the young captain yelled to drop anchor.

"Hello, old friend," the captain from the Potosi called across the water.

"Come aboard," the young captain called in return. The captain from the *Potosi* was a middle-aged man, slightly overweight, but conniving and quietly ruthless. The two captains had pillaged from the trade ships for only a few years, but worked well together. The one strong thing they had in common was their mutual hatred toward Vargas.

"Ay, I see you have a new crew member," he said, looking at Lebreaux as he stepped over the side onto the main deck.

"Captain Edward Cardona," he bowed toward Lebreaux. She gave him an inscrutable smile as they made their way to the captain's quarters.

"Show me this map you found," Captain Cardona asked, walking in. The young captain pulled the compass rose from the wall and reached into a secret compartment, pulling out the map. He rolled it out onto the table and backed up for Captain Cardona to examine. "After all these years, my great-great-grandfather's map. And the coin?" He looked back at the young captain and Lebreaux. She handed him the coin. He ran the coin over the map until it reached a hole that it fit, and after snapping it into place, he stood up and smiled, "Are ye ready?"

"Ay!"

The two ships sailed slow and quiet through the waters of Barataria Bay as they set course for the Spanish Barge Treasure. Lebreaux leaned on the railing, watching the *Potosi* navigate around the small grassy islands of the marsh. She felt the warm hands of the young captain run over her shoulders and turn her to face him. He gently placed both hands on the side of her face and drew her in for a kiss, but her eyes remained open, staring into the tranquilizing green eyes of the man she had given her heart to. He placed his arm around her shoulders, pulling her into his body. As they gazed into the darkness of the marsh, she felt the safety of his heart beating through his vest.

A young sailor approached the couple, saying "Captain, we're on course, but the night is making it difficult to see the islands."

He shook his head, saying "Send word to the *Potosi* that we will drop anchor till first light."

"Ay, Captain," the sailor replied and ran back to the bow of the ship.

Lebreaux reached down and took the young captain by the hand, escorting him to his quarters. The door swung shut, and as the captain threw his hat on the table, Lebreaux turned and ran her hands under his coat, taking it off and laying it across the back of a wooden chair. As she turned back to him, he snatched her off her feet and carried her to the bed, where he gently set her down. She felt chill bumps cross her body as he unbuttoned her dress and let it fall to the floor beside the bed.

The faint sign of light peered through the stained glass window above the headboard, waking Lebreaux, who was sleeping in her lover's arms. "Light," she whispered in his ear.

Without opening his eyes, he smiled, whispering back, "Today we become rich." She ran her hand across his chest as he stretched his arms.

Sitting on the side of the bed, he rubbed his head and reached down for his clothes. "Can't it wait a few more minutes?" Lebreaux tried to lure him back under the covers.

"After today, we will have all the time in the world." He stood and retrieved his coat from the chair.

Stepping out onto the main deck, the young captain looked over at the *Potosi* to see her crew busied around the mizzen mast. He whistled toward the crew, and one of the crew members gave him a thumbs up.

"Pull anchor, mateys! Today we get rich!" he yelled across the decks. The loud outburst brought Lebreaux out onto the stern castle deck.

"Captain!" one of the crew members shouted, drawing everyone's attention.

"That island," he pointed, "I believe that is the island," he called, pointing down at the map. *Have we anchored near our treasure?* The captain beckoned to the sailor holding the bamboo map and examined the terrain.

The young captain shot a firm stare at the *Potosi*, and as if Captain Cardona were reading his mind, a smile formed across his face. "Lower the tenders!" both captains shouted simultaneously. After a short row around the small saw grass island lined with black mangroves, the two crews were drifting over a wooden structure. Captain Cardona ordered two of his men to dive below and survey the area, and after a short time one of the men surfaced with a handful of silver coins.

The two captains began barking orders and shouting back to the ships for more tenders and men, and the area became chaotic with the excitement of the discovered treasure. Lebreaux joined them as they set up camp on the small island, and empty crates and wooden barrels were bought to load the silver, gold, and other valuable goods being brought up from the shallow depths.

After two days of hauling up treasure, the two ships were loaded beyond capacity. "Captain, there is much more," one of the sailors said, treading water beside a tender.

The young captain looked at Captain Cardona for advice. "We take what we have and sail to Spain. We will come back next spring for the rest," Captain Cardona replied.

The young captain nodded his head in agreement. "We stop at Port Royal for supplies, then head east."

They loaded the remaining treasure and tenders onto their ships, unaware of the vessel watching in the distance. Pulling anchor and turning south, the little vessel quickly sailed ahead of the slow-moving treasure ships toward Grand Terre.

Chapter 53

The following morning, Spencer walked into the aroma of fresh baked bread and coffee from the kitchen. Dusty was sitting at the table having a conversation with the cook about south Louisiana dishes versus Spanish dishes. "Well, good morning," he said with a devilish grin.

"Good morning," Spencer replied trying to ignore the insinuation about him and Toni.

"Where's our fireball?" Dusty asked.

"I guess still hugging her pillow," Spencer said, pouring two cups of coffee. "I'll be right back," he said, setting his cup down to cool off.

Cardona met Spencer in the hall. "I hope you slept better last night knowing everyone is safe."

"I did. I want to thank you for everything you have done for us. I know it's put you at risk with Vargas."

"We've been at risk with each other for many years, nothing new. Let's reconvene in the kitchen in a few minutes," he said.

"Are you sure you don't want part of the treasure?" Spencer asked.

"I'm sure. Money and treasure have caused me great pain in my life. Just make sure they don't cause you the same."

"I won't. Thanks."

Spencer quietly opened the door leading to their bedroom, finding Toni lying across the bed, tangled in the sheets and sound asleep. He climbed into the bed beside her after putting the coffee on the bedside table and gently rubbed her back to wake her. "I don't do mornings," she mumbled through a pillow.

"I brought coffee," he said.

She repositioned herself lying across his lap, and with her head still buried, mumbled, "Keep rubbing." Spencer chuckled at the thought that if this was what he was to expect from her in the mornings, he wouldn't mind.

"We have to get started this morning," he said, reaching for her coffee. She flung back the covers and poured out of the bed, heading to the bathroom without saying anything.

Returning with a kiss, she climbed back in bed and sat up with her back against a stack of pillows. "I can get used to this," she said, blowing the steam from her cup.

"Waking up to me?"

"Coffee in bed," she smiled, blowing the steam from the mug.

"OK ..."

"I'm just kidding." She set her cup down and forced him down on his back, climbing on top of him. Her hair fell on both sides of her face as she leaned over to kiss him. "Can't we just stay in bed today?" she whispered as she kissed his ear.

"I wish. But we have to get back home to find a treasure."

"Promise me that after we find it, we go somewhere where we can stay in bed all day."

"Promise."

She climbed back out of bed, announcing, "I'm going to take a shower." Spencer nodded with his cup in front of his face. She left the door halfway open, and after a few minutes Spencer saw an arm reappear from behind the door, dropping her clothes on the floor. He wasn't sure if that was a tease or not. He sat in the bed with the thought of his childhood crush evolving into a heart-pounding love, the thought intoxicating him.

"Hey, come here," Toni yelled from the shower.

Not very flirtatious, he thought, walking in the bathroom with steam already sinking from the ceiling. "Can you hand me my face soap? It's in my bag," she asked from behind the shower curtain.

Face soap? As he handed it to her, she pulled back the curtain, revealing her arm and face.

"Thank you," she said in a soft tone.

"I'm going to meet with everyone in the kitchen," he said.

"OK, I'll be right there."

Back in the kitchen, Spencer replenished his cup and talked with Dusty and the cook for a few minutes until looking at the clock above the stoves, he noticed the time. "She should be out now—I'll go get her," he said. Walking out of the kitchen, he met Toni in the hall. "That was a fast shower."

"I know we have a lot to do today," she said, looking at the oil painting of two men climbing out of a small boat onto a sandy beach.

"I've seen this before," she said.

"Huh, where?" Spencer asked, looking over her shoulder.

"I swear I dreamed this."

Cardona walked through the hall, so Toni asked him, "Where did this piece come from?"

"My great-grandfather had it made after his great grandfather described a similar painting he once had in his possession. Nothing of value," he said, continuing down the hall.

"He has a lot of things here that I've seen before too. Kinda creepy," Spencer said.

"You think?" she agreed.

Walking back into the kitchen, Spencer was greeted by Cardona, Dusty, and four of his men. "We have a plan to get you guys safely back to the States," Cardona said.

"You're not coming?" Spencer asked confused.

"Vargas doesn't know I am involved, and we can play this to our advantage. You and your friends will take my private jet today, but I need you to buy three tickets for departure in three days. This should buy you some time back home," Cardona said.

"We need a distraction for when Vargas's men do show up in Louisiana," Dusty piped up.

"He's right. Two days isn't enough. Even though we know where the treasure barge is, it's going to take some time to dig it up and unload it." Chills raced up Spencer's back with the thought of them finally knowing where the treasure was.

"I know who we need," Toni said from the doorway.

She caught the attention of everyone in the room. "Who?" Spencer asked.

"Jimmy," she replied.

"Jimmy? I don't know if we want to include him," Spencer said.

"I don't know; I think she's right. He can keep them at bay, and we don't have to tell him about the treasure," Dusty said.

"Good, then use this Jimmy fellow," Cardona said.

"Why so many holes on the map?" Toni asked.

Cardona spun in his chair to face her. "Why are you asking?"

"I was just thinking last night, all the holes are different shapes. Why so many?"

"I believe they are just a distraction to make the map harder to read," Cardona replied. Toni nodded her head, understanding, and took another sip of her coffee.

"Vargas's men are swarming the train depots and airport," Arturo said, walking in the kitchen.

"I need you to buy those tickets now. I am sure they have someone in the airport that can confirm your flight information for them," Cardona said.

"You can use my computer," Arturo said.

"Put word on the street that our friends are staying at a local hostel," Cardona added. Turning back to Spencer, he said, "We can keep them on a wild chase for a few days. I would pack—we will fly you out this morning."

After eating, Toni and Spencer walked back to their room to gather their things. "You are definitely not boring to have around," Toni said, walking into the room.

"Well, I didn't expect to be in the middle of all this, either."

After zipping up her bag, Toni stepped in front of him. "Promise me something else."

"What's that?"

"That when this is over, we go see the world."

"I assure you that when we find the treasure, we'll be able to do whatever we want," he answered.

"Sounds good to me," Dusty said from the doorway.

"We have to get it first," Spencer said, drawing his attention away from Toni.

"We'll find it. You guys ready?" Dusty asked.

"Yep," Toni replied, and followed Spencer and Dusty out through the foyer, where Cardona was waiting for them.

"Where did that come from?" Spencer asked, pointing to the iron lantern.

"I'm not sure, I inherited it with the estate," he answered. Spencer smiled, nodded his head and walked out to the car that was waiting for them. Toni followed. wondering what Spencer was thinking. Something obviously had stirred his curiosity.

They had a short ride to the airport and to a private hanger where a Falcon 7X was waiting for them. "Cardona has some class," Dusty said, looking at the white jet with orange and yellow stripes.

"Good morning," a young flight attendant met them as they exited the car.

"Hello," Toni answered.

"We will get your bags for you, so you can board." She held her arm out toward the jet.

"First class," Dusty added.

Within a few minutes, they were lounging in plush leather chairs as the Falcon 7X rapidly climbed to its cruising altitude. Toni leaned over to Spencer. "Can we buy one of these when we find the treasure?" she whispered, smiling.

I don't think there is enough treasure to buy one of these, but I guess Cardona really doesn't need the treasure, Spencer thought while observing the gold-trimmed teacups sitting on a silver tray.

"On behalf of the flight crew, Hola and Welcome," came a pilot's voice over the speakers. "We have clear skies, and our flight time is just over ten hours, so sit back and enjoy the flight." Spencer reached over for Toni's hand, and she looked at him curiously, wondering what he wanted. Then she looked down at his hand to find it open and holding the Potosi coin. "You hang on to it for a while," he said, smiling.

Chapter 54

"We will begin our descent into New Orleans soon," the captain announced over the speakers.

"Man, that was much faster than flying to Spain," Dusty said.

Toni looked out the window at the approaching coastline, thinking, *I loved Spain, but I'm so glad to be back home.*

"Dusty, how did you get to the airport?" Spencer asked.

"My truck," he answered.

"It might be safe to leave it and rent a car to drive back to Buras," Spencer said, planning their undetected escape from the airport.

"OK, but I had your boat docked at Lafitte."

"Perfect," Spencer replied.

After a slight bump and the screech of the tires on the runway, they were back on US ground. The jet taxied to a local hanger, and as the engines shut down the door was opened by the flight attendant. "Thank you," Toni said as she walked down the stairs.

"Mr. Cardona took the liberty of having a car here waiting for you," the attendant pointed at an Audi A6 that was parked in the hanger.

"Man, he doesn't miss anything," Spencer said out loud.

A gust of wind blew through the hanger. "Looks like another storm is coming," Spencer said, looking at the radar on his phone.

"We better head on. It's going to be a choppy ride to the camp from Lafitte," Dusty said, tossing his bag in the trunk of the black Audi.

After making it through customs Toni slid in the back seat as the two men climbed in the front and drove out of the New Orleans International Airport.

"Well, now the phone call," Spencer said, picking up his phone. After dialing, he placed it to his ear and looked in the rear view mirror at Toni. "Jimmy! Hey, it's Spencer."

"Mr. Cardona, phone call." One of Cardona's men handed him a cell phone.

"Hola," Cardona answered.

"No, I do not know who that is. No, I am not involved. If I had the map, I would not be here. I will keep an eye out for the three of them." Cardona hung the phone up and looked at the young man standing beside him. "Vargas is looking for the three of them and is clueless that I am helping."

The young man chuckled and walked out of the library, passing two other men in the hall. They gave each other a nod as one of them pulled out a Glock 17 and screwed a silencer to the end of it. After they disappeared into Cardona's library, there were two piercing clicks, followed by a heavy object falling to the floor.

Once the trio arrived in Lafitte, they parked the car in the marina lot and unloaded their bags. "She looks good from here," Spencer commented on his boat floating in a stall. A gust of wind blew through, sending Toni's hair in her face as she stepped down into the boat.

On the canal leading from Lafitte to the bay, the waves had picked up, tossing the other boats tied to the dock and telling Spencer it was going to be a rough ride to Dusty's camp.

"I'm going to grab a few things before we head out," Spencer said, pointing to the store.

"Wait up." Toni dropped her bag in the boat and jogged to catch up with Spencer.

The boat ride out was everything Spencer thought it would be, rough and long. He steered close to the marsh islands to break up the rough ride, but still waves sprayed over the hull as they made their way south. The sky was a somber blue with cumulus clouds forming high above the water, and to the south, the clouds began growing darker, with an occasional bolt of lightning. "How long till it gets here?" Toni yelled above the engines.

"Tonight. It's not a big storm, so it should be gone by morning," He shouted back as a blast of brackish water splashed him. He quickly ducked back behind the console.

After the long, rough ride, they pulled up to Dusty's camp, where the waves were crashing on the front of the island, sending a mist of water over the camp house. "I say we put this back were you had it." Dusty held up the waterproof case with the map inside.

"Here, I'll put it back," Spencer said, holding his hand out.

"No, I got this. You better make sure your boat is tied," Dusty answered. Toni helped Spencer tie extra ropes to the 42' foot vessel as Dusty waded under the dock, pushing the case far up into the crossbeams.

Thunder could be heard in the distance as the sky grew darker with clouds slowly crawling into the bay. "Don't you find it unusual and even weird that Cardona had so many artifacts that we both have dreamed about?" Toni asked Spencer as they walked to the house.

"At this point, nothing surprises me anymore," he answered.

"Well, you can bet one thing. There won't be anyone out on the bay tonight," Dusty said as a gust of wind blew against the screen door he was trying to close.

"Well, we should be good for a couple of days. Enough time to find the treasure and haul it up," Spencer said.

"When we do haul it up, where are we going to put it?" Toni asked. Spencer and Dusty looked at each other with a blank stare; they had planned everything to a tee, but failed to make a plan about where to stash it.

"Here?" Dusty said.

"Nobody would expect us to hide it within a half-mile of where we found it. Perfect!" Spencer exclaimed.

The camp house creaked and rocked as the winds picked up and the thunder became louder as the storm was quickly approaching. The three of them gathered in the kitchen, and Dusty finished cutting the shrimp Spencer had bought and added it to their gumbo cooking on the stove.

"Not as extravagant as Cardona's," Dusty pointed around the kitchen.

"Man, he is set up," Spencer added.

"Wonder why no Mrs. Cardona?" Toni asked.

"I don't know," Spencer answered.

Falling back unto the couch, Toni blew on her gumbo, trying to cool it down. She took a sip from a cold longneck they had picked up from the store. "Well, I still believe this is the life," she said. Both men agreed.

"You know, last time we were out here together I kicked your butt in Booray," Dusty taunted Spencer.

"You think?" He raised an eyebrow.

"I want to play," Toni said in an innocent tone. Spencer and Dusty smiled at each other, believing she would be an easy push over.

An hour later and with most of the match sticks piled in front of Toni and her cards, Spencer decided to check on his boat. "You're killing us! I'll be right back," he said. Toni acted like she wasn't paying attention. Spencer put on a rain jacket and walked out with a flashlight in hand. He reached in his pocket, and covering his cell phone under his jacket he called Cardona's number, but after several rings he hung up. Checking his boat and pulling on the ropes to make sure everything was tight, he hustled back to the camp house. Walking in, he dried off his hands and sent Cardona a text:

"We are back. Tried calling you. I'll try again in the morning."

Looking at a blood-stained phone, Vargas barked, "They flew back today! Call our men in the States and tell them they're back in that small southern town." He paced back and forth on the tile floor of his mansion, quickly coming to a decision. "Get the jet ready! We are flying out tonight!" he demanded, then disappeared into his wing of the enormous home.

Chapter 55

As it grew later into the night, the storm became more intense, the wind picked up blowing against the small camp house nestled within the saw grass of the island, a few strong blasts of wind sounding like the old camp was blowing over. With the system only a small tropical depression, Dusty and Spencer were certain that the third-generation house would make it through the night. Toni, on the other hand, jumped with every gust that forced itself on the structure. "You sure we are OK out here?" she asked, clinging to Spencer's arm.

"Yes, I wouldn't have brought us out here if I didn't think it was safe tonight," his voice had a calming tone to it.

"Well, you cleaned us out of matches. Remind me never to play you with money," Dusty grumbled, walking to the kitchen to retrieve another longneck from the cooler. Opening the bottle, he flung himself back on the couch beside Spencer. "What's this I overheard you two saying about dreaming about this treasure stuff? That voodoo woman didn't put a hex on y'all, did she?" he chuckled. Spencer looked at Toni, realizing they hadn't been as quiet as they thought.

"It's a long and crazy story," Spencer said.

"Hell, LeJeune, it's not like we're going anywhere. Let me hear it so I can make sure I want in on this voodoo pirate treasure." He took a long sip of the beer.

"Do you remember that day when we were kids and we left the marina with Lebreaux?" Spencer asked.

"Yep, I also remember your dad wanting to skin your hide for that." Spencer shook his head, remembering the same.

"She told us about the Spanish treasure barge and the story that went with it."

"And I always thought that was a legend. Here I am chasing the damn thing now," Dusty grumbled again.

Toni sat down beside Spencer on the armrest. "She told us that it would be us two that would find the treasure. She gave us the silver coin that day," Toni added.

Dusty looked serious. "No kidding?"

"Well, we buried the coin under a tree on Perino Road, but with our luck Hurricane Andrew took it," Toni said.

"But here's the creepy part. While I was in Seville Spain looking for the manifest on a ship called the *Compostela*, I hired a young Spaniard to interpret the historian I was questioning, and it turns out he was a relative of Vargas. They followed me to Vigo, where I met an old woman who gave me the coin back."

Dusty's eyes widened. "Lebreaux?"

Spencer smiled. "I don't know who she was."

"Now that's creepy," Dusty said.

"But ever since the day Lebreaux gave us the coin in the bay, Spencer has been having dreams about her and her lover." She looked down at him.

"I wrote my books based on my dreams."

"So, she has been leading you to the treasure?" Dusty asked.

"Yes, but there's more. I can't put my finger on it, but there's something else," Spencer said.

"I have the strongest feeling that is has something to do with her lover," Toni said.

"Who's her lover?" Dusty asked with the eagerness of a child hearing a bedtime story.

Spencer shook his head. "We don't know."

A strong gust shook the camp house, startling all three of them. "Well, that is one crazy story, and if we weren't Cajuns, I wouldn't believe it. But we live in some crazy stuff." He turned up his beer and finished it off. "Well, you two kids behave yourselves. I'm turning in." He pulled himself up and waved goodnight, heading to one of the bedrooms.

Toni slid down onto the couch with Spencer. "What do you think it means that Cardona has artifacts that we have dreamed about?"

"I don't know," he replied. "I've been trying to wrap my head around it. It's like we're just adding pieces to a giant puzzle, and hopefully it will all add up soon."

She nuzzled under his arm and pulled her legs up. "It's been a long day."

"Yep, weird thing. I've called Cardona and sent him a text. He hasn't replied."

"Isn't it early there?" she asked.

"Yeah, but he said to call him."

"I'm sure he's just sleeping," she said in a calming voice.

Spencer wrapped his arm around her and pulled her in closer to him; she snuggled against his side. "Crazy how we got here," he said.

She pulled herself up and flung one leg over his lap, straddling him, "Crazy?" she said, facing him.

"You know what I meant." She grinned and leaned in to kiss him, and he started to say something when she placed her finger on his lips with a smile and a "Shh." She playfully nibbled at the side of his neck, and he struggled to place his beer on the end table with her in his lap. She took that as a hint and lay down against his side. He eased the palm of his hand against the side of her face and softly pecked her lips, whispering, "If you're going to kiss me, then kiss me!" She slid her body under his, causing him to lie on her and journey into a long, passionate kiss.

With their bodies intertwined together, Spencer occasionally stole a glimpse of the light from a candle flickering and dancing on the old wooden walls cluttered with pictures. The rain began pounding on the tin roof, making it almost deafening in the small living room.

A flash of lightning with a crack of thunder made both of them jump, and Toni looked up and smiled at Spencer. Their stares locked, and for the first time their thoughts were the same.

Spencer found himself hypnotized by the same hazel eyes he had learned to love at such an early age. She had obviously changed over the years, but her eyes remained as innocent as they were when they were ten. Toni was fixated on the dimples that formed on Spencer's face every time he smiled, a figure she loved. "Spencer ..." Toni began to say when another flash of lighting stretched over the bay, followed by an enormous clap of thunder.

"That was right outside! I better check on the boat," Spencer said, jumping up from the couch. Putting on his rain jacket. "You were about to say something?" he asked.

"It can wait."

Chapter 56

The silver Gulfstream Jet belonging to the Vargas family stopped shy of a waiting black Mercedes on the tarmac of New Orleans International Airport. Vargas exited the jet with four other men following him. "You find them yet?" he asked one of the two men waiting on him.

"No sir. They didn't come back to Buras."

Walking out of customs, he ordered, "Get my things!" to one of the other men, and climbed in the back seat of the Mercedes. As they pulled out of the airport, the first light of the sunrise was breaking through the clouds to their east.

Spencer eased out from under Toni, who had fallen asleep on his side where they had slept on the couch during the night. He stretched his eyes wide, trying to clear the blur from his morning vision. Walking into the kitchen, he started his usual pot of coffee and peeked outside to see the storm had quickly blown through. He could see light forming over the small town of Buras. Once he had enough for one cup, he poured a Styrofoam cup and headed outside. *I can't believe Dusty isn't up yet.*

As he cranked the four 350s, white smoke formed over the water rolling in all directions, creating an eerie fog. *I should go wake up Toni, but I'll just make one pass and then come back for them.* He set his cup in a cup holder on the console and untied. He idled out and aimed toward a small island he remembered seeing on the map. The coin had fit the cut out hole on the south side of the island.

As the boat idled slowly north, Spencer opened a compartment under one of the seats and pulled out his computer, then retrieved the towfish from another compartment. He was completely set within minutes and hammered down the throttles, jetting toward the small grassy island. The water, still choppy from the storm, was cold, murky, and barely had any visibility. A few ducks flew low to the water and cut in front of Spencer as he rounded an island.

The small island came into sight, so Spencer pulled back on the throttles and drifted in closer while rigging the towfish. He set his boat on the southeast side of the island and prepared to make a pass within feet from the grass. He looked over at another small island just a few hundred feet away from where he had found the injured crane. After dropping the towfish overboard and tying the line, he eased back to the wheel and watched the computer screen resting on the console.

Everything was black on the screen as he approached the island, the water holding at 14' in depth. Then as he had once seen before with his father when looking for *the Griego,* a wooden structure came into view. Not the shape of a barge, but it still was definitely something man-made. Now, nearly 400 years later, the truth was about to be unburied. Spencer swung the 42' boat around, and pulling up where the towfish had painted the picture on the screen, he threw out an anchor.

Excitement ran through his veins, and his heart was pounding as he pulled his dive gear from in front of the console. He was so enamored with the thought of finally finding the treasure that he forgot the towfish was resting on the bottom of the bay. Cranking the air on, he tested his regulator, and after a few blasts from the mouthpiece, he set it in the floor of the boat. He could barely muster up enough spit to clean the lens of his mask with his heart pounding in his chest. He lifted the tank over his head and slipped into the BC, then turned and sat on the side of the boat. Putting his mask on and the regulator in his mouth, he leaned back and hit the water.

Not surfacing, he headed straight down, and with two fin kicks he was on the bottom of Barataria Bay. He ran his hands through the silted floor and immediately felt something hard and long. Scratching with his fingernails, he could feel it was wood. The visibility was already low, and his hands stirring up the bay floor caused even more murkiness in front of him. He broke off a piece of the wood and came to the surface. Examining it above the water line, he could tell it was similar to the piece he had taken to the research lab at LSU. He cleared his regulator once again and kicked for the bottom.

This time he pulled back another piece of wood and felt beyond it, expecting a void under the piece of broken wood. Instead he felt another structure; it was solid, but broke apart when he ran his fingers through it. *Rocks?* he thought. He removed one and headed back to the surface to examine the find. Pulling his mask down around his neck, he washed off the object, and opening his hand to look, his heart stopped. There facing him was something many people and even countries had been looking for: Lying in his hand was another silver coin.

"Yes!" he screamed so loud that a few cranes took off from their perches. This coin, which was more round than the one Lebreaux had given them, bore the cross on one side and a chest on the other side. Spencer could make out only the letters HILIP, but on the other side of the chest the letter P was clearly stamped out—Potosi mint.

He started to put the coin in his BC pocket and head back down for more when a bloom of thick black smoke caught his attention. The cloud of smoke was coming from Buras, and his first thought was *Whatever is on fire, it's big*. He figured he had better head back to the camp house and see if Dusty and Toni were up. He climbed out and laid his gear to the side, and pulling a towel out from under the seat, he realized he had left the towfish out. Once he had secured his gear, he threw out a small buoy with an anchor attached to mark the spot, and then he spun the boat around and slammed the throttles wide open toward the camp house.

When he sailed around an island to bring Dusty's camp house into view, he could see someone outside on the dock. He couldn't help but laugh out loud with the excitement still running through his veins. While he was trying to figure whether to tell Toni or just hand her the coin, he could see that both Toni and Dusty were standing on the dock.

☠ Chapter 57 ☠

"It will be slow sailing to Port Royal," the young captain said to Lebreaux as they walked back to their quarters.

"Are ye sure it was safe to give da other captain da map?" she questioned his decision.

"It's useless to me now. His ancestor made it. It belongs to him," he replied, opening his door. He led Lebreaux into the captain's quarters, her eyes twinkling in the light from the lantern swinging above the table, and untied the lace on the front of her dress. As the dress fell to the wooden floor, he lifted her into his bed.

Moments later, a blast echoed through the captain's quarters, causing them to shoot up out of bed. The captain's heart pounded with panic, not knowing the cause of the explosion. He stood beside the bed looking confusedly at Lebreaux; no one was yelling or running through the ship, so it was almost as if they dreamed it. Then part of the wall exploded, sending splinters of wood throughout the quarters as a cannon ball tore through the ship. With ears ringing, he could hear his crew now shouting and making their way to the main deck.

He pulled his pants to his waist and slipping into his jacket without a shirt, he yelled, "Stay here!" to Lebreaux, who was under the covers, hiding her ears from the loud gun fire coming from outside. He crouched down, walking onto the stern castle deck with two other men. "Who is firing on us?" he yelled.

The two men looked paralyzed with fear and as confused as he was. "The only ship that was near us was the Potosi," one of them answered.

The Potosi*? Why would Captain Cardona be firing on me?* He crawled to the railing and peeked over.

To his horror, he saw the *Potosi* in flames and its crew bailing overboard. *Who is attacking us?* He stood to his feet and saw the ship he most feared, a ship that had been captured months earlier from the British Empire. *Lafitte!*

"To the cannons!" he ordered. The crew scrambled while Lafitte was occupied finishing off the Potosi. "Bring her around!" the young captain yelled, then ran to the railing, looking at the *Potosi*. The flames that engulfed the large ship intensified as it reached the powder kegs stored in the hull. Lafitte's ship began swinging portside and moving away from the young captain's position. *Hold steady, ye wench!* He spun the wheel counter clockwise, trying to get ahead of their target. *Why won't she swing?* He looked up and saw the damage to their mast. In a quick decision gained from his wisdom on the seas, he ordered, "Drop anchor!"

They began taking gunfire from the fast-approaching ship, causing the crew to scramble to the sides seeking cover. "Drop anchor!" he screamed again, but the crew remained pinned against the railing. Lafitte's ship turned broadside, "Fire!" the young captain ordered. His ship rocked with the explosion of cannon fire toward their opponent. Their first shot seemed ineffective, and the captain ordered reloading.

The first exchange of cannon fire hadn't seemed to affect either side, but the unrelenting gunfire from Lafitte caused the crew to load their cannons slower.

Another volley of cannon fire echoed across the water with the young captain's ship firing only a few cannons this time. Lafitte's ship swung in for another pass, this time within feet from the other vessel. Lafitte's crew swung aboard with fire from their flintlocks and swords drawn, so the fight was now on the main deck of the young captain's ship. Within minutes, his crew surrendered.

After tying the ships together, Lafitte's crew dropped a plank on the railing, allowing the tall and slim captain to cross over. "Well, ye did the hard work for me," Lafitte said to the captain, who was now standing in front of his crew.

"Take it!" the young captain replied, knowing that more treasure lay in the bottom of Barataria Bay, and the only map was burning a few hundred feet from their ship.

"Oh, I'll take it," Lafitte snarled, "and the girl too," he added.

A gruff, burly man pulled Lebreaux out on the main deck. "Here," he growled, throwing her down on the wooden floor.

"I said ye can't run far," Vargas smirked at her as he made his way over on the plank.

"Captain, the *Potosi* is going down. In these depths we'll never be able to retrieve the treasure," one of his crew members said.

"We have this ship," Lafitte replied.

"We? I told you I didn't want to lose any of the treasure, and now a third of it is going down with the *Potosi*!" Vargas snapped at the captain.

"You have my blessing to go and get it," Lafitte said, pointing to the sinking ship.

Lebreaux climbed to her feet and ran to the side of the young captain, but before she could wrap her arms around him, the burly man pulled her back. Lafitte's crew laughed.

"Don't touch her," the young captain stepped forward, only to find himself staring down the barrel of Lafitte's pistol.

"This is how it's going to work," Lafitte began to explain, when another one of his men yelled from below.

"She's sinking!" he ran shouting onto the main deck.

"The *Potosi*?" Lafitte demanded.

"No sir. *This* ship," the sailor answered in a shaky voice.

"I'm losing my treasure!" Vargas yelled.

"How long?" Lafitte asked.

"Minutes, captain."

Lafitte looked back at the young captain, only to have him reply, "You sank all the treasure."

"Ay, matey. I don't need this treasure." He turned and stepped back onto the plank leading back to his ship with a curt command: "Bring the girl!"

The young captain leaped forward, grabbing Lebreaux by the arm and lowering his pistol on Lafitte, who was standing on the plank. Lafitte swung around in his step and stared down the young captain. "Pity!" he commented as Vargas fired point blank. The air filled with white smoke as the bullet entered the chest of the young captain, spraying blood as it exited through his left shoulder blade. He swayed in place for a second, then collapsed to his knees. "No!" Lebreaux screamed. She fell to the floor with him, his pistol now lying on the wooden deck. His face turned pale as he gasped for air.

"No! Please, no," Lebreaux pled as she tried holding him upright, but with the color leaving his green eyes, so did his life. The young captain lay lifeless in the arms of the woman he loved.

Everything around her faded into a fog with no sound, and she began remembering his face in the tavern the night they met. His green eyes entrapped her into a deep love she had never felt before. The way he touched her face with the back of his fingers and the warmth of his breath on her ears as they made love. The strong beating of his heart against her chest as she lay across him, thinking about their future, a future she was just robbed of.

She clung tightly to his body, swaying back and forth with tears flooding his blood-drenched shirt. "No, don't leave me!" she begged, "Please don't leave me!" She felt the strong hands of one of Lafitte's men pulling her away from her love, and as they pulled her away, she reached out once more, praying to the spirits to remain with him.

"Put her below in the barracks," Vargas said, stepping aside and giving the man room. He looked back at the crew standing around their dead captain, and in a sober voice, said, "Kill the crew."

Chapter 58

Spencer pulled back on the throttles and drifted into the dock at Dusty's camp, where Toni stood on the pier with her arms folded and a frown on her face. "I thought you were going to wake me up?" she asked, upset.

"You were sleeping so well I didn't want to bother you," he defended himself.

"You asked us to be part of this, and that's what we want to be—part of this!" she snapped back. Clearly she was upset, and it wasn't making Spencer feel any better with Dusty quietly standing beside her.

"OK, it won't happen again. I'm sorry," he said.

"Man, I'm not sure what's going on, but that's a large pillar of smoke coming up," Dusty said, pointing toward the town. Spencer looked at the thick bloom of black smoke rising from town, clearly a big fire. He thought that maybe the fire department was doing some controlled burns—the levee board would burn the grass on the levies from time to time—but that smoke would be spread out, while this pillar seem to be more centrally located.

"We better head into town and see what's going on," Dusty said, heading back to lock up the camp house.

As Dusty disappeared through the screen door, Toni turned back to Spencer, "You're starting to worry me about this treasure. You seem to be getting out of control and leaving others out."

"Can you blame me? Every time someone gets involved, something happens. That's why I didn't want to include anyone. It wasn't that I wanted to keep the treasure all to myself—I just don't want others to get hurt," he answered. Before she could say anything else, Dusty jogged down to the dock and stepped in the boat.

Heading toward town, Dusty got busy on this phone, then said, "We can park this at the Perino Pier. My buddy said his truck is there, so we can use it." It wasn't easy hiding a 42' boat, but Spencer thought since they had a few days, everything would be ok.

That was his thinking before he got a text from Jimmy: "Where are you?"

"Heading to town. What's up?" he texted back.

"Your house is on fire!"

What? My house! At first Spencer didn't put things together. He pulled up on the throttles, throwing Toni and Dusty forward with the unexpected stop.

"What's the matter?" Toni asked, regaining her balance.

"My house is on fire," he replied, dialing a number.

"What? Who are you calling?" she asked.

"Cardona," he replied. After the third ring, Spencer could hear someone pick up on the other end. *Finally!* he thought, but it wasn't the voice he was expecting.

Both Dusty and Toni could tell by his expression that something terrible was going on, and with his question they knew. "What have you done with Cardona?" Spencer asked the voice on the phone.

"Let's just say he is reunited with his ancestors. Now you have something that belongs to me, and I expect it now!" Vargas barked.

Spencer thought for a moment, "Well, you see, that's the problem with cell phones in these parts. We don't get good reception." He hung up.

"Did they—" Toni started to ask.

"I believe so," Spencer interrupted her question, knowing she was asking if Cardona was dead. She sat down on the cushion seat in front of the console.

"Man, this is getting deeper," he said to Dusty.

"You've got this far," Dusty replied. Spencer sat down in the captain's chair and looked at the floor, thinking.

Toni walked around the console. "We aren't even sure the treasure is still there," she said. "Maybe if we just give them the map and coin, they will leave everyone alone."

"That's not going to happen," he said, still looking down.

"You don't know that."

Without looking at either one of them, Spencer reached in his pocket and pulled out the silver coin he had just found. Both Toni and Dusty drew back in surprise and stared at the coin.

"You found it?" she asked.

"This morning." Toni took the coin from Spencer's hand and examined it.

Dusty looked over her shoulder. "This raises the stakes," he replied. Then like a coach firing up his team before a game, Dusty exclaimed, "I signed on to find this treasure, and no fifth-generation pirate is going to ruin our plans! And he sure as hell isn't going to beat us on our own turf!"

The sure words from Dusty hit Spencer—*fifth-generation pirate? Why would we let a pirate like Vargas have a treasure that doesn't belong to him to begin with?* Spencer looked at Dusty, saying, "Let's end this!"

"I'm on board, Captain!" he shot back to Spencer. Without warning, Spencer slammed the throttles down, and the big red boat shot out of the water heading toward the town where three Cajuns would avenge this unwanted war.

"OK, here's the plan," Spencer started to explain as the boat idled inside the no-wake zone heading toward Perino Pier.

"I'll drop you two off at the marina to get your trawler."

"I'm staying with you," Toni interrupted.

Spencer thought for a moment, then said, "Fine. Dusty, take your trawler and meet us in Adams bay. I'll send them on another wild goose chase, and while they're doing that, we'll dig up the treasure."

"I'll have to gas up first. But that should work," Dusty said, stepping onto the pier and tying Spencer's boat.

Spencer waved his keys at them, explaining, "I'm hiding the keys under the captain's seat." Together the three of them walked toward the friend's truck, climbed in, and headed down Hwy 23 toward the marina and Spencer's house. Within a few miles of the marina, they could see the pillar of smoke turn from a thick black to a grayish, almost white color. Toni held tightly to Spencer's arm.

"Pull over here," Dusty said, and they let him out at the road leading down to the marina and harbor. Spencer and

Toni proceeded down Hwy 23, and turning left on Spencer's road, they could see the extensive damage. After surviving several storms and floods, Spencer's childhood home, where his greatest memories of his mother were made, lay in ashes. They stopped a block away in fear of being recognized by one of Vargas's men.

"Spencer, I'm sorry," Toni said, rubbing the inside of his arm. He didn't say anything, just stared at the pile of smoldering rubble.

"It can be rebuilt," he finally replied, thinking back on how many times his father replaced the roof, siding, and other things damaged by storms. Then something suddenly struck him—the pile still had some flames showing. "Where is everyone?" he asked.

"I don't know," Toni said, realizing the same thing. They knew that the volunteer fire department lived for structure fires and would stay around until the last flame was extinguished, but they weren't anywhere to be seen. No sirens. No police. No fire trucks.

"That's weird. Nobody is here. Not even nosey neighbors," Spencer said, pulling up closer to the pile of rubble.

"Don't get out!" Toni said, realizing Spencer was putting the truck in park and opening his door.

"I don't think anyone is around." He made his way up the lot. He kicked a few boards out of his way and tried to get closer, but the flames were still shooting up through the rubble, making it too hot to get close.

Toni walked up behind him. "Spencer, look!" she said, pointing to another pillar of black smoke blasting into the sky.

Lee DuCote

"That's Mr. Gentry's store!" he exclaimed.

Chapter 59

Spencer and Toni cautiously snuck through town, aiming toward Gentry's store. Their question about the absent firefighters at Spencer's house was answered once they rounded a corner and faced Gentry's store fully engulfed in flames. Toni cupped her mouth with her hands as Spencer shook his head in disbelief. They pulled into a lot across the street and parked beside another truck, watching as the firemen ran from their truck to the store pulling more fire hose. A neighboring fire department had just arrived to aid in extinguishing the old store when Spencer and Toni were startled by a knock on Toni's window.

"What are you two doing?" Jimmy asked, almost yelling.

"We figured we'd just be in the way if we went up there," Spencer said.

Jimmy nodded. "Sorry about your house. This is crazy, and now Mr. Gentry's? What the hell have you gotten yourself into?" he asked. Spencer wasn't sure how to answer the question. "Listen, I know I can be an ass from time to time, but if you want my help, I need to know what I'm getting myself into. I've already been shot at by foreigners, your house was incinerated, and now Mr. Gentry has lost his store," Jimmy added. Spencer was prepared to explain everything when a fireman yelled from the front of the store.

The words sent shivers up Spencer's spine, and he played the words over and over in his head, hoping he misunderstood: "We have a body over here!" Jimmy left them sitting in the truck and jogged over to the store.

Toni opened the door. "Toni! Stay inside," Spencer called out, but she looked back at him with a demoralized expression. "People are dying over this!" she said, shutting the door and running over behind Jimmy.

Spencer exited the truck and scanned the area. He knew that if they saw Toni, they would know that he was also there.

He walked across the street and stopped a fireman. "Is it Mr. Gentry?" he asked.

"Sorry, too hard to tell. The body is burned up pretty bad. We did find it behind the counter, so we think it was Mr. Gentry." Spencer walked up behind Jimmy and Toni, finding they had received the same news.

Jimmy spun around to Spencer. "I'm not sure what the hell is going on, but after I kill a few foreigners, you have some explaining to do!" He stormed off.

"Jimmy!" Toni ran after him. "Please think this through. We don't know how many there are." Trying to stop him, she called back to Spencer, asking for his help, but Spencer didn't say anything. Jimmy squinted his eyes at Spencer and took his silence as a hint to go after them.

Spencer felt his phone buzzing in his pocket, and pulling it out, he saw it was Cardona's phone number. He answered it, put it to his ear, and didn't say a word. The voice on the other end said, "I am someone you do not want to mess with! Hang up on me again and witness another fire. Maybe this time it'll be a veterinary hospital."

"What do you want?" Spencer asked, knowing the answer.

"The map and coin!"

"If I turn them over, will you leave us alone?" he asked.

There was a short pause on the phone, and then the words: "Turn them over and we will see."

Not the answer Spencer was looking for.

He glanced over the area looking for anyone out of place, and even though he knew he was being watched, he didn't see anyone. "Fine! I don't have them with me," he answered.

"No more waiting, get the map!" Vargas yelled.

"It's in my boat."

"You have thirty minutes! Meet me at the marina." The phone went dead.

Spencer turned to Toni. "We've got to get out there and get this treasure."

She looked at him with a baffled expression. "No!" She shouted at him. "Mr. Gentry is dead because of this treasure and probably Cardona. No more," she said, searching for the right words, her expression full of anger and confusion. He grabbed her hand, only to have her jerk it out of his grasp.

"Toni, these people will never go away. We have to finish it."

"At the cost of people's lives?"

"We have to finish," he repeated his words. She took a step back, bumping into someone.

"So, Mr. Gentry is dead?" Dusty asked.

"What are you doing here?" Spencer asked.

"I saw the smoke and knew it was Mr. Gentry's store. He was inside?" Dusty asked.

"Yes," Toni said, crying.

"What's the deal?" Dusty asked with a more serious face.

"If I don't give them the map and coin, they will burn down the vet clinic next," Spencer said.

Toni's face turned pale, and then her hands fell to her side. "I'm done!" she said, and turned to walk off.

"Toni, it's not safe," Dusty said.

Spencer stepped in. "Let her go. It's me they want."

Dusty looked back at Spencer with a disappointed look. "You're responsible for that girl," he said.

Spencer watched Toni walk off, and the vision of her riding off on her bike twenty years ago played all over again: *Go after Toni or go after the treasure.* He remembered Lebreaux's words, "The girl or the treasure." *Can't have them both?* He couldn't understand why.

He looked back at Dusty. "I wish I could tell you what to do," Dusty said. Spencer looked back at Toni vanishing around a building on the corner.

"But I could tell you what to do with Toni," Dusty added.

Spencer looked at him. "What?" he asked in a solemn tone.

"I'd go after the girl!" Dusty smiled.

Vargas watched from the inside of a vacant building as Spencer left Dusty and headed toward Toni and not his boat. "Get him back on the phone!" Vargas ordered one of his men. The man handed Vargas the phone. Spencer felt the phone vibrating in his pocket, and jogging toward Toni, he pulled out the phone and saw it was Vargas again.

He stopped and answered. "Listen, I'm going to give you the map, coin, and everything else. But first I am going to get what I want!" Spencer barked into the phone.

Vargas pulled back the phone at looked at it. No one talked to him in that tone. "Twenty-five minutes!" he said and handed the phone back to one of his men.

Looking back up, Spencer realized Toni was nowhere in sight. He jogged to the road, but seeing nothing, he quickly walked back to the side street. Still no Toni. He pulled out his cell phone and called her phone, but it went straight to voice mail. Then the fear of her being taken again hit him, and he knew this time they would kill her. He dialed Cardona's number.

Vargas's man looked at Vargas, "It's the guy." He looked puzzled.

Vargas snapped his fingers for the phone. "Hello!"

"Did you take her?" Spencer asked, his voice rising in anger.

"Take? No, I didn't take the girl," Vargas answered.

"You wouldn't be lying to me?" Spencer snapped back.

"If I say something, then you can believe me." He hung up on Spencer. *Huh, this guy has guts.* Vargas thought, looking at the phone.

Spencer realized where he was, one block from the longest pier in Buras and also a pier that both of them would visit from time to time. Stepping onto the pier, he saw Toni sitting at the end, with her legs dangling off the edge—a vision that had returned again and again from twenty years ago, when she found him after the death of his mother.

☠ Chapter 60 ☠

It had been a few days, and with little water and no food, Lebreaux was at her weakest. She had tried to think of a way to end her life so she could be with her love, but the cell was small and had nothing in it. She sat leaning against the rusty bars with both arms drooped at her sides and hands motionless. Her face was filthy with dirt that had collected with the tears that had dried the day before.

The door leading down into the hull and cell swung open, allowing light to enter the damp and stenchy area. "I have someone who would like to meet you," Vargas said, standing in the doorway. "Get her out and bring her to the main deck," he ordered one of the men. After opening the cell door, the man picked up the weak and frail woman, carrying her out to the open air. Once they broke into the bright sun, the man dropped her body onto the wooden deck, and she felt the pain radiate through her bones. She shielded her eyes from the sun and tried to peek through her hands to see where they were. The figure of another woman was standing in front of her.

"Lebreaux," the female spoke. She recognized the voice, but with her eyes not yet adjusted to the sun, she couldn't see the person speaking. She desperately struggled to remember where she had heard that voice, but nothing was coming to her mind. Then she fought through the brightness and pulled her hand down to see in front of her the face of Cecile Fatiman, the voodoo priestess who helped lead the ceremony at Bois Caiman, and the most feared mambo in all of Haiti.

Her skin crawled as the mambo touched her arm. "Child, ye have disobeyed da spirits. And ye should know calling on da loa to free ye comes wit a price." Lebreaux cut her eyes at Vargas.

"Laffite said he knew a little about voodoo," he smiled.

"Give her water, I need her strong for dis," the mambo ordered. "For?" Lebreaux asked as they pulled her to her feet.

"Ye loyalty lay in da wrong person," said the priestess, "and now ye must be punished for going against dis man." She pointed to Lafitte, who was standing on the deck above them.

"Kill me," she replied.

"Oh no, we ain't going to kill ye," Vargas said, stepping forward.

The mambo held up a hand that stopped him in his tracks. "Death ye'll never see." The mambo reached down and picked up a cloth sack, and reaching in, she pulled out a snake. The crew, including Vargas, took a few steps back. Lafitte continued watching from the deck above, feeling queasy.

Then with a knife, the mambo cut the top of her arm, and drawing blood from the cut, she dipped the snake's nose into the bright red liquid. She approached Lebreaux, and in a chant she attempted to summon the spirit Erzulie Freda. Lebreaux closed her eyes as she was approached by the snake, the hands gripping tighter around her arms as she tried to flee. The snake's nose touched Lebreaux's forehead, making a bloody cross. "Ye shall never die, ye shall never leave dees waters, ye shall never see ye love again," the mambo chanted.

Lebreaux opened her eyes again to see she was in the waters of Barataria Bay. The men pushed her to the side of the ship.

"Ye take something from me, I take something from ye," Vargas said. "Over." He motioned for the crew to throw her overboard.

Struggling to the surface, Lebreaux fought to stay above water, and one of the men threw a small barrel over. She clung to the barrel, trying to catch her breath.

"Good bye!" Vargas said, peering over the side.

"Pull anchor and set our heading to Tortuga," Lafitte barked, walking down the steps.

"She'll keep the curse forever?" Vargas asked the mambo.

"All curses can be broken," she replied.

"This one?" he asked.

"If she finds two young souls and causes them to fall in love, then the curse will be broken."

"That's not impossible!" Vargas grew angry at the simple suggestion.

"Ay, but one of them must lose the other and then trade places with Lebreaux in order for the curse to be broken."

"Ha, she'll never find that," he laughed.

Sailing away, Lafitte watched with a satisfied expression as Lebreaux struggled to swim to land.

Lee DuCote

Chapter 61

"Seems like you were walking down this dock twenty years ago to console me," Spencer said, walking up behind her. She turned with tears still in her eyes.

He sat down beside her. "I remember. Your mother had just died," Toni replied, looking back out over the marsh.

Spencer looked out. "Yeah, that was a rough time."

"She was a good woman," Toni said. They sat watching two dragonflies chasing each other over the water.

"Mom was a smart person. I still remember the things she used to tell me when I would complain about other kids." He looked down at the water. The wind had picked back up and was sending small ripples under the pier.

"One thing she told me over and over was that nothing was worth more than relationships."

Toni looked over at him with her head cocked sideways. "And?" she asked.

He smiled. "You can't put a value on friendship." She held her foot out for one of the dragonflies to land on. "Toni, when I left here, I wanted to start over and not be that geeky kid any more. I thought moving to Florida was the greatest thing—I was on the swim team, ran track, and did everything I couldn't do here."

He took another deep breath. "My dad was the most important thing to me, and I wanted to be around him all the time; I wanted to *be* him. Nothing was more painful than when I lost him. Before he died, we found the *Griego* together, and it was one of the happiest times in our life. I promised him before he died that we would find the *Compostela*." He took a deep breath. "I love you, but I have to find this treasure in his honor."

"Spencer," she interrupted him, her voice soft and hesitant. "The week you left, I realized I had let that school consume me. I was trying to be someone I wasn't. I cried for weeks after you left, but felt that you would never want to speak to me again, so I didn't call." Tears started forming again in her eyes. "I quit cheer and everything that led to popularity, but it didn't fix that empty feeling. Went to college, started my career, and still no fix. I thought I had found it with Clint, but he became so obsessed with his music that I didn't matter anymore. And then when I ran into you a few weeks ago, that empty feeling went away. For the first time in years, I felt complete again. But you're letting the treasure consume you. An obsession." He moved his hand on top of hers.

"You have nothing to prove with me, Spencer. I love you, but I can't be with someone who is fixated over something else. I don't want to compete with something else." She gazed back over the marsh at a few low-flying pelicans.

"I understand."

"This isn't going to work, is it?" she asked in a soft voice.

"I don't think so," he lowered his head with Toni's hand slipping out of his.

A commotion behind them caused them to turn and find Jimmy walking toward them on the pier. "With all the fires and gun fights, you two are sitting on the end of the pier like nothing is going on. LeJeune, can you tell me why I'm shooting foreigners?" Spencer paused, trying to think of something to tell him. "This isn't about that stupid Spanish barge legend?" Jimmy pressed on. Spencer looked at Toni, who nodded toward Jimmy, hinting to tell him.

"Jimmy," Spencer began, but then stopped and looked at the smoke coming up from behind him. He glanced at Toni, who caught his glance toward the smoke.

"Please tell me no," she said.

Jimmy spun around. "Damn, these guys won't stop." Toni ran in the direction of her clinic with Spencer and Jimmy following. Only a few blocks from the pier, they found flames shooting out the front windows of her clinic.

"Help me get the animals!" she screamed, running across the street. Spencer and Jimmy looked at each other with the same thought: Where are Vargas and his men?

In Toni's mind, she didn't care. Her only concern was to rescue the animals that were put in her care. When she fumbled with her keys to open the back door, Spencer took them. "Which one?" he handed the keys out. A loud crash thundered behind him, and he turned to see that Jimmy had kicked in the back door.

"Take them to the pens out back!" Toni yelled over the barking as smoke bellowed out the door. They grabbed their first round of dogs and cats and ran them to the kennels that were in the back away from the building.

The three of them ran back, and as Spencer entered he saw a fire truck pull into the parking lot. Two more trips and all the animals were out of the building, with only the fire fighters inside battling to put out the flames.

"LeJeune!" A voice yelled over the engine on the fire truck. Spencer turned to see the sheriff walking to him. "Three fires in one afternoon that started with your house! What the hell is going on?" Spencer froze with the question.

"He's the victim of false identity! These people think he's somebody else!" Jimmy said, stepping in.

"I should have known you'd be involved, Jimmy," the sheriff replied.

"Now, LeJeune, a lot of weird things have been going on since you got back in town. I want an explanation, or I am going to place you under arrest." He pointed at Spencer.

"Arrest? For what?" Toni shot back.

"Benoit! You stay out of this," the sheriff snapped, pointing at her.

There were many things that got on Toni's nerves, but one of her downfalls was not to let the little things go, and someone pointing a finger in her face was one of those things. Before the sheriff knew it, he had a 125-pound pissed off Cajun girl in his face. "You better put that finger down. His house burned down, my friend Mr. Gentry is dead, my clinic is burning down, and your answer is to arrest him!?" She pointed at Spencer. She took two more steps toward the sheriff, and he wasn't sure whether to let her vent or pull out his Taser. Spencer wrapped his right arm around her waist and pulled her back.

"Sheriff, I'm going to fix it." Spencer reached in his pocket, but realized he had lost his cell phone. He looked back at Toni. "My phone!"

"Is it on the pier?" she asked.

"I bet so. Sheriff, I'll be back!" He sprinted around the fire truck, unaware that Toni and Jimmy were pursuing him.

Running back onto the pier, he saw his phone lying next to where he was sitting at the end of the pier. He sprinted to the end and was reaching down for it when a shadow caught his eye from behind. Standing, he saw Toni and Jimmy halfway down the pier, but it wasn't their shadows that caught his eye—it was the trio that stepped onto the pier behind them—Vargas and his men.

Chapter 62

Without warning, the first shot rang out, missing Toni by inches. Spencer grabbed her and fell behind a few 55-gallon drums of grease. Jimmy dove behind a few crates and quickly scooted his back against them for cover. They could see each other across the pier, and Spencer was out of options. Four more shots ricocheted off the barrels as Spencer covered Toni's head and drew her against his chest.

Spencer's right ear began ringing with two shots exploding out from Jimmy's direction. Spencer looked over at Jimmy, who was now holding an automatic Colt .45 in his left hand. Vargas and his men quickly scrambled for cover at the front of the pier. "Mr. LeJeune! You have nowhere to go," Vargas yelled at them.

Spencer looked down at Toni. "I can call the sheriff," he said.

"No!" Toni exclaimed.

"Why?"

"This is going to lead into a blood bath, and he is already suspicious of you!" she answered.

"What do you have in mind?" he asked.

"I don't know, but you better think of something," she said. Spencer looked back over at Jimmy and held his hands out for any suggestions.

Jimmy held up his index finger. "Hey, Vargas," he shouted, "If I turn over these two over, will you let me go?"

"What are you doing?" Spencer asked.

Vargas was kneeling behind a container but heard Jimmy's question. "What is this American doing?" he asked. One of his men shrugged his shoulders.

"OK?" Vargas answered, confused at Jimmy's question.

"Well, come get them," Jimmy yelled back.

Spencer and Toni shot a blank stare at Jimmy. "I don't think that is going to work," Toni said.

"I don't know. I was just trying to lure them out," Jimmy said.

"How many rounds do you have?" Spencer asked Jimmy, keeping his voice down.

He reached in his pocket and pulled out four more clips. "A few," he whispered back. Spencer was thinking about who he could call; he wasn't interested in inviting anyone to a gun fight.

One of Vargas's men started creeping down the pier unnoticed by the three of them, but halfway he stumbled over a rope, causing his steps to be heard and noticed by Jimmy. Jimmy fired three shots at the man as he ran back to cover, making it in time before Jimmy hit him. A hail of bullets rained over them as Vargas and his men fired randomly at their barriers. Jimmy reached over the crates and fired another clip back at them.

"Stop shooting, Jimmy, they just want to run us out of ammo!" Spencer yelled over the thunder of gunfire. Jimmy pulled his gun down and slammed in a full clip. *Dang it!*

Think! Spencer scanned both sides of the pier, finding nowhere to go.

While contemplating their plan Spencer felt the entire dock tremble as if an earthquake had just hit. The three of them quickly turned to find Dusty's trawler rammed against the end of the dock. "Y'all come on!" he screamed.

Vargas saw Dusty waving at them and opened fire, blocking their way. "Go! I'll hold them off!" Jimmy yelled at Spencer and Toni.

They froze, not wanting to leave Jimmy. "Go!" he screamed at them again.

Dusty ducked into the wheelhouse to avoid the onslaught of bullets ripping through his trawler. "Ready?" Spencer looked at Toni.

"No! We can't leave him," she yelled back.

Spencer knew she was right, but it was their only way. "Get her out of here!" Jimmy demanded.

"We'll draw their fire away—they're after us, not Jimmy. It's the only way." He looked back at Jimmy and gave him a nod, and Jimmy stood to his feet and took aim. His first shot clipped one of Vargas's men, causing him to fall behind the barriers with Vargas. Spencer grabbed Toni's arm and jumped for Dusty's boat, the two of them landing on the bow as Dusty slammed it into reverse, swinging the boat around and shielding them from the gun battle.

"Jimmy!" Toni screamed again. Jimmy turned to see Toni hanging off the front railing of the trawler. Spencer, Toni, and Dusty helplessly witnessed Jimmy running through the smoke from his Colt as he rushed Vargas and his men. The pier disappeared from their sight as they rounded a corner.

"What's the plan?" Dusty asked Spencer as they steamed south.

Spencer looked at Toni. "I'll help, but then I'm out," she replied.

Spencer looked back at Dusty. "Burn him!" he replied.

"I want to go home and get my baseball bat and teach Jimmy a lesson!" Spencer exclaimed through his tears and throbbing eye.

"I don't think so. The fight is over," Steve answered, pulling out of the Benoits' driveway.

"No, it's not," Spencer fumed.

"Son, it's over."

"It's not over till I'm done with Jimmy. I can't let him win." The truck slowed down as Steve looked for traffic, and then he pulled it over on the side of the white seashell road.

"Win? There's no winning to a fight," Steve said.

"Last man standing is the winner," Spencer replied.

Steve took a deep breath. "Why do you think Jimmy was picking at Toni?"

"Because he's mean."

"Then why didn't he kill the two ducks?"

Spencer sat quietly for a moment, thinking the question over. "I don't know," he finally answered.

"I'm going to bet it's because he likes Toni."

"What?"

"Sometimes guys don't know how to show they like someone, so they pick on them."

"That's stupid," Spencer said under his breath.

"But I'm proud of you!"

"Why? I lost, and it's pretty clear you're not going to let me get my bat," Spencer said sarcastically.

"You fought for what you believe in, and sometimes losing the fight is winning the battle," Steve replied, pulling back out onto the road. Spencer looked at his dad like he was crazy. "There are going to be times in your life when you come across people and situations that don't make sense. But always standing up for what you believe is right is actually winning; there are just times when you have to come away with a few scars and bruises."

"Well, I still want to get my bat," Spencer replied.

"For what, revenge?" Steve asked.

"Yeah! Revenge," Spencer said with a second wind.

"Revenge is an act for the one who lost the battle," Steve answered.

"Toni stayed with you. You dropped her off at her house, not Jimmy," Steve went on, trying to prove that Spencer had won.

"Toni thinks I'm a big geek like everyone else."

"I think Toni sees you a little differently than everyone else."

Chapter 63

The waters of Barataria Bay had an eerie calm as Dusty's trawler eased into the Buras Marina. Spencer and Toni stood on the bow, scanning the area for anyone who looked out of place or the slightest resemblance to one of Vargas's men. The intensity level was thick between the three of them as they prepared for their plan. The marina had a placid feel to it, with only a few fishermen who were cleaning their catch and the parking lot empty. Spencer knew that would change with Vargas on his way.

Toni and Dusty stepped off the trawler onto the dock, and she turned toward Spencer. "Please be careful," she asked. He watched as the two of them jogged to her father's boat and fired up the engines. Dusty gave him a thumbs up. Spencer slowly backed out of the dock and cut the wheel toward open water. Once out of the marina, he headed south to the one boat he knew would help with their plan, *Waterproof*.

Their plan was simple. Spencer would run out to Dusty's camp house and retrieve the map. Once the map was in hand, he would swing by Adams Bay and give Toni and Dusty his diving gear. After he gave the map to Vargas, the next part of the plan was to lead them on a long trip to retrieve the coin from Lebreaux's house. This would buy

Lee DuCote

Toni and Dusty enough time to remove as much of the treasure as they could in the short time they had.

Pulling up to Perino Pier where *Waterproof* was tied, Spencer looked for any signs of Vargas and his men. Satisfied that he was the only one on the pier, he tied Dusty's boat to the rusted cleats on the dock and quickly made his way to his own boat. Within a few feet of stepping down into the fiberglass floor of the boat, two men dressed in slacks and button-down shirts blocked his way with guns drawn.

"We figured you would be here," one of them said. The other holstered his gun and pulled out a cell phone. "We have him," he reported. Spencer knew the call was to Vargas, but what worried him was if they were talking to Vargas, where was Jimmy? "Hold him, and if he tries to get away … shoot him!" Spencer could hear Vargas's voice through the phone.

Spencer found himself in a quandary and wasn't sure he would be able to figure it out in time; the three of them stood frozen in place, waiting for Vargas. Spencer stepped to the side, knowing he would provoke a response. "Don't move!" his guard ordered, stepping to the side with Spencer, the one movement that Spencer was hoping for.

Now facing each other on the dock, Spencer looked toward the parking lot. "What? No black Mercedes?" he said, lying.

The man looked for a brief moment to find nobody there. The next thing he felt was Spencer's hands on his chest, pushing him off the dock. He fired two shots before splashing into the water, hitting nothing, while Spencer quickly kicked in the knee of the other guy holding only a cell phone. With enough time to run and dive into his boat, he scrambled to the console and fired up the engines.

Two more shots rang out as Spencer wasted no time slamming down the throttles with the intension of breaking the rope that had the boat tied. What happened next even Spencer couldn't have planned—the power of the engines and strength of the ropes pulled the dock into the water, causing both of Vargas's men to wind up in the water. Spencer reached into a compartment on the console and grabbed a knife, and after cutting the line he throttled forward, running over part of the collapsed dock as he headed toward open water.

He heard four more shots while ducking behind the captain's chair, thinking, *I'm in the clear!* Little did Spencer know that one of the four shots clipped a fuel line on the back of his boat. A flurry of thoughts ran through his head as the boat powered away—*Now the plan, how many guys does he have?* He slowed down to make a call to Toni.

I smell fuel, he thought as his hands shook trying to hit Toni's number on his cell phone. Before she had time to answer his call, the windshield exploded, raining glass over him and the boat. The two men were now in another boat heading straight toward him.

The cell phone hit the floor of the boat and Spencer leaped for the throttles, putting his weight into the silver handles. *Waterproof* shot out of the water, and his first thought was *I know they can't catch me,* but feeling resistance against the boat, he looked back to see two of the four engines weren't running, and the holes that ran through the engine covers told why.

Struggling to outrun Vargas's men, Spencer sailed across the choppy water desperately trying to reach his cell phone, but the bullets raining through his boat prevented him from coming out from behind the captain's chair. He steered toward Adams Bay, hoping that Dusty could help fend off the unwanted boat that was gaining on him.

Pulling into the bay, Spencer searched the area for Toni and Dusty, but came up empty. *Where are they?*

Dusty and Toni had heard the shots and knew that Spencer was in trouble, so they had doubled back to help and were hot on the tail of the men chasing Spencer into Adams Bay. Dusty pulled out his old rusted Smith and Wesson and took aim at Vargas's men in front of him. "Is that thing safe to shoot?" Toni asked. Her question was quickly answered when the gun went off with an explosion, causing pieces to fall into the floor of the boat.

"Damn it!" Dusty yelled, shaking his now throbbing hand.

One of the men spun around, and seeing Toni and Dusty behind them, he tapped on the shoulder of the pilot and instructed him to circle back to finish off the two Cajuns. Toni spun the wheel for a sharp right turn, throwing Dusty against the side of the boat. "You OK?" she yelled.

"Yes, get us the hell out of here!" he shouted back. But with the sharp right turn, the motor sputtered a few times and died.

"Start the motor, Toni!" Dusty said with a strong sense of urgency. He watched as the boat in front of them circled around and was now headed straight toward them. With no gun, no motor, and no defense, Toni and Dusty found themselves helpless. The first shot missed Dusty by only inches as it passed through the fiberglass sides. Toni dove to the floor with her hands shielding her head.

One of the Spaniards smiled at the other and pointed their boat directly at Toni and Dusty—they knew these two would be an easy kill. As they approached the stranded boat, both men took aim with their Glocks and began to squeeze on the triggers.

Out of nowhere, *Waterproof* shot in front of them, and they swung the wheel of their boat to keep from hitting Spencer, breaking their course on Toni and Dusty to go speeding after Spencer. Running only on two motors, *Waterproof* was no match for the pursuers' boat, and soon Spencer could hear the gunshots raining on him again. Toni and Dusty watched helplessly from their derelict boat.

Spencer looked back at Toni, the two locked eyes from a distance, and everything in her body went numb. She couldn't scream. She couldn't move. She saw her life flash before her eyes, with Spencer's voice whispering in the air, "My only obsession is you!" In that moment, a single shot pierced the open fuel line on the back of Spencer's boat, and in a ball of flames, *Waterproof* exploded. It was as if Toni was caught in a movie watching in slow motion as her childhood crush and the man she had fallen in love with vanished in a glow of orange flames.

Chapter 64

With everything unfolding around her, Toni watched the two Spaniards circle the wreckage searching for any sign of Spencer. "Please God! No!" Her knees buckled, causing her to fall to the fiberglass floor of her father's boat. Dusty stared as the boat that once bore the name *Waterproof* sank into the bay in a ball of fire. "Dusty, tell me he jumped," Toni pleaded as she pulled on his shirt, but he remained motionless. "Please!" she begged. Tears hadn't yet formed over the shock that was radiating through her body.

The two Spaniards aimed their boat toward them, and Dusty pushed Toni behind him to shield her in whatever was to come. Their boat drifted alongside Toni and Dusty, and one of the Spaniards said, "Get in," waving his gun toward their boat. Toni couldn't get up—the weight of her body felt like a thousand pounds, glued to the floor of her father's boat.

Dusty reached down and grabbed her under her arms. "Come on," he whispered into her ear.

"Dusty, they killed him." She looked up at him, her hazel eyes finally filling up with tears.

"I know," he softly spoke. The pain of his agreement penetrated deep in her soul, and her will quickly left.

"Get in the boat!" The man shouted again. Dusty picked up Toni against her own will, and with her fist bouncing against his chest, he placed her in the Spaniard's boat. "We're not leaving!" she screamed, reaching toward the last few burning pieces of the wreckage of Spencer's boat.

"Come on, let's—" Dusty began to say, but with a sudden pain to the back of his head, he collapsed.

"If you move you will get the same treatment," snarled the man who had just knocked out Dusty.

"Now, where is the map?" he demanded. She pulled herself up to Dusty, who was still out cold on the bottom of the boat.

She shook him, "Dusty?"

The man walked up and buried the barrel of his Glock 23 in Dusty's dirty red hair. "Tell me!" he barked. She pointed away from the shore.

"Where are you pointing?"

"The camp house. Head that way," she said, numb.

Dusty felt the boat come off its plane and drift into a structure, and through blurred vision he saw his camp house. "Well?" one of the men asked Toni.

"It's under the dock." The man motioned to the other to jump in and investigate. He handed him his gun and leaped over the side of the boat. Pushing his way through the thigh-deep water, he made his way under the old dock.

"Ha! Got it!" he said from underneath the dock. He waded out and handed the waterproof case to the other man.

"And the coin?" He looked at Toni. The plan had been to lead them on a wild chase to Lebreaux's house in Lafitte for the coin, but it was only a bluff. She reached in her pocket and presented the silver coin.

"This is it? It's not even round," the man said. She remained silent about the shape of the coin.

Dusty was sitting up holding the back of his head as the boat fought through the choppy water back to Buras.

Toni rested against Dusty's side. "They're going to kill us, aren't they?" she asked.

"I don't know. We'll figure a way out," he assured her.

The boat hit a large wave, sending a shocking pain through his back. "They don't even know how to drive a boat," she said.

Once back at the marina, Toni saw the black Mercedes parked at the end of the pier. "Say anything or try to run," their captor threatened, "and I'll kill you both. Understand?" Both Dusty and Toni nodded. The Spaniards barely tied the boat before they stepped out onto the dock, ordering Toni and Dusty to head to the car. The man pushed them. No one was on the dock, no one in the parking lot, no one in sight—Vargas's men were getting what they wanted.

Both Dusty and Toni climbed into the back seat of the Mercedes with one of Vargas's men sitting in the passenger seat, aiming his gun at Toni. The car slowly backed out of the parking lot and headed south on highway 23 toward the Oyster Bar. Stopping in front of the closed bar, the men ordered Toni and Dusty to get out and walk in. *Why are we here?* She thought.

Their eyes hadn't had time to adjust to the darkness of the bar, but with only a few lights on, Toni could see Vargas sitting at the bar. "Many people have tried to outwit my family for over 400 years for this treasure. So I understand you trying," he said with a smirk. "But today the Vargas family finally gets what belongs to us." He waved for the men to hand him the map.

"My great-grandfather told me about this map, and now after many years, I get to see it." He unrolled the bamboo map on the bar. "He told me that Nicholas Cardona made the map where only he could read it. He should have kept quiet about his own key," he added. "The coin!" he demanded.

The same man handed him the coin. "Ah, a sixteenth-century Potosi coin. You see, during that time they rushed out their silver, not taking the time to round their coins." He showed the coin to his men.

He scanned the map, and then with a snap he placed the coin in the only fitting place, over the treasure. He sat back and smiled. "Give me the other map," he ordered one of his men. They handed him a modern-day map of Barataria Bay. "You!" he said, pointing to Dusty. "Show me on this map where the treasure is." He pointed to the modern-day map. Dusty walked up to the bar and pointed to the location. Vargas studied both maps for a moment, "You tell the truth." "Vamonos!" Vargas motioned everyone out.

With his men leaving, he turned toward Dusty and Toni. "You gave me what I wanted, so I will spare your life. But if you pursue me or call your authorities, I'll come back after you. Claro?" He squinted his eyes.

"Clear," Dusty said in a solemn voice.

"Here, a little memento from me." He threw Dusty the bamboo map and coin. The door opened, blinding them for a moment with the bright day while Vargas left.

"We need to call the sheriff," Dusty replied.

"No, let them go." Toni put her head down on the bar on top of her arms.

"We can't let them get away," he pushed.

"No, someone else could get killed," she said through her folded arms. Dusty agreed.

Visions of Spencer danced through her head, and she flashed back to the age of ten. She remembered the times they rode through Buras on their bikes in search of treasure. The times that they went out on the marsh with Steve in search for dolphins. The times they spent running from pier to pier in search for fish. The times they spent searching for excitement, treasure, and adventure—she started crying again.

"We'll get through this," Dusty tried to comfort her.

She looked at him briefly. "Tell me this is all a dream," she asked.

"I wish it was," he replied.

Chapter 65

"Let's go get my family's treasure!" Vargas ordered his men as they walked to the Mercedes. His men stood in a small circle with blank expressions. "What?" Vargas held his arms out.

One of the men spoke up. "We don't have the equipment to recover the treasure."

"What?" Vargas asked, his temper rising.

"We were going to use Mr. LeJeune's equipment, but it was lost in the explosion."

Vargas rubbed his chin. "Yes, this is true. We'll go get more equipment!" he decided.

"Considering we burned down half the town," the man who had spoken said, "I don't think anyone here is going to help."

"What do you suggest we do?" Vargas asked.

"We head to New Orleans and get the equipment we need, then rent a boat first thing in the morning." The man's voice shook with fear over his plan.

"Not what I wanted to hear," Vargas replied, thinking for a moment.

"To New Orleans," he finally agreed, waving for everyone to load up.

Sitting in the driver's seat, one of Vargas's men asked, "You sure those two won't talk?"

Vargas looked at the door leading in the bar. "No, we are good. Let's go." He put on his sunglasses and pointed forward. With a cloud of dust, the black Mercedes and two Land Rovers sped out of the small south Louisiana town.

The night was the longest Toni had ever been through. Their plan was to wake up early and salvage through the wreckage in both the burned buildings and Spencer's boat on the bottom of Barataria Bay. Dusty had planned to call the sheriff and explain everything first thing in the morning, but morning was struggling to get there, with the night just as long for Dusty as it was for Toni.

With the sun beginning to rise over the Mississippi River and the waterfowl leaving their roosts heading toward the marsh to feed, Toni, who had yet to sleep, started making coffee in her kitchen. She quietly sat at the table, blowing the steam from her mug. She caught the shadow of a small animal peering from the hallway, "Tucker. Come here," she whispered. The inquisitive raccoon stuck his head around the corner cabinet. "Shh. Don't wake up Dusty," she whispered again.

"I'm not asleep. Just lying here," the voice came from the couch. Dusty sat up with his hair a mess and in the same clothes he had on from the day before. "What time is it?" he asked.

"It's almost 6 a.m.," she replied.

"Well, you ready to start our day?" he asked.

"No," she replied, walking toward her room to get ready to leave.

"Me either—I'll ask the sheriff to meet us at the Oyster Bar at 9 a.m.," he said.

The water on the bay was like glass with only a few shrimp boats trolling the outer banks for their catch. A small group of brown pelicans glided over the marsh in a V-shape pattern searching for fish. With the sun well into the sky, everything seemed normal in the south Louisiana bay with the exception of Vargas and his men heading toward the Spanish barge treasure.

They had spent most of their evening and night putting together dive equipment and other machinery to haul out the treasure. Vargas knew that Dusty and Toni would call the local authorities, and he hoped that his one-day set back was long enough for them to extricate the treasure and be gone before anyone questioned them.

Their boat pulled up, and two of his men were pointing and arguing in what direction to go. "Give me the map." Vargas snatched the map out of their hands. He studied it for only a minute and pointed in a direction. "That way." He sat back down. His men were well trained and extremely smart, but it was times like this that made him doubt their common sense.

Their boat rounded a small island with an old rusty oyster boat on one side, and the lonely captain gave a simple wave. Vargas returned with a wave that suggested he really didn't care about the captain and his rusty old trawler. The old man at the wheel looked back at the boat full of well-dressed men, something unusual in the marsh.

Once Vargas's boat was far enough out of sight, the old captain took off his hat and jacket. "Those stupid sons of bitches ain't got a clue!" Jimmy commented, walking out of the wheel house.

"I believe you're right," Mr. Gentry replied to Jimmy, who was wearing two gold chains and playing with a handful of Potosi silver coins.

Mr. Gentry put the old trawler in gear and pulled away from the small island, giving them a view of Vargas and his men, who were now stopping at the island near a small buoy that once marked the treasure. Jimmy, who was still wet and still wearing his wetsuit bottoms, opened a bottle of water. "You sure you put enough out there?"

Mr. Gentry smiled. "Boy, I was setting mortars and C4 before you were a gleam in your parents' eyes."

Jimmy, who was now biting into a sandwich, said, "I sure would like to see their expressions."

"This is it!" Vargas was saying with an excited tone. "Get the equipment ready and get in the water. It looks like Mr. LeJeune left us a mark." He pointed at the small floating buoy. Nobody in the boat moved. "What are you doing? Let's go!" Vargas clapped his hands.

One of his men pointed to the small grassy island. "That's not all he left us."

Vargas pushed the man out of his way to get a better look at the object that was staked in the grass. Not one, two, or even three, but *twelve* stakes of C4 littered the small island. Vargas looked behind him and noticed more metal objects in the water surrounding their boat. "Son of a—"

"Jimmy, I learned this in Vietnam." Mr. Gentry pulled out an old hand-held remote and lifted the antenna. "Wave goodbye!" the old man said, looking toward Vargas as he pressed the exposed red button. A mushroom cloud formed above the ball of flames and what used to be a grassy island and a fifth-generation pirate. As their boat sat in the water a quarter mile away, a sudden rush of wind created by the blast blew past them. Mr. Gentry started to dance in place.

"Damn! I guess you did have enough," Jimmy said, still eating his homemade sandwich.

Chapter 66

Jimmy joined in with Mr. Gentry on his outdated happy dance, and together they celebrated over the treasure nestled in the holding tanks of the rusty old trawler. People gathered on the shore of Buras and other surrounding areas watching the mushroom cloud dissipate into the sky. "Can't this lug go any faster?" Jimmy yelled over the engines.

"She's weighted down!" Mr. Gentry shouted back while patting the console.

A boat appeared from behind an island and aimed toward Mr. Gentry and Jimmy. Jimmy took off the gold chains and looked at Mr. Gentry. A few minutes later, a Wildlife and Fisheries boat rolled up beside the trawler. "Mr. Gentry! Strange to see you out here," one of the officers said.

"Oh, just taking a stroll through the marsh," he smiled back.

"Mmm huh! With Jimmy Pastadoria?" he asked.

"What? We're old buds," Jimmy said, putting his arm around Mr. Gentry.

"Let me guess—you don't know anything about that explosion?"

"Explosion? Was there an explosion?" Mr. Gentry said.

The officer pushed off the old trawler with a smile. "Have a good day," he waved and headed in the direction of the explosion they had created.

Jimmy started dancing again out of excitement. The officer looked back at the trawler to witness Jimmy and Mr. Gentry dancing. "Nothing out here surprises me any more!"

"So where are we going to hide this lug?" Jimmy asked.

"In plain sight," Mr. Gentry said, heading toward the marina.

"Boy, I can't wait to see the look on everyone's faces when they see we got the treasure and that you're alive."

Mr. Gentry lit a cigar. "Hard to kill an old geezer!"

Dusty pulled out his phone and answered a call from the sheriff, "Yes, sir. I will. Call when you're done." He hung up.

"What was that about?" Toni asked, sitting at the bar inside the Oyster Bar.

"Sheriff said he has to go investigate an oil platform that exploded in the marsh."

"Great! That's all we need is another oil spill," she said, sipping on a large cup of coffee.

Toni's eyes were bloodshot, her hair messed up, and she was still wearing the same clothes from yesterday. She had just survived the longest night of her life and worried what today would hold.

The door exploded open to the Oyster Bar, and Dusty jumped, expecting Vargas or his men to enter. Dusty placed himself between the door and Toni, but she pushed him to one side with the back of her hand. Jimmy and Mr. Gentry walked in. "It's time to party!" Jimmy yelled.

"Mr. Gentry!" Toni jumped up from her bar stool.

"I thought you were dead!" she replied.

"Honey, it's going to take more than a few foreigners to take this old man down. Maybe a jealous husband," he laughed, punching Dusty in the side with his elbow.

"But there was a body in your store?" Dusty asked.

"Yep. I capped me one of those fellows when they came in threatening me. I escaped through the side door," he smiled.

"Jimmy, how in the hell did you get away from Vargas on the pier? We were going to draw their fire, but we saw you storm them on the dock," Dusty asked.

"Soon as y'all took off, they ran for their car. I was just blowing holes in the car. Your plan worked perfect," he replied.

"I'm sorry about your store," Toni said, releasing Mr. Gentry.

"Oh hell, I'll just build it back. Done it many times," he said.

"Plus he's got this to do it with!" Jimmy slammed a duffle bag of silver coins on the bar and opened it.

Dusty's eyes widened. "You guys found the treasure?"

"Yep! And you should see what's in the boat," he replied.

"But wait, how did you guys know where to look?" Dusty asked.

"Spencer!" Jimmy answered, confused why he asked.

Toni sat back down—it was obvious Jimmy and Mr. Gentry weren't aware of the news. "What's the sad face for?" Jimmy asked her.

She took a deep breath and through forming tears, managed to whisper, "Spencer's dead."

Jimmy and Mr. Gentry looked at each other, confused. "Dead? When?" Jimmy rattled off the questions.

"During the afternoon," Dusty said placing his hand on Toni's shoulder.

"Well, then, I must be seeing a ghost," Jimmy said, pointing behind them. Toni spun around to find Spencer standing by the bar.

"Spencer?" she asked in disbelief.

"Yep," he said with a deep breath. She stared with thoughts of hallucinating or possibly a ghost, but receiving a soft smile with dimples, she knocked over a few bar stools to get to him. He wrapped his arms around her, lifting her feet off the floor. Spencer felt his shirt getting wet again, this time from the tears of his childhood crush and the woman he loved. She started mumbling something with her face still buried in his chest. He pulled her back. "What?" he asked.

"I saw you die in the explosion. How?" she cried.

"Let's just say with the help of an old friend," he whispered in her ear.

"Wait!" She pulled back.

"How did they know where to look?" she asked, pointing at Jimmy and Mr. Gentry.

"I called Jimmy," Spencer answered.

"When?" she asked.

"Yesterday evening," he answered.

"And you let me think you had died!" she said, backing up from him.

"I wasn't sure what Vargas had planned, and I didn't want you two in danger." He pointed to Dusty.

"How did you get to shore?" Dusty asked.

"After you guys got in their boat, I was able to restart Toni's father's boat. I followed Vargas's car here and slipped in the back." He pointed to the back door he had just entered. "I was prepared to shoot Vargas, but when I heard him say he was letting you go and that they had to go to New Orleans for gear, I had time," he said.

He looked at Toni. "I'm sorry, I just wanted you safe."

"So how did you know this old luger was still alive?" Dusty asked pointing to Mr. Gentry.

"I didn't until Jimmy told me." Dusty shook his head, and then a big smile formed across his face. They turned their attention to Jimmy, who was happily displaying the silver and gold coins from the duffle bag.

Spencer started to walk over to join the others, but Toni pulled on his arm. "I thought I lost you," she began crying again.

"It's OK. I'm here now." Spencer pulled her head back into his chest. "You're my obsession, Toni, not the treasure or anything else." He pulled her face close to his. "I promise."

"I've heard that before," she answered.

"Let me prove it."

He kissed her with an audience looking on. "About time!" Mr. Gentry said.

Chapter 67

The day before, during the boat chase, Spencer swung the wheel on *Waterproof* as hard as he could, luring the two Spaniards away from Toni and Dusty. He watched as the two Spaniards broke course and aimed toward him, and through the water spraying off the back of his boat, he could also see their pistols aiming in his direction. He ducked below the captain's seat after hearing bullets ricochet off the console. *I still smell fumes!* He had a little time to think.

He turned the wheel slightly to the left, directing his boat to a small opening between two islands, and caught the sight of two hazel eyes staring back at him. Locking eyes he mouthed the words, "My only obsession is you!" Then a bright flash of light surrounded him with an intensive tsunami of heat that drew the breath out of him, and he closed his eyes, expecting the end.

Within the cloud of heat Spencer felt the grasp of a hand pulling him into the water and then through blurry eyes he saw a ghostly figure shielding him from the blast. The percussion from the explosion sent a thunderous wave through the water, knocking him unconscious.

After a few blinks he sat up, sitting on the side of one of the small islands, and gazing over the bay, saw only Toni's father's boat, unoccupied. "Boy, I got you," a voice came from behind him. He spun around to see only a shadowed figure with the sun beaming from behind.

"You saved me," he replied rubbing his head.

"Ay, let me look at dat." She glanced at the cut on his head, saying, "It's a good cut, but it'll heal."

"Lebreaux?" Spencer asked.

"Yes." A smile formed across her face.

He looked back out over the bay. "Where's Toni and Dusty?"

"Dey have dem," she replied.

He looked back at her with her long gray hair and embroidered coat. She looked the same from when they were kids. "You're a spirit?"

"Some might say dat, and others would say a ghost."

"Why?" he asked, unsure of what to say or ask.

"I was cursed to Barataria Bay for betraying a man," she answered, knowing it was time to tell him.

"Vargas!" Spencer answered, remembering his dreams.

"Yes."

"Who cursed you?"

"A powerful mambo."

"Voodoo ... then you can be set free," he said, remembering his study on the religion.

She smiled, looking at the dirt. "By letting you die in da explosion," she answered him without looking up. "Da mambo cursed me with a powerful voodoo loa, an da only way to break it is for someone to lose der love in the midst of my hands." She held her hands out, and Spencer instantly remembered her holding Toni's and his hands in the bay years earlier.

"But you saved me …"

She looked up at him. "Dis curse I wish on no one. You and da girl are meant to be together." She stood and grabbed his hands with hers. "Marry da girl, take her on adventures, take her to da end of da world and back, have babies and love dem as your father loved you. I see dis and it makes da curse worth having. Now go, you don't have much time!" She pushed him toward Toni's father's boat.

"How can I ever repay you?" he asked.

"Choose da girl!"

"I'll never forget this, and we'll break your curse," he replied, diving back into the water.

"I know you will," she said with tears forming, running down her face. Then looking back over the bay, she whispered, "Louis-Michel, I will always love you!"

"I don't mean to break up what should have started twenty years ago," Jimmy said to Spencer, "but this treasure was supposed to be so big that three ships couldn't carry it. We loaded it in a few hours in one oyster boat," he added. Everyone stopped looking at the coins and turned their attention to Spencer.

"Well, that's true. And if I had found it like it is now, I would have been disappointed," Spencer said, looking at everyone. "But I learned something from a letter that was given to me in Lafitte, Louisiana, by an old man."

Toni looked back at Spencer, remembering the letter at Lebreaux's house. "So here's a ghost story." He sat down on the bar stool with his arms around Toni, who was leaning against him.

"The story is much more than just about the barge and the one surviving Spaniard. Nicholas Cardona and Gaspar Vargas searched for the treasure for years, but during their time Vargas turned against Cardona."

"Go figure," Dusty interrupted.

"Yeah, right. Well, Cardona found the treasure, and before he could haul it up, Vargas caught up with him. He made this map, and with the one coin that the Spaniard, who had gone down with the barge, had taken, Nicholas made the key piece. Now, fast-forward over a hundred years, and a young buccaneer is looking for the treasure. He is part of Jean Lafitte's group of pirate captains. He falls in love with a Haitian woman we all know as Lebreaux Papillion."

"Whoa! Ghost story for sure," Jimmy replied.

"What makes it more interesting is that Lafitte hired Vargas's great grandson to help him find the treasure. Word got out in Spain, so Cardona's great-grandson joined the search with the young buccaneer and persuaded him to turn against Lafitte and Vargas's great-grandson. Together they found the treasure and loaded their two ships with most of the treasure and sailed to Port Royal, leaving what we found last night. But Lafitte and Vargas got wind of their plan for keeping the treasure and waited for them at the mouth of the Mississippi. Lafitte caught them in the gulf, and a battle broke out. Unfortunately, the buccaneer's ship was badly damaged and sank, and rumor was that he was killed."

"OK, so to be clear. Lafitte sank the buccaneer's ship and Cardona's great-grandson's ship?" Dusty asked.

"Yes."

"So Cardona's great-grandson died too?" Dusty asked.

"No, that's where the story gets better. Cardona's great-grandson lost his ship, but saved two things, the map and the coin. He then marked the spot of the buccaneer's ship and his ship on the map and added a new key piece," Spencer answered.

"Another coin?" Toni asked.

"Yes."

"Cardona marked the map of the new wreckage with a different coin. A gold Potosi," Spencer went on.

"So what happened to the other ship?" Mr. Gentry asked.

Spencer pointed at him. "I learned from Cardona in Spain that his ancestor's ship was named the *Potosi*, which threw me for a loop on the clues that Lebreaux left us until the old man at Lebreaux's house gave me the letter from her naming the ships and the story. Lafitte sank The *Potosi* only a few hundred yards from the *Compostela*, something he didn't mean to do."

Dusty pulled the map toward him, "So are you saying that one of these holes represents the Spanish barge and another one represents the *Compostela* and the *Potosi*?"

"Yes."

"And the *Compostela* and *Potosi* have the rest of the treasure?" Dusty asked.

Spencer smiled, "Yep. A lot of treasure."

"So we divide this treasure and then go after the rest," Jimmy replied.

"Where would we start? Without this gold coin, we would never know where to look," Toni said.

"There's probably eight figures of treasure in that old oyster boat," Mr. Gentry said proudly.

"Split five ways, it still is a lot of money," Dusty said.

"Yep and it's only a third of the treasure. The other two thirds is still on the *Compostela* and the *Potosi*!" Spencer replied.

Everyone got quiet and drew their attention back to Spencer. "What are you saying? We going after the rest?" Dusty asked.

"I'm done," Spencer smiled.

"Done?" Dusty asked, surprised.

Toni stood from leaning against him. "What do you mean, *done*?"

"I have to make a decision, and well ... I made it," he said to everyone.

"The girl or the treasure," Dusty said. Spencer smiled.

"That's great, but where does that leave us?" Jimmy asked.

"Rich." Mr. Gentry said, pulling the map toward him and rolling it up. "Without the gold coin, there is no other treasure. Don't let greed take you folks over."

Nobody replied.

"Well ... I say it's time to celebrate!" Jimmy yelled, breaking the silence. He jumped over the bar and grabbed a bottle of champagne.

"Jimmy, we can't take their stuff," Toni said.

"Take? Hell, I'm buying this bar!" He didn't hesitate to pop the cork and hand out glasses.

Everyone held up their glass. "To new adventures!" Mr. Gentry said, with the clinking of glasses and a simultaneous chant of "New adventures!"

"I wish we had known Lebreaux's lover's name," Toni said to Spencer.

"Louis-Michel," he replied.

"How do you know that?"

"I found it in one of the letters."

She paused for a moment. "You're really giving up?" she asked Spencer.

"I'm not giving up; just choosing something different."

"What?" She drew back and looked at him.

"I choose you, Toni Benoit. No treasure in this world is worth more than you."

She set her glass down, flipped her hair behind her, and looking up with her hazel eyes, replied, "Mr. LeJeune, I love you!"

Looking down into her eyes, he replied in a raspy voice, "Ay, matey, calm seas lie ahead of us."

"Captain, I'll follow you to the ends of the world," she whispered before kissing him.

Chapter 68

Twelve years later Spencer and a gray-whiskered raccoon sat in his recliner watching the last quarter of the LSU football game. "Always a fourth-quarter team," he observed out loud.

"But they keep it interesting," Toni replied, sitting in his lap. She fought her way out of her entanglement with Spencer and the recliner, still in her scrubs. "Do you want more tea?"

"Sure," he gave her his empty glass.

A loud commotion broke out down the hallway in one of the bedrooms. "Kids, you better not be breaking anything," Toni yelled, walking to the kitchen. A little dark haired-girl exited the room and ran down the hall.

"Daddy, Steven won't leave me alone," she said to Spencer.

"Steven!" he called, not taking his eyes off the TV.

"Dad, I didn't do anything," a little boy said, walking toward them.

"You two go get your shoes on and then head outside," Spencer said.

"See what you did?" the little girl said, pushing the boy.

A light knock came from the sliding glass door, and Spencer looked over as Toni opened the door for Katie Pastadoria.

"Hello Mrs. LeJeune, can Hailey play?"

"She can if you take Steven with you," Spencer replied from his recliner.

The little blonde haired girl gave him an annoyed smirk, "OK."

Toni stood at the sliding front door and watched as the three kids ran down the stairs and grabbed their bikes. Peddling as fast as their bikes would allow them, they disappeared around the corner. "Who would have thought our kids would be playing with Jimmy Pastadoria's little girl?"

"I still don't know where she got her cute looks from."

"Behave!" Toni threw a pillow at him.

"Steven, you know Mom and Dad are going to get mad at you for climbing on that wall!" Hailey said, referring to one of the concrete barriers that protruded into the Mississippi river.

"I'll be fine unless you tell on me!" he said, watching his footsteps as he ventured out farther onto the wall.

"My brother is such a jerk!" Hailey said to Katie.

Katie looked over her shoulder at the ten-year-old boy carefully balancing himself on the twenty-foot wall. "He's not always a jerk," she said with a glimmer in her green eyes.

Steven stopped short of reaching the end and looked down at the fierce river pushing past the wall, creating a strong rip tide. He eyed the violent water, looking for fish that it would capture and push along the current. Leaning over to look past the wall, he felt his right foot slip on a few loose pebbles. He flung his arms backwards trying to catch his balance, but the momentum had started him on his downward plunge. In fear he tried to scream, but the shock of losing his balance drew the wind out of his lungs. As he watched the violent waters come closer, though, something snatched his arm and quickly pulled him back to the top of the wall.

With the two girls oblivious of what was happening, he panted, trying to catch his breath.

"Boy, I got you," a voice came from behind him. He spun around to see only a shadowed figure with the sun beaming from behind.

"You saved me," he replied, rubbing his leg.

"Ay, let me look at dat." She studied the cut on his leg. "It's a good cut, but it'll heal."

"Who are you?" he asked, fascinated by her long gray hair and embroidered coat.

"A friend," a smile formed across her face.

"Well, thank you," he said, looking at the mysterious woman.

"Say, do ye like adventures?" she asked.

"Sure."

"Take dis and show no one but da girls." She pointed to the two girls who were playing with something in the dirt, still unaware of what was going on.

The woman took Steven's hand and placed something in his palm, closing it before he could see what it was.

He looked back up at her with a confused expression. "What is it?"

"That's for ye to find. Remember … da mark is on the *Potosi*!"

He opened his hand, revealing an oblong gold coin with a cross on it, and looking back up, he found the woman had vanished.

"Katie! Hailey!"

For more books by Lee DuCote
www.leeducote.com
Follow Lee
www.facebook.com/authorleeducote
@leeducote – Instagram
@leeducote - Twitter